THE JAZZ MASTER

THE JAZZ MASTER

DEVASHISH

InnerWorld Publications
San Germán, Puerto Rico
www.innerworldpublications.com

To study Buddhism is to study ourselves. To study ourselves is to forget ourselves.

— Dogen-zenji

Prologue

HANGING ON THE WALL in my study is a simple wooden plaque given to me by my teacher, Shunryu Suzuki, a few months before his death in December 1971. Engraved on the plaque are four Chinese characters copied from his calligraphy that roughly translated mean: *this day will not come again; each minute a precious gem.* It is a reminder to me that the Zen student lives in the present moment, his beginner's mind open to the endless wonders of the world around him. Roshi-san had a smile on his face when he translated the characters for me, the same smile that appears in the photo I keep on my desk. For me that smile is as timeless as those words, the Buddha's own smile reminding me of my Buddha nature. Whenever I catch myself getting lost in the dark alleys of the past, an ever-present danger for a jazz historian, I have only to glance at his picture or at his calligraphy to find my way back to the secure mooring of the here and now. It's hard to believe that it's been seven years since he left us, but as Roshi-san himself once said, life and death are the same thing. He is as present now as he ever was, keeping a watchful eye out for me as I begin these pages, trying to reverse the flow of time as Dogen-zenji did in the mountain solitudes of Mount Tiantong when he cast off his mind and stepped into the trackless void.

Earlier this summer my old friend Diana Sartori invited me out to Naropa to accompany her in an evening of poetry and jazz. The poems were new, a long cycle she had recently completed entitled "Samsara and Nirvana," but the night was a throwback, a reprisal of our performances in the late fifties in the clubs and coffeehouses of North Beach where we carried on a tradition that had begun with Kenneth Rexroth and Lawrence Ferlinghetti. It had been years since we'd performed together, but we picked up right where we'd left off nearly two decades earlier, piano and voice cavorting onstage like soul mates in a pagan marriage rite. The crowd was every bit as enthusiastic as the bohemian angels who followed us from coffeehouse to coffeehouse back in the magnificent, scarred fifties when my Zen-inspired jazz had been the perfect complement to Diana's nonintentional poetry, and afterward we repaired to the nearby house that Burroughs shared with Corso for an after-hours party of full-on nostalgia, a chorus of old-timers swapping war stories from the birth of the counterculture while a bevy of twenty-somethings crowded around us in the living room, sipping beers and passing around the occasional joint. Corso was his normal provocative self, the precocious poet playing devil's advocate to Ginsberg's laid-back dharma angel; Burroughs was as irreverent as ever, half mystic philosopher, half alien; and Amiri Baraka did his best to keep us grounded with his maximum-density materialism and his periodic rant against the capitalist machine. But in the end it was a chorale of Buddhist voices that carried the night—myself, Allen, Diana, Orlovsky, even Burroughs in his own way. As the night wore on, it became clear to me—and I think to all of us—that the voice that had cried out in the wilderness of the fifties against a repressive culture, in anger and despair and hope and joy, had been the voice of a spiritual longing that had sought its inspiration in the esoteric wisdom of the East, much as the transcendentalists had done more than a century earlier.

Though Allen was the ringleader, Diana and I did our fair share of the talking. She had always been a marvelous storyteller, and I guess I had picked up a certain ability from my years of writing about the colorful characters that people the off-kilter world of jazz—or else my companions that night made a special effort to cede the stage to me since I was only there for a short visit. Allen asked me to tell the story of how I met Elijah, and with Diana providing counterpoint, I must have spent close to an hour entertaining the gathering with my introduction to Buddhism through the offices of the most unusual jazzman I've ever met, the man who taught me that blue is the color of nirvana, and that a tenor sax's true purpose is to empty the mind of all but the wind and clouds and rain.

The next afternoon, Peter, Allen, and Diana took me to the air-port—three New Yorkers and a lone Californian—and the three of them ganged up on me, as New Yorkers often will when they outnumber their West Coast cousins. Allen was adamant that it was my spiritual duty to write up my early experiences as a kind of Buddhist memoir, and Peter and Diana provided a convincing chorus. Confronted with such overwhelming odds, I opted for Hakuin's answer when faced with the winds of destiny: "Is that so?" And so it proved to be, especially once Diana returned to San Francisco at the end of the summer, determined to remind me of my duty every time we got together at Zen Center for zazen and crumpets.

This book is dedicated to Elijah, my first mentor on the road to nirvana, and to my teacher, Shunryu Suzuki, the embodiment of all that I hope to be, but it never would have been written without Diana's invitation and her affectionate prodding and constant encouragement. To them my thanks and my love. They are the harmonious background to a world of breathtaking imbalance, the spaciousness in which these words dwell.

1

My introduction to Zen began with the sound of a horn. To be more explicit, the sound of a tenor sax. It was the first Saturday in January, 1956, two days before the beginning of my second semester at UC Berkeley, where I was enrolled as a music major, and I had just moved into my first apartment, a fifteen-by-twenty garret over a detached garage with a cubicle for a bathroom, a small gas stove, and a 1903 Hornung Bros. upright against the back wall that had been recently tuned. It had a skylight, which I found very cool, and a window on either side, one facing north toward the campus and the other south toward People's Park. And it was sufficiently isolated that I could play my instrument without unduly disturbing the neighbors. The perfect pad for a single-minded young jazz musician sold on the virtues of practice and dedicated to his art.

I was unpacking my books when I heard the faint sound of a sax coming from somewhere down the block. Still giddy from the elixir of having my own place, I didn't pay much attention at first, but after a few minutes my curiosity kicked in. I went to the north window and opened it. Whoever it was, he was practicing a minor scale, but there was something odd about it, a Middle Eastern or oriental color I wasn't familiar with. I stood there and listened until I figured it out: a minor scale with a sharp fourth, a flat sixth, and a sharp seventh, something I had never run across before. I went to the piano to confirm what I'd heard and played around with it for a few minutes, intrigued by the possibilities.

When I went back to my unpacking, my unknown colleague had moved on to practicing patterns, modulating one by one through the different keys. That's when I realized he had some major chops, well beyond what I or any of my fellow students were capable of. He was too fluid, too fast, and even from that distance I could tell that his tone was stronger and fuller than that of any of my classmates. One of my teachers, perhaps, or a local musician, maybe even someone I had seen playing in one of the Fillmore clubs. It seemed a happy coincidence, moving into my first apartment and having it turn out to be just down the street from a first-rate saxophonist.

I went on with my unpacking until he started soloing over imaginary changes, and moments later I lost all interest in the apartment. A few bars were all it took to realize that he wasn't one of my teachers. We had a couple of professors in the department who could really blow, but this guy's style was too distinctive. Nor was he one of the local saxophonists, someone who had made a name for himself in the San Francisco jazz scene. By now I had heard them all and I would have recognized his style if I had heard it before. In fact, as I sat down by the window on the twin-size mattress that I had bought secondhand the previous day to stand in as a bed, it dawned on me that I couldn't remember ever hearing anybody quite like him. He was using the same scale, for the most part, giving his lines an ethereal, Arabian Nights flavor, but it wasn't the scale that impressed me—it was the ideas. They were as inventive as any I had heard on vinyl and as stylistically unique. I had spent countless hours trying to cop the style of every great saxophonist who caught my ear, beginning with Bird when I was still learning my scales and most recently Stan Getz and Paul Desmond, who were the epitome of that West Coast Cool that was all the rage among the jazzophiles at Berkeley. But except for Bird and Prez and maybe one or two others, I could always hear echoes of other musicians' ideas in the solos I was learning—a little Charlie Parker, a little Lester Young, an echo or two of Coleman Hawkins. But whoever it was, he didn't sound like anybody I had ever heard. I had no clue where his ideas were coming from. It was like he was his own school of jazz, and before long I found his improvising so arresting that I gave up trying to dissect it and just lay back on the bed and let the distant music flow over me like an invitation to another world. My mattress became a magic carpet, floating me up and out of my window, carrying me into whatever landscape he was imagining as he played, making me feel as if I were overflying the earth with an unaccompanied tenor sax for a soundtrack. When he finally stopped, at precisely one-thirty, I felt like the wind had suddenly failed, sending me plummeting back to earth where I was rudely deposited once again in my Berkeley apartment.

I had missed my lunch break by more than an hour, but I didn't care. Somewhere down the block a master of the music had just finished practicing his horn, and that was all I could think about. I even got on my bike and took a quick ride around the block on the odd chance that I might run into some hip jazz angel exiting a suburban Berkeley house with a tenor sax under his arm and an aura of majesty on his face but I had no such luck; nor, I realized, did I have any real idea where the sound had been coming from, though I knew it couldn't have been very far away. When I returned home and wolfed down some leftovers from the fridge, I was barely aware of what I was eating. Who could it have been? An up-and-coming East Coast saxophonist that the music department had invited to Berkeley for the spring semester as a visiting professor? Some hot new sideman that I had yet to discover, getting ready to burst onto the jazz scene like a comet shooting across the heavens? Did he actually live somewhere down the block—a stroke of luck seemingly too good to be true—or was he just passing through, staying in a friend's house whose walls were still smoking from the music? I was dying to find out, but there was nothing I could do except hang around the apartment until the unknown sax man broke his silence. The thought that it might have been a one-time deal, that I might be less than a hundred yards from a truly great saxophonist and not have the chance to meet him was almost excruciating, but there was nothing I could do other than marshal my patience and let my chips ride.

As it turned out, I had no cause for worry. I spent the rest of the afternoon practicing my sax and then the piano, and in the evening I got in my car and headed over the Bay Bridge to San Francisco where I visited some of the local clubs, wondering if I might run across him smoking up the bandstand. I didn't hear him or anyone else of any particular note that night, at least not anyone on his level, but the next morning, just after ten-thirty, I heard the sound of a tenor sax present itself at the open window, breathing life into an altered scale. This time I was ready to seize the moment. I waited until he started playing patterns with that unmistakable fluidity. Then I put on the fur-lined jacket and scarf my parents had given me for Christmas and descended the stairs to the street like a five-year-old enthralled by the enchanted timbre of the pied piper's magic flute.

It didn't take me long to locate the source of that enchantment. At the other end of the block, on the same side of the street, surrounded by a plank fence covered with ivy and flowering vines, stood a dark-green, two-story Victorian with a steeply pitched roof, spired turrets, gable dormers, and a wraparound porch with spindlework banisters. It was a beautiful relic from a legendary era, the glory days of the gay nineties, that I had stopped to admire when I first checked out the apartment. The music was coming from out back so I took the liberty of letting myself in through the side gate. I followed a white-stone walkway that ran alongside the house to the backyard where I emerged into a landscape that startled me almost as much as the unseen sax had the previous day. There in the middle of Berkeley, hidden to the eyes of anyone passing by on that small suburban street, was a secluded Japanese garden, as finely sculpted and meticulously cared for as any you might find in Kyoto or Osaka. The walkway continued on past gracefully trimmed shrubs, flower beds, and oddly shaped boulders of different sizes sitting in beds of raked sand. There were several bonsai perched on pedestals and a small pool with brightly colored fish, ringed by stones. A rivulet flowed into the pool from a cluster of tall boulders, like a mountain river emptying into a secluded lake. On one of those boulders, flatter and wider than the rest, sat a stone Buddha about three feet tall, his hands folded on his lap and his eyes half-closed, sunk in some mysterious inner silence. At the rear of the property, flush against the back fence, was a small redwood cottage that someone had remodeled to make it look like a medieval Japanese temple. It had a curved tile roof, a shaded front porch, a slatted sliding door fitted with opaque paper instead of glass, and a red paper lantern decorated with Chinese characters hanging above an engraved wooden sign that read: leave your ego at the door. For a moment I thought I must have misread it, but a second glance confirmed my initial reading. Leave your ego at the door. Whoever was in that cottage playing that otherworldly tenor clearly had a sense of humor.

It was a chilly, overcast day, in the midforties at best, and the music he was playing seemed to reflect the weather: grave, penetrating, as weighty as the oppressive cloud cover that sapped the day of any vestige of warmth. I didn't dare interrupt, not with the closed door and that unusual sign, so I sat down on one of the steps that accessed the raised porch to listen to the rest of his session, marveling at the warmth and clarity of his deep, rounded tone. It was elegant and sad at the same time, solemn and thoughtful, and the weight of that tone seemed to anchor me to the music, as if it were the center of gravity rather than the earth beneath me. He was playing free-form now, long sinuous melodies that seemed as oriental as the garden, as if he were a thousand miles from Berkeley wandering through unfamiliar landscapes that rose up in the shadows of my imagination, filling me with a bittersweet longing that was almost too poignant to endure.

When he finally stopped, at exactly one-thirty, I felt a shock, as if I had just been ushered out of a movie theater, forced to readjust to the harsh light of the outside world. I sat there for several minutes trying to get my bearings, a little unsure of myself now, until I heard the sound of running water coming from inside the cottage. I got up and was about to knock when a voice called out: "You can come in now, but be sure to leave your shoes outside." That I could do. My ego I wasn't so sure about. I slipped off my shoes and slid the door open to find an imposing black man in a loose-fitting robe standing over a small sink, washing vegetables with his back to the door. He had a shaven head and looked to be in his early thirties, and he was at least six foot four with a powerful frame, the kind of person I might have instinctively steered clear of had I passed him on the street, but the robe—a coal-black Japanese kimono with wide sleeves and silver borders—made him seem surprisingly benign.

Oddly enough, he didn't turn around to see who it was. "You hungry?" he asked without lifting his head from the sink.

"I don't want to be a bother," I said, surprised by his offer. "I just stopped by to introduce myself."

"Okay, but I'm accounted a pretty fair cook." He spoke in a musical southern drawl and his voice was soft and measured, not what I would have expected from a man built like an NFL linebacker. "I've put on some rice to steam and I'm about to stir-fry some vegetables. It'll be ready in ten minutes. You're welcome to join me, brother. Or not. Your call."

"Okay, sure, why not? I'd love to."

"I'm Elijah," he said, finally turning around to look at me as he took the vegetables out of the sink and set them on a cutting board, "though most folks round here call me Preacher. And who are you, exactly?"

"My name's Dan, Dan Hennessey. I just moved in down the block. I could hear you playing from my apartment. It was pretty impressive."

"You a student at the college?"

"Music student."

"I heard somebody playing a sax yesterday. Was that you?"

"That was me."

"Didn't I hear a piano also?"

"That was also me."

"Thought so. Well, why don't you have a seat, Brother Dan. It'll be done before you know it."

I looked around for a chair but there wasn't one. Apart from the tiny kitchenette where Elijah was deftly chopping vegetables with a butcher's knife, the room was empty, just a bare floor covered with tatami mats, a small bookcase with a few cushions stacked up beside it, a tenor sax in a stand in the far corner, and a single wall hanging—a Japanese scroll with some elegant ink calligraphy, what I later learned was called a *tatemono*. There was a back room divided off from the main room by a slatted wall with the same opaque paper, and a bathroom no bigger than mine next to the kitchenette, but no furniture whatsoever. I grabbed a cushion and sat down rather awkwardly on the floor while he stir-fried the vegetables in a large wok. I was no cook—after three days on my own I still hadn't gotten past warming up a can of chili beans—but the big man looked like he knew what he was doing, and the pungent aroma that wafted from the sizzling wok reminded me how hungry I was.

When the vegetables were ready, he pulled out a folding table with foot-high legs that was tucked in between the refrigerator and the stove and set it up in the middle of the room. From beneath the counter he took out a tray with lacquered bowls and tableware inscribed with Chinese characters and proceeded to set the table in a meticulous, almost ceremonial manner. There was something very graceful about his movements that I wouldn't have expected from a man that large, but it seemed to fit with his unusual dress and the exotic surroundings, a sense of quiet solemnity that made me reluctant to interrupt the ritual with any irreverent chatter, despite the questions that were buzzing in my head. I had no idea how well-known he was, but after a second straight day of listening to him play I certainly knew how good he was. And he was black, like virtually all the great jazz musicians that I had grown up idolizing and unlike any of my teachers at Berkeley — the first honest-to-God black jazzman I had ever met. There were a million things I wanted to ask — had he recorded any albums, who had he played with, was he in a combo I might have heard of or had he ever been in one, how had he developed his unique style — but other than the quick lesson he gave me on how to use chopsticks, I spent the entire lunch answering his questions while I fidgeted on my cushion, trying to keep myself from rambling: What kind of music did I listen to? Who were my favorite musicians? Why the piano, why the sax? What was the music program at Berkeley like? Where was I from and what got me started playing an instrument? What did I think of San Francisco after growing up in the Valley? Here I was, a nineteen-year-old kid from an all-white suburb who had led a thoroughly uneventful life sitting on the floor across the lunch table from a shaven-head black saxophonist in a Japanese kimono who had as unique a sound as I had ever heard — and he was asking me questions? Listening to my every word as if nothing else in the world mattered? Wanting to know the tiniest details — the name of my high-school band director, what tune we played for the finale of my senior-year concert — and nodding at my answers as if he had just acquired a piece of priceless knowledge? I had no idea how to react, other than to continue rambling on about my high-school dreams to one day become a professional jazz musician.

After we cleared away the meal, he invited me out to the porch, where we sat on a couple of wooden benches and looked out on the garden. I was still rambling when we sat down, explaining how my real teachers had been the records I'd listened to, but my long dissertation had drained the nervousness out of me, and eventually I collected myself enough to ask him a question that had been on my mind since I first heard his sax floating in through an open window.

"There was one thing I wanted to ask you, if you don't mind. Actually there are a lot of things, but one thing I really noticed was your use of space when you play. Most of the guys at school seem to feel like they have to fill up the bar with as many notes as they can. I'm the same way. Even my teachers are, for the most part. But when you play, the music really breathes. Is that something you think about when you play, something you've worked on, or does it just come naturally? I've only heard you a couple of times, but it seems to be a real trademark of your style."

"I don't think about it when I play, brother. The whole point of playing an instrument is not to think. But if the music doesn't breathe, if you can't hear the silence behind the sound, then how can you hear anything? It's the silence that makes the music."

I don't know what I expected for an answer, but that wasn't it. When I expressed my puzzlement, Elijah tried to simplify it for me.

"Do you see my hand?" he asked, holding it up in front of him.

"Sure."

"And do you see what surrounds it?"

"Yes."

"Well, without that background you wouldn't be able to see my hand. If it were all ground, no background or foreground, there would be no perception. No perception, no hand. It's the contrast that differentiates the ten thousand things into this and that. You follow?"

"Yeah, I think so."

"Silence is the background of sound. Without silence there is no sound. According to the Hindus, silence and sound is the first duality. So if you really want to understand music, then you have to first understand silence, because without silence there *is* no music."

I was still baffled but some small ray of understanding made it through a chink in my mind. "Now that I think about it, when I was listening to you, it felt like the space was adding resonance to what you were playing. I don't know if that's the right way to say it. Could that have something to do with what you're talking about?"

"Absolutely. If you just string a bunch of notes together without any space, it won't mean anything to anybody. Not really. That's the resonance you're talking about, brother. Music has to breathe to be comprehended. It has to grow out of silence. The silence you bring with you."

Again his words threw me. Was this the way southern jazzmen talked when they got together with other musicians? I certainly hadn't heard anybody talk about music that way at Berkeley.

"So then you *are* conscious about it when you play—at least on some level?"

"I guess that depends on what you mean by 'conscious,' whether you are talking about big mind or small mind."

"Big mind?"

Elijah smiled and added one of his trademark pauses. He was a big man, an imposing figure, but when he smiled it was as if he had slid back the cottage door to reveal the gentleness within. It was as great a contrast as silence and sound, this man with the body of a bouncer who was as gentle as a Buddha.

"Let's try something," he said. "You see that cloud over there?"

"Yes."

"Fix your gaze on the cloud and watch what it does, but don't lose sight of the sky. Take your time."

We were silent for the next few minutes, both of us watching a solitary cumulus floating high above the Victorian roof in a lake of iridescent blue. I didn't know exactly what I was looking for or why, but I had a peaceful feeling while I watched the cloud gradually change shape as it drifted in a southerly direction.

"Now, tell me, brother," Elijah said softly, breaking the silence, "was the cloud stationary or did it move?"

"It moved."

"And was the sky in any way disturbed by its movement?"

"Disturbed? No."

"Would it be disturbed if it were a lightning flash or a flock of birds passing by?"

"No. The sky is the sky."

"Exactly. The sky is always the sky, no matter what the weather. Just like the ocean is always the ocean, no matter how strong the waves. You may think that the waves are separate from the ocean but they are not. They are just the motion of the water. Just as the clouds are contained in the sky. That's big mind. You may think that the things you see, the things you hear, are outside you, but that is an incorrect understanding. They are just waves in your mind. They are not separate from you; you just think they are. And as long as you think they are, you are a prisoner of your small mind. But when you experience everything within you, like waves in the ocean, then you are looking at the world from big mind. And that's when the music takes off. That's when you really cook. When there's no one in the kitchen."

My confusion must have been painfully evident. Elijah looked at me and laughed, not in amusement but in commiseration.

"Take another look at the sky, brother. Does the cloud decide where it's going to go? Does the lightning choose where it wants to jump?"

I shook my head.

"No, they don't. And that's the secret of their freedom. They have no small mind to bother them. The best jazz improvisation isn't planned. You don't think it into being. It leaps across the sky like lightning—beautiful, perfect, utterly spontaneous. It makes no difference whether it comes from your horn or mine or from no horn at all. Music is just music, like the clouds are just clouds. Is it any clearer now?"

"No," I said, shaking my head in complete bewilderment.

"No matter. If you don't understand now, you'll understand later. In the meantime, just play. Feel the horn in your hands, listen to the way your breath becomes sound and the way the sound dies and becomes silence. Listen to the space between the notes, but above all, to the space behind the notes, and let the music play itself. Then come back and tell me how it went."

My head was swimming when I got back to the apartment. By then I had realized that Elijah hadn't been speaking some kind of hip jazz lingo that I wasn't familiar with due to my ignorance or my inexperience, but a language of his own that I simply didn't understand. And yet, even though I had no real idea what he had been talking about, those incomprehensible words set my imagination on fire. As I opened my sax case and started assembling my instrument, I saw images of myself on a bandstand, listening to the silence behind the music as my alto borrowed my fingers to let loose an elegant cascade of notes worthy of Elijah himself. The images dissolved quickly enough once I picked up my horn and began to practice — it was still me, after all — but there was a difference in my playing that was not imagined. I made a concerted effort to focus my attention on the space between and behind the notes, and that one little shift in perspective made my playing come alive. The music began to breathe, similar in some small measure to the way Elijah's music breathed, and I could hear musical ideas forming in my mind during the pauses, getting ready to leap out when I bit down again on the reed. There was only one possible explanation for my sudden change in fortune: Elijah. I was a full-time music student in a first-class university with excellent teachers, but the world of academia — white academia — and the world of authentic jazz improvisation were worlds apart, the difference between black and white. Through blind happenstance I had stumbled onto a bona fide jazzman, a black master of America's greatest and most original art form, one who was capable of teaching me the secrets of the music I loved, and all I could think about when I finally put down my horn was how long I should wait before I went back to visit him. It hadn't occurred to me when I first lay down on my mattress to listen to that dazzling river of notes from an unseen sax that the unseen musician might be black. But now that I knew he was, it made a universe of difference. Through blind dumb luck or the unerring eye of karma, however you choose to explain it, I was now living down the street from a true master of the music, the first I had ever met face to face. This world that had never completely made sense to me before was about to take on a whole new meaning.

2

It was in the 1940s that the American dream officially relocated to the suburbs, and my family was right there in the vanguard. My father moved us from Sherman Oaks to Northridge in the spring of 1939, into a vast expanse of newly cleared farmland that was on its way to becoming one of the San Fernando Valley's most affluent and prestigious communities. We were the first family to buy a house in our development and the third to move in, proud owners of a four-bedroom ranch house on a full half acre with an area set aside for a pool that was completed a few months later. My earliest memory has me standing in the driveway of our new house the day my mother received a brand new 1939 Chevrolet sedan for a birthday present. My father had taken us out to a restaurant in Van Nuys, and when we returned home the car was sitting in the driveway with a huge red ribbon around it. I was only two and a half and I don't remember the restaurant, but I remember the enormous red bow and my mother's infectious laughter that seemed to sum up our charmed existence: a single-family home with a separate bedroom for each child; a well-manicured lawn out front and a pool and patio out back where my mother sunbathed on her chaise lounge each afternoon; periodic dinner parties and barbecues with the neighbors, whose kids were in our pool nearly as often as we were; and the yearly trip to Yosemite, where we were inevitably reminded of our bounteous good fortune. "This is what everyone in America dreams of," my father would tell us, with a healthy display of self-satisfaction. "I hope you kids know how lucky you are."

But that was our parents' dream, not ours. I suspect we imbibed some of their self-satisfaction through simple osmosis, but for me and my brother Jack, who was two years older, and for Pauline, who came along three years after I did, life in the suburbs was nothing special. We hadn't moved up in the world; we had just landed in it: acre after acre of empty lots with cookie-cutter houses rising from the barren ground by the power of prophecy, the story of Genesis reenacted each day between sunup and sunset, rolling out a sacred suburban welcome to the new recruits, rosy-cheeked kids who looked and acted just like us. Like the young Siddhartha, whose father went to great lengths to hide the sufferings of the world from his son, we were safe within the borders of a privileged all-white suburb, unaware of the privations and the prejudice that stalked children of color only a few miles away in places like Pacoima and South LA. I was two years old when World War II began and eight years old when it ended, but it was too far away to have any real impact in my daily life, beyond the patriotic clamor of a few movie reels and our morbid obsession with killing Germans and Japanese when we got together with our friends in an empty lot to play soldiers. That there could be another kind of war going on just a few miles away, in the cities and towns of America—a war in which basic human dignity was at stake—entirely passed me by.

That all began to change when I was ten years old, and I had a black man's music to thank for it. My father was a supervising engineer in RCA's West Coast Missile and Surface Radar Division, but his first love had been the trumpet, and his idea of a relaxing evening was to put on a Harry James record and sip a beer while he read the evening paper. He was a swing aficionado who got my brother and I started on music lessons at an early age, an enthusiastic follower of the big bands that used to tour the country in the thirties: the Dorsey brothers, Woody Herman, Harry James, Glenn Miller, Benny Goodman, and our favorites, Stan Kenton and Artie Shaw, both Southern Californians based in LA who were the idols of every kid on our block with an ear for music. All-white bands, of course, but that was all anybody listened to in the Valley in those days, and by the time 1947 rolled around I was a pretty fair pianist, a mainstay in our school band in which Jack played lead trumpet. One day that summer Jack brought home a seventy-eight RPM recording by a group called Charlie Parker's Reboppers. I had heard of bebop, but I had never actually sat down and listened to it. It hadn't really caught on yet on the Coast, and if there were any radio stations playing that kind of music, my father wasn't about to tune them in. I had been taking sax lessons for about a year by then, and my idea of a great jazz side was Stan Kenton's recording of "Painted Rhythm," which Jack and I had nailed note for note. But when my brother fired up my father's turntable and put on side A—"Ko-Ko"—my world spun out of orbit. I remember jumping off the couch near the end of Bird's first chorus with ears as big as saucers, unable to control my excitement, caught in the vertigo of those two minutes and fifty seconds that would redefine my world.

In the weeks that followed I literally wore that record out, trying to cop Bud Powell's distinctive style—he was the first piano player I'd ever heard who put the rhythmic pulse in the right hand—and dreaming of the day when I would have the chops on the sax to fly like Bird, which was about as close to nirvana as a white boy in the Valley could get in those days. After that, my brother and I saved our entire spending allowance for bebop records. Bird and Dizzy led us to Hawk and Monk and eventually to the Duke, opening our eyes to the real history of the music. It was a real-life adventure that outdid anything in the Hardy Boys mysteries that my brother had turned me on to a few years earlier, but as with most real-life adventures it was not without its perils and its disillusionments. I remember mentioning Bird and Dizzy to my father when I was in the early throes of my fascination with the new music, and I'll never forget his disparaging remarks, how they and their jungle music were a bad influence that I'd do well to stay away from. The reaction we got in school wasn't much different, not only from Mr. Kruger, the band director, a German traditionalist who had come under his own share of suspicion during the war, but also from our friends and bandmates, whose attitudes ranged from dismissive to downright hostile. At first I couldn't understand it. My parents and teachers were from a different generation, but did my friends really have so little ear for music that they couldn't hear how far ahead of everyone else Bird and Dizzy were? I dug Stan Kenton and Artie Shaw as much as anyone, but it didn't stop me from recognizing real genius when I heard it. Music was the language Jack and I spoke best, and it was obvious to us that the black modernists like Bird and Dizzy spoke it better than anyone else alive, just as it was gradually becoming obvious that the white bandleaders our friends and neighbors idolized made their living imitating the black man's music. But my friends couldn't hear it. Or rather, they refused to hear it, refused to open their eyes and ears to their own prejudice. Jack and I learned quick enough to keep quiet about the change in our musical tastes, but it didn't stop us from learning where the music came from and why the men and women who invented it and were changing the way it was being played were looked down on — if they were seen at all — by the smug inhabitants of the all-white communities of the San Fernando Valley.

Siddhartha would have to escape his sheltered existence and confront the realities of human suffering before he would be ready to seek out the path of illumination. In my case, the borders of Northridge proved a good deal more porous than the walls of the future Buddha's Indian palace, but I experienced a similar awakening when I followed my brother to North Hollywood High in the fall of 1951, albeit with far less transcendental consequences. It was in my first few weeks of high school, in social studies class, that I learned about the housing covenants in force throughout the Valley that didn't permit property owners to sell to blacks or Mexicans, and in many places to Jews, a de facto segregation policy that was universally supported but rarely talked about. Housing covenants weren't racist, my teacher was quick to point out. This was California, the most liberal state in the union, not the antediluvian South. Housing covenants were necessary for the public good, a conclusion the US government itself had clearly arrived at, since it was the official policy of the Federal Housing Administration to withhold loans from areas not covered by real-estate covenants — on the grounds that they prevented racial violence. There were whispers among my classmates of how they prevented property values from falling as well, but the party line, the one we got from our teachers and our parents, was that they promoted social welfare. Spoken in perfect earnest in a high school that didn't have a single black or Mexican student, in a state where a Mexican woman and a black man had to go to the California Supreme Court to get a marriage license just two years earlier, the first successful challenge of the antimiscegenation law that made mixed marriages illegal in the Golden State. I hadn't known about housing covenants or anti-miscegenation laws, but I had learned a fair bit about racism in Northridge, the kind practiced by my parents and my neighbors, the understated, cleverly camouflaged intolerance that abhors the KKK but is perfectly comfortable with Jim Crow. Equality for blacks and other people of color—as long as they don't trespass on hallowed ground. What I hadn't known was how institutionalized it was, a realization that made me acutely uncomfortable, as did much of what I learned in high school about the world I had been born into.

Somehow the fact of boarding a bus each morning and traveling beyond the borders of my little hometown opened up the floodgates and allowed the outside world to come pouring in. Not only was I thrown together with kids from all over the Valley, I had a sense that I was finally being allowed to see the adult world that I would soon be joining, a world that our parents and teachers had done their best to keep from us. It wasn't just the unacknowledged but thoroughly institutionalized racism of an all-white world—it was the growing realization that fear was a constant and accepted presence in our lives, like the San Francisco fog that soaks you so insidiously and surreptitiously you don't even realize you're getting wet. We had Joseph McCarthy and the mass hysteria of a public witch-hunt against the country's best and brightest thinkers, a political establishment that played upon our fears of the "communist menace" to give full vent to its own megalomaniacal tendencies, and the pending prospect of nuclear annihilation that hinged on the posturing of politicians from both sides who were drunk on their own hubris. People were afraid to open their mouths, lest somebody accuse them of being anti-American, and they were terrified of the bomb, sure that Southern California, whose vertiginous growth had been fueled by the defense industry, would be the Soviets' top target after Washington. I was a sophomore when we detonated the first hydrogen bomb in the Pacific, an incoming junior when the Soviets tested their own

H-bomb, and a senior when Ho Chi Minh marched into Hanoi and Eisenhower pledged to help South Vietnam stand up against communist encroachment. When the prim, smiling blond asked Marlon Brando in *The Wild One*, "What are you rebelling against?" and he answered, "Whad'ya got?" he was speaking for all of us, even those of us who put on our best Ozzie-and-Harriet smiles each morning and washed down our repression with milk. Something was radically wrong with our world, and the anger was building, even if it was buried under a few layers of landfill. In time that anger would send us to the streets, erupting in the bittersweet chaos of the sixties, loosing a tidal shift in consciousness that would eventually end the war and fuel the victories of the civil rights movement. But that was later. It would take another decade before the silent generation would find its voice.

I turned eighteen in November of 1954, and that weekend my brother took me to Billy Berg's on Vine Street in Hollywood for one of its last shows before the historic venue closed its doors. It was the first time I had ever set foot in a jazz club, and no birthday before or since has meant as much. Billy Berg's was the site of Bird and Dizzy's legendary appearance on the West Coast in December 1945, only a few days after they recorded the Savoy sessions in New York that had served as my initiation into the delirium of bebop. That was the gig when Bird didn't show up for opening night until the end of the second set — not because he was strung out, as some writers have claimed, but because he was in a back room casually working his way through two complete Mexican dinners, the specialty of the house. When he did make his entrance, it was in high style: emerging from the crowd with his sax to his lips, blowing his way through the changes to "Cherokee" with the same verve and brilliance he had shown on "Ko-Ko" and the other Savoy sides. My brother and I were both jazz-history buffs, but that was not the only reason he took me to Billy Berg's for my birthday. The headliners that night were Wardell Gray and Dexter Gordon, the dueling tenors who had left another major milestone for jazz aficionados with their 1947 recording of "The Chase" in which they traded choruses, half choruses, quarter choruses, and four-bar turnarounds over seven breathless minutes and both sides of a ten-inch shellac seventy-eight that my brother and I regarded as one of our greatest treasures. They had reprised their duel — a tradition among jazz soloists where each tries to outdo the other to prove who is the baddest, the fastest, the hippest — on a number of occasions in different venues, and though we didn't know it then, this was to be their last: six months later Wardell was found dead in the desert outside Las Vegas with a broken neck, rumored victim of a mob boss from whom he had borrowed money to support his heroin habit. I knew nothing about his habit at the time, and very little about the widespread use of heroin among jazz musicians. All I knew was that he was like a genie who had been let out of his bottle, a born enchanter who cast a spell with his horn. He was called the "thin man" for his gaunt figure and delicate build, but his playing was all lightness and joy, reminiscent of Lester Young, who had been his model, but more spirited and unlike any saxophonist who had come before him. Seeing him onstage next to Dexter Gordon was a contrast in appearance as much as a contrast in style. Dexter was tall and imposing. He wore a wide-brim black hat and a baggy yellow zoot suit with a black shirt, and even though he stooped when he played he towered over Wardell. But no matter how impressively he blew, Wardell barely felt the breeze. He came back at him chorus after chorus, spinning dazzling, complex lines that made even the most jaded rednecks in the audience grin with delight.

But as great as the music was and as thrilled as I was to see the inside of what was for me the jazz world's most important nightclub after Minton's Playhouse in New York, it was the audience that made the biggest impression. Billy Berg's was a rarity in Jim Crow LA: a totally integrated club. Los Angeles wasn't the Deep South but it wasn't New York either, and Hollywood was only one of many predominantly redneck communities. Interracial couples were routinely stopped by the local police in most parts of the city and were often brought to the station to be searched. A black man with a fancy car was an automatic suspect, as likely to be pulled in for questioning as he was to be given a ticket — no matter that he hadn't broken any traffic laws. In Glendale it was still illegal for a Negro to be in town without a permit after six—black musicians who played the clubs there were escorted to the city limits as soon as the gig finished. I had heard these and many other stories from my brother, who had abandoned me to the straitjacket culture of the Valley when he began attending UCLA in my junior year, so I was surprised to see how relaxed the atmosphere was inside Billy Berg's oasis. Black couples, white couples, interracial couples, chatting and laughing together at the same tables while they grooved to the music of an all-black band. I was dazzled by the sense of sophistication they radiated, by their clothes and the snatches of conversation I overheard. It was the first time I had ever seen whites mixing freely with blacks, and it was a confirmation of everything I felt was wrong with my world. Billy Berg's was only twenty miles or so from Northridge by the newly opened Hollywood Freeway, but it might as well have been the moon in the days before Sputnik, and I knew right then and there that I had to get out—the farther away the better. My father was pushing me to follow Jack to UCLA, but Jack's experience of that racially divided city and the freedom that I'd breathed inside Billy Berg's, a freedom that I knew didn't exist outside its walls, sealed the deal for me. I was going as far away as my father would allow. Leaving the state was out of the question—he had already put his foot down when it came to paying out-of-state tuition—but there was a Baghdad-by-the-Bay to the north that had a reputation for freedom that no other city in the West could match. The next day I told my father that I had decided on Berkeley because of the strength of its music program, but all I really cared about was its proximity to San Francisco and the promise of a life that was entirely different than the life I had known up until then.

3

I SPENT THE REST OF the weekend in San Francisco, hanging out in the jazz clubs and walking around North Beach, where I dipped in and out of my favorite cafés, listening to snatches of poetry and folk music, but much of my time was spent screwing up my courage to ask Elijah for sax lessons. My first semester at Berkeley hadn't disappointed—the school had an excellent music department, as advertised, with a healthy respect for jazz, even if the professors were all white, and I had taken advantage of my newfound freedom to spend most of my weekend hours in San Francisco, listening to whatever musicians were in town and soaking in the bohemian atmosphere of a city that seemed intent on drafting a new narrative for American culture, a city in which blacks and whites, Asians and Mexicans, mingled in the streets with apparent disregard for one another's otherness. But I was still on the outside looking in when it came to the jazz culture that I had idealized while growing up. I had made friends with some talented musicians in school—one of them was even black—but what I really needed was a mentor, an insider in the way that none of my professors or fellow students were. And from the moment I slid open the door to Elijah's cottage, I was sure I had found him. Who knows, perhaps even from the moment I first heard his tenor sax blowing in my window. The question was: would he see it the same way? Throughout the weekend and the first day of classes, I kept reliving our meeting, hopped up on the thought that I now had an authentic black jazzman for a neighbor, wondering whether or not he would be willing to take me on as a student, an idea that began as a hopeful fantasy and ended up as a burning determination to convince him by whatever means possible, even if it meant getting down on my knees and begging at his door.

I didn't have afternoon classes that semester on Tuesdays and Thursdays, so after my last class on Tuesday I jumped on my bike with my sax dangling from the handlebar and pedaled straight to Elijah's cottage. Normally I would have eaten lunch on campus and grabbed a practice room in the basement of the music building, one with a piano whose sound I liked, but all I could think about at that moment was the possibility of taking lessons from a master jazzman. I could hear Elijah improvising as I pulled my bike up to the side gate, and my excitement mounted as I locked the bike and entered the garden with my sax in hand. It would have only taken a few extra minutes to leave my bike at home and walk back, but I didn't want to miss a single minute of his practice session. I took a seat on a porch bench this time and focused my attention on the music. As far as I was concerned, I already was his student and this was lesson number one: listening to the master at work and trying to figure out what he was doing. I can't say I had much success—I still had no explanation for his unfathomable creativity—but I knew I couldn't have found a better model for my own aspirations. If I could ever learn to play half as well as he did, I told myself, I would consider it a life well spent.

Moments after the last note sounded, the door to the cottage slid open and Elijah emerged wearing the same kimono he had been wearing three days earlier.

"I see you brought your sax," he said with a sidelong glance as he looked out at the garden and flexed his fingers.

I took a deep breath, trying to fight back my nervousness. "I was hoping you might agree to give me private lessons. I'll pay whatever you ask. I get a pretty healthy allowance from my father, and I always have something left over each month."

"Private lessons?"

There was a note of curiosity or perhaps surprise in Elijah's voice as his attention rounded on me. For a full minute he examined me in absolute silence, his body perfectly motionless while I fidgeted on the bench, waiting for him to pass sentence. Then he gave a slight nod. "Let's eat," he said. "We'll talk about it after lunch. This time you can help me prepare the meal."

I followed him inside and waited while he washed some rice and put it on to steam. Then he pulled out a wooden chopping board and a stainless steel cleaver and selected some vegetables from a wicker basket beside the sink.

"The first observance when cutting vegetables is to have proper respect for the knife. Treat the knife with respect and it will treat you with respect. That way your fingers will stay attached to your hand." Elijah held a carrot under the faucet and washed it with a stiff-bristled brush. "Now watch carefully, brother," he said, setting the carrot on the board. "This is called a roll cut. The left hand rolls the vegetable, the right hand stays in place. As you get to the fat part of the carrot, you increase the angle to get more surface area, so that each piece cooks evenly." Within seconds perfectly shaped orange slivers slid from the cleaver into a neat little pile. "Now you try. Slowly and with complete attention. As long as you have the knife in your hand, your universe is confined to this cutting board."

I washed the rest of the vegetables and cut them under Elijah's careful tutelage while he chopped up some ginger and whipped together a quick peanut sauce. Then I stood by and watched while he showed me how to stir-fry vegetables: heating the wok until a bead of water vaporized within a second or two, swirling in the oil, then adding the ginger, the soy sauce, and the vinegar, and finally the vegetables in order of hardness. It was remarkably easy, remarkably fast, and remarkably tasty, which made me wonder why I had never bothered to learn before, especially now that I was responsible for my own meals.

Elijah brought out the folding table and the lacquered tableware, but this time, instead of watching with an amused smile while I did my best to accommodate myself on a cushion, he took a few minutes to correct my posture.

"You've spent too much time sitting on chairs, Brother Dan. Learn to sit on the floor; it'll keep you grounded. The earth gives us strength and stability. Learning to sit properly will help you tap into that strength. You'll need it if you want to play a musical instrument. In Japan they say that an artist is suspended between heaven and earth. If you lose your connection to either then your art won't flourish.

Lose your connection to the earth and whatever you create will lack substance; lose touch with heaven and it will lack inspiration. Now let's eat. You look hungry."

That was the beginning of my apprenticeship: learning how to sit—oriental-style. After the meal we went out to the porch and talked for half an hour or so while we digested our food. Elijah wanted to know more about my musical education and exactly what my aspirations were. When he asked me why I wanted to pursue jazz as a career, I told him about the joy I'd felt when I listened to Bird for the first time in my parents' living room. "I want to know what it's like to fly like Bird," I said when I finished telling the story, and I think that was the first time I had ever put into words the longing that had been chasing me since childhood, harrying me toward an as-yet-unknown destination. He must have liked my answer, because he smiled and asked me to put together my sax and play something for him. I thought about playing a Bird solo but it felt a little pretentious; plus I hadn't warmed up yet and the few Bird solos I knew required some serious chops. So I played the solo from "Daddy Plays the Horn" that I had been working on all week, the title track from a Dexter Gordon LP that had just hit the record stores. Elijah stopped me halfway through the second chorus, causing a momentary sense of panic. I was afraid my playing had turned him off, but to my surprise he ducked into the cottage and came out with a pair of cushions.

"The first thing we are going to learn is how to breathe from your abdomen, like a baby breathes. In Japanese the navel area is called the *hara*. It is the source of the body's energy and vitality. If you can make the *hara* your center of gravity, then your upper body will automatically relax and your mind will become steady and decisive. If you can learn to play from your *hara* then your music will have a source of inexhaustible energy to draw from. Master the right posture and the right breathing, and the instrument will play itself. So we'll start there. Now sit like I taught you: back straight, legs crossed. Bring your chin down a little. Okay. Now sway a little from side to side and front to back until you find your center of balance. Okay, good. Now focus your attention just below the navel and imagine that the pit of your belly is the center of your universe..."

I had learned about diaphragmatic breathing in my very first sax lesson, but this was far more involved. For the next twenty minutes I followed Elijah's careful instructions, sitting on the porch with my eyes half-closed, concentrating on my breathing. By the time he ended the exercise, I was astounded just how firm and grounded I felt, how much steadier and calmer. I had no idea what he meant by "the instrument will play itself," but after twenty minutes I was convinced he was right.

"The first step toward learning to master your instrument," he continued, "is learning how to breathe. The next step is learning how to listen. That's what we'll work on for the rest of the lesson."

Just hearing him say the word *lesson* sent a thrill through me! But this was a lesson unlike any I had ever had. Elijah asked me to stretch my legs and make a quick circuit of the garden. Then he had me resume my posture on the cushion and listen to my environment with my eyes half-closed and my gaze lowered and unfocused. There was no further instruction, so I started cataloging the different sounds, making a mental inventory of everything I heard. It was amazing how many different sounds I heard in those next few minutes: at least five different bird calls, the water gurgling into the pool, the rustling of the leaves and bushes, street sounds that I could actually locate floating in over the fence. But after I opened my eyes and told him what I'd heard, he recited a long list of sounds I had missed, including the sounds of my own body — my breathing, the beating of my heart — and the sound of my thoughts, the incessant chatter of my own inner voice. It was a revelation, not just how much was going on around us, but how acute Elijah's hearing was. Then he asked me to focus on specific sounds — a particular bird call, the plashing of the water — and to describe them: their timbre and pitch, their rhythms, even the melodies they made, for each sound indeed was melodic in its own particular way, even if that melody didn't correspond to the twelve tones of our Western scale. And again he pointed out qualities I had missed, qualities that I only heard after he pointed them out. Finally he asked me to listen to the entire tapestry once again, but this time without identifying or differentiating the different sounds, without thinking about them in any way, simply letting them wash up against me, allowing myself to become fully immersed in the aural landscape. I had been listening to music all my life, but I had never really listened to the world itself, to the ocean of sound in which I passed every single second of my day. It was an exhilarating experience, especially once my thoughts quieted enough to let me really appreciate the endless variety of the sonic world.

The lesson lasted an hour and a half, and other than my two choruses of "Daddy Plays the Horn" I didn't touch the sax a single time. But I wasn't frustrated or disappointed. Quite the opposite. Never in my life had I paid so much attention to either my breathing or the act of listening, and by the time the lesson was over I couldn't understand why none of my teachers had ever bothered to train me in those two supremely important faculties. The sax is a wind instrument, after all. It only makes sense that you should learn to master your breathing if you want to master the instrument, but other than a few words about the diaphragm during my first sax lesson and some basic instruction in circular breathing, I had never been taught a single breath-control exercise. I had spent much of my life listening to music with a passion, and I had heard the adage many times that to be a good musician you had to develop a good ear, but other than a few exercises in recognizing intervals, I had never heard any of my teachers talk about the art of listening, much less offer any training in it. Until Elijah. So for all the strangeness of a sax lesson that didn't involve an instrument, I was elated. I felt like I was finally being initiated into a higher understanding of the art.

When the lesson was over, Elijah gave me my assignment for the week, and again it had nothing to do with the saxophone. "I want you to get up early each morning and ride your bike out to the marina. Bring a cushion with you and find a secluded spot where you can sit on the rocks facing the ocean. Practice your breathing exactly as you did today for twenty minutes with proper posture. Concentrate on your *hara* until nothing else exists, just the air filling up your belly and flowing out again, like the waves against the shore. Watch the inflowing and outflowing breath exactly as you might watch the sea rolling in and out, with your body as stable and as firm as the land you're sitting on. Then turn your attention to your ears for the next twenty minutes. Listen to the ocean, to the sound of the waves. Don't think, just listen. Listen to that sound until you feel the waves washing up inside you. Until you *are* the waves. Then come back next Tuesday at three and bring your sax. Depending on how you do with your exercises I may even have you play it."

When I asked Elijah how much I owed him, he gave me an enigmatic smile that I would come to know well in the coming months. "Don't worry, brother," he said. "I'll collect when the time comes, and I give you my word—it won't be more than you can pay. Just don't count on money being involved. You won't get off as easily as that."

4

I WENT HOME THAT AFTERNOON in the throes of an adulation
that rivaled what the average Berkeley freshman felt for James Dean
or Frank Sinatra. My heroes had been jazz musicians for nearly
as long as I could remember, most of them black, and now I had
added another name to the list. I still dreamed of flying like Bird
but now I wanted to blow like Elijah, to cast the same spell over
people that his horn had cast over me. But this was no childhood
dream or adolescent fantasy. Elijah was a real flesh-and-blood jazz
genius and as unlikely as it seemed, he had agreed to take me on
as his student. The jazz Elysium of Bird and Duke and Dizzy that
had seemed so far away to a young kid in the Valley had shown
up wearing a kimono in a cottage at the other end of the block,
and I had just been given permission to sit in. Until then my only
real access to the magical world of modern jazz had been through
records. Even my professors at Berkeley, all accomplished musicians
in their own right, were outsiders when it came to the tradition
that had grown up with King Oliver and Louis Armstrong in New
Orleans and reached its apogee in New York in the forties with
the birth of bebop. But Elijah was the real deal, the music in its
truest incarnation—a black man with a horn—and he had seen
enough in me to agree to teach me the secrets of the art form. It
was something I had fantasized about back in Northridge, like I had
fantasized about playing one day in a biracial band where the only
color anyone cared about was the color of the music, the bluer the
better, but where I grew up the chance of that actually happening
was as unlikely as the chance that I'd grow up to be president. If
anything, the color of my skin was enough of a barrier to keep me
forever on the outside looking in.

I remember fantasizing during high school that I had a split personality divided by instrument. The piano was the instrument of my public persona, that of the promising young pianist who anchored the North Hollywood High band and was accepted into Berkeley during his senior year as a music major with a concentration in composition. Because I could play a mean Dave Brubeck, everyone assumed that he was my idol and my biggest influence—I remember the enthusiastic congratulations I received from my buddies the day before my eighteenth birthday when he became only the second jazz musician ever to appear on the cover of *Time* magazine, almost as if it had been my picture on the cover. I liked Brubeck, his compositions and his flair, and I was even more impressed with him when I found out a few weeks later that he had told Duke Ellington, with whom he was touring when the magazine hit the newsstands, that it should have been him on the cover. But I found his block chords clunky, and anyhow no white pianist I knew of could hold a candle to Bud Powell or Thelonious Monk, whose soulful playing was almost antithetical to the instrument. There is something about the piano that tends to keep you tied to the intellect. I don't know if it's the orderly arrangement of the keys, strapping you to a mathematical grid, or the fact that it's a harmonic instrument, but the piano is inherently cerebral and it's something you can see in most piano players, however hip they may be. There are exceptions, of course—Monk used to get up in the middle of a tune and turn circles in front of his piano with his eyes closed, like a Sufi drunk on devotion—but Monk was from a different planet, and even he thought his way through the music for the most part; he just did it in a way that was utterly idiosyncratic and fiercely innovative. But a horn, like the human voice, is emotional by nature. Your tone reveals something fundamental about your soul, and for this reason you can lose yourself in the music easier than you can with the piano. I was too young to understand this but I could feel it, and as I grew comfortable enough on the sax to start copping solos from my favorite players, I would lock myself in my room and imagine my skin turning as black as Bird's. With the sax you can bend notes, something you can't do with the ivories, and by bending them it was as if my soul could bend its way into an alternate reality, into the community of men and women who had navigated the centuries of oppression and suffering that had given birth to the blues and then to jazz. The survivors of the enforced Calvary that had given the music its emotional ground and its unimpeachable intensity. There were white players in the fifties who could really play, Stan Getz for one, but neither he nor Desmond nor Chet Baker, whom my brother idolized, could reach the emotional depths that the best black horn players could—at least not to my ears. And if they couldn't, then how could I ever hope to do so?

But Elijah wasn't like the other great horn players of his day, black or white. There was something in his playing and in his person that stepped outside the idiom and outside his skin, a spaciousness that would have attracted me even without the music, and which would lead me to understand soon enough that the freedom I was seeking had nothing to do with the color of my skin or the limitations of my culture. It was a quality that resided in the soul and expressed itself even in something as simple as sipping a glass of water. That quality in Elijah was just as evident when he talked as when he played: in his liberal use of silence, just enough and at the right moments to lend his words—or yours—the resonance they deserved; in the way he gave you his full attention whenever you were with him, as if nothing else in the world mattered. He didn't speak with passion but with an awareness and a presence that passion would have undermined, a mindful elegance that was intrinsic to his music, even when he played the blues; and he listened even more eloquently than he talked, not only to your words but to the ripples they raised in the lake of silence. The saxophone, as he liked to say, was merely an instrument. All I saw at first was the music and my unbelievable good fortune, but Elijah's words and the quietness from which they sprang were already working their way inside me, preparing to put an end to my preconceived notions of what the music—and life—were all about.

$$5$$

5

THE MARINA WAS A good three miles from my apartment, and the assignment Elijah gave me didn't exactly mesh with my habit of getting up half an hour before class, jumping in the shower, and hopping on my bike after a banana and a bowl of cereal. So I allowed myself a liberal interpretation of his instructions and went in the late afternoon instead. I stayed to catch the sunset those first few afternoons, and between the beauty of the sun flaming out over the bay and the novelty of the exercise, I thoroughly enjoyed spending the dying hour of the day listening to the sea at the secluded southern edge of the marina, down past Shorebird Park, though there were always other Berkeleyites around at that hour taking in the scenery. But it was when I went early Saturday morning that I had what I consider my first true meditative experience.

I had gone straight to North Beach after my last class on Friday, and as usual I eventually ended up in the Fillmore district, home to the best jazz clubs in the city. Phineas Newborn and his trio — Oscar Pettiford on bass and Kenny Clarke on drums — were headlining at Jackson's Nook, and after the final set I hung around near the bandstand and was rewarded with a chance to talk with Newborn while he was relaxing with a drink. He was a brilliant technician who used both hands when he soloed, something I had never seen before, and I probably learned more about jazz piano in those twenty minutes than I had learned in my first semester at Berkeley. I was pretty hyped up by the time I got to my car, so instead of going straight home I stopped off at the marina. It was getting on three by then and the marina was heavy with fog, cold and lonely — perfect conditions to put a damper on all that nervous energy. I walked down to the same flat-topped boulder I had sat on the previous afternoons, feeling the salt mist wetting my face and the chill gusts from the bay ripping through my jeans and jacket, exactly what I needed to clear my head. I practiced my breathing for about ten minutes, until my agitation subsided enough to turn my attention to the sound of the water, that syncopated, hypnotic wash that has a way of drowning everything else out. Or it would have if not for the foghorns. I knew about the foghorns, of course, that inescapable and oft-cursed presence in every San Franciscan's night—I'd even heard of city residents becoming addicted to sleeping pills solely on their account—but I didn't live near the bay and they had been mercifully quiet during my afternoon practice. But on a foggy marina night there was no escaping them. They were like the soloists in the ocean's big band. You couldn't *not* listen. They dominated the soundscape, rising above the swells and playing off each other like the brass in Basie's band: one directly across the bay at Point Bonita in Sausalito, one on Alcatraz, one each on either side of the Golden Gate Bridge, and two more guarding the entrance to the bay. Point Bonita was the closest and the loudest: a one-second blast on Gabriel's horn followed by two seconds of silence, then a two-second blast and a twenty-five-second rest. When Point Bonita put down its horn, Alcatraz stepped up, a bit farther away and off to the left: two seconds on, two off, two on again, and then twenty-four seconds of silence. Behind them and farther away, the other four horns played a supporting role, each with its own distinctive pattern providing counterpoint to its colleagues, all woven together in the early morning silence that wasn't silence at all but an undulating tapestry of sound underpinned by the omnipresent backwash of the water scudding against the shore. The foghorn blasts were jarring at first, seemingly intent on sabotaging my concentration, but once I began to listen to the entire soundscape as I would listen to a piece of music, they began to blend in as any soloist would who had a feel for the rhythm section. It didn't take long before I discovered that what I was hearing wasn't a meaningless disordered jumble of sounds but a kind of orchestral performance that had a logic all its own—not that much different, really, than the logic of any musical ensemble. In the case of the foghorns, there was noticeable human intent—a deliberate pattern of sounds divided by location, time, and timbre that helped mariners navigate their entrance or exit from the bay on a night shrouded by fog—but the quieter my thoughts, the more the natural sounds, those devoid of human intention, seemed no less deliberate, no less patterned, just subtler, more intuitive, as if they were the product of a far greater musical imagination that lay beyond the reach of my understanding. But understanding wasn't the point of the exercise, at least not any kind of intellectual understanding. The point was the sounds themselves, to let them wash over you and through you, until, as Elijah put it, "they are sounding inside of you rather than outside, until you are the sound and the sound is you." I didn't quite get there but I got close, close enough to glimpse what Elijah was talking about, to give myself up, shivering as I was, to the music of the world around me, until for a few tantalizing moments I forgot myself entirely.

It was exhilarating and calming at the same time. When I made it home that morning, I was even more excited than I had been after my lesson, but it was a different kind of excitement, the kind that comes from a quiet mind and pleasant waters. I had realized—not on an intellectual level but on an intuitive level, through experience—that there was a lot more to what he had taught me than just learning to control my diaphragm and fine-tune my ear. This was a whole new approach to music—a whole new approach to life, in fact, though I don't know if I thought of it yet in those terms—and before my next lesson I returned twice more to the marina in the early morning hoping to replicate the experience, with varying degrees of success.

When Tuesday afternoon rolled around, I couldn't wait to tell Elijah. He was sitting on a porch bench when I arrived, wearing an ash-gray kimono this time with a printed pattern of brown and green bamboo shoots. Next to him on the bench were a couple of cushions. The first thing he asked me was how my practice had gone—the same question that would begin all our lessons from there on out—and I wasn't shy about telling him. Under different circumstances I might have been intimidated by Elijah, by both his musical and physical presence, but for whatever reason I felt perfectly at home on his porch, as if I had known him all my life—or even longer. Elijah didn't say much while I was talking, a brief question or two and an occasional nod of the head, but he listened with such unwavering attention that I felt sure he heard not only everything I said, but much of what I didn't say, those facets of my experience that went unvoiced because I hadn't yet understood them myself. When I finally ran out of steam he broadened his smile and said, "Well, I think I'm going to have you play the sax today, after all. But just one note."

"One note?"

"If you can play one note well, then you can play any note well. But playing one note well is not as easy as it sounds, brother. First let's do some breathing practice and a little listening."

This time, instead of guiding me through the breathing and listening exercises, Elijah sat on a cushion next to me and joined me in my practice, but instead of the simple cross-legged posture he'd adopted the two times I had joined him for lunch, he placed his legs effortlessly in the full-lotus posture, the right foot resting on the left thigh and the left foot on the right. He was a big man, but when he sat on his cushion he was the image of elegance, like a living statue. It would be many months before I could sit in full lotus, but I was so impressed with his posture I made a conscious effort to emulate his graceful ease and obvious relaxation.

Once we finished our practice, I assembled my sax, curious about what kind of unusual lesson awaited me—I had already learned to be on the lookout for the unusual with Elijah—but I had another unexpected hoop to pass through before he would let me play that single note. First he wanted to review my fingerings. There was nothing unusual about this, although he did insist that I learn all the alternate fingerings for the altissimo notes, but when he was satisfied, he had me play through all twelve diatonic scales without touching my lips to the reed.

"For now I just want you to be aware of your fingers. Not the fingerings—the fingers. Think of it as a dance. Your fingers are like dancers moving across a stage. The more graceful their movements, the more artistic the dance. But you can't force grace. It comes of its own accord when you fully give yourself up to the dance. And to do that you have to learn the steps to the point that you can forget about them and let the dance take over. Your fingers know what they have to do. They don't need you to think for them. They know the choreography. Just sit back and appreciate the dance. If you notice any tension, any jerkiness or stiffness, just be aware of it. Don't try to correct anything. Your fingers are on their own. You're just observing, getting to know them, in the same way that you got to know the birds and the water. And really, they're no different. Your fingers are just as much a part of nature as the birds and water are. So breathe and watch your fingers in the same way that you breathe and listen to the world. Okay?"

It was an interesting exercise. It took some real attention not to think about the scale I was playing but to divorce myself, so to speak, from the saxophonist and step back into the audience. Fortunately it wasn't that much different than my listening practice, and I soon got the hang of it. As Elijah said, it was very much like a dance, a clackety form of modern dance with keys for castanets.

After ten minutes or so of silent scales I finally got my chance to blow—a single sustained note that Elijah had me repeat over and over again in different registers. "Tone," he emphasized, "is all about character. Have you ever heard a singer's voice crack because they can't contain their emotion? Sadness, joy, compassion, apathy—it's all there in the voice. The same is true with wind instruments. The sax is not only an extension of your breath, it's an extension of your voice—that's why no two instrumentalists have the same tone. Some people think that tone depends on the reed, the embouchure, and the quality of the instrument, but actually it depends on who's playing the instrument. Physically it comes from the larynx but really it comes from the soul. That's why you'll never sound like Bird. You can imitate a person's voice, but anyone with any ear at all will hear the difference. The same goes for the saxophone. Each person's tone is unique. It's a product of their character, the tenor of their mind, the depth and quality of their emotions. The purpose of this exercise is to find your tone and settle into it. If you can blow one true note, true to yourself, then you will have found your voice. The rest is just what you have to say on that particular day, and that's as variable as the wind. Remember, brother: it's not only what you say that matters, it's who's saying it."

Elijah went inside to get his tenor and I found myself thinking of Billie Holiday, how you could hear the unmistakable pathos in her voice, a quality so searing it left an indelible stamp on whatever tune she sang. Her tone was everything. I had never really thought about it before, but I realized immediately that the same was true for Miles and Bird and Dizzy. I could always tell right away who was playing, even if I hadn't seen the record jacket or heard the tune before, just from their tone. When Elijah came back with his sax, he asked me to blow a middle register B-flat and hold it for a full minute while staying as relaxed as possible. Holding the note wasn't difficult—I had been practicing circular breathing since grade school—but maintaining what I considered a good tone was a different matter. Then Elijah blew the same note. Only it wasn't the same note. It was rounder, fuller, lighter, and far more relaxed, imbued with a reflective calm that brought out the beauty of the instrument. I could hear the bay at night in his sax, overtones of the Orient drifting in above the fog like nectar for the imagination, and I found myself closing my eyes to drink in the rich timbre of his single note.

Elijah let the note die out and then waited for me to open my eyes. "There's an ancient Chinese text that says that a satisfying tone should convey happiness, elegance, sadness, sweetness, subtlety, resonance, and strength. Those qualities have to be inside you before you can bring them out. And they're there. It's just a question of allowing your humanity to flower. Now blow that B-flat again, brother, and this time don't try so hard. Don't try at all. Just relax and listen to the sound of your horn the same way that you listen to mine. Don't try to control it, just listen. If you listen well, you'll hear yourself in your instrument."

And so I blew, and blew some more, always the same note, and gradually I began to hear myself in my sax: my sense of insecurity, my ambitions, the mental disquiet that made my tone thin and unsteady, so unlike Elijah's full, confident, relaxed sound. But it was mine, as Elijah emphasized several times, mine and no one else's. "Listen to yourself play," he told me, "and it'll help you discover who you are.

As you grow, your tone will grow, and if you can grow your tone, then you will grow your self. It works both ways." I wasn't about to ask him what he meant. I knew he wanted me to experience it for myself, and I already had enough trust in Elijah by then to believe that eventually I would.

The last part of the lesson was the most unusual but in some strange way the most comforting, perhaps because I felt privileged that Elijah shared it with me.

"Now I want you to sit here and watch," he said, "and try to get a sense of what I'm doing." Elijah went back into the cottage and emerged with several large sticks of lighted incense. He walked slowly and solemnly to where the Buddha presided over his miniature lake. With the same sense of elegance with which he sat, he knelt in front of the statue with his head lowered and began waving the incense in graceful circles while chanting in a low monotone a long string of syllables that I assumed to be Japanese. After five or six minutes of this exotic and intriguing ritual, he placed the incense sticks in the stone incense burner just in front of the statue, touched his head to the ground, and came back to the porch where he sat down in silence, his face a picture of repose.

"The practice of any art form," he said, breaking the silence several minutes later, "is fundamentally an aesthetic and spiritual discipline whose goal is the attainment of freedom. When you learn Chinese calligraphy, you practice each individual brush stroke over and over and over again, so that when the time comes to draw the complete character you can do it without thinking. It's only when you can draw without thinking that great art becomes possible; otherwise, the mind gets in the way. Music is no different. Every element of the art form must be refined to the point where you can do it without thinking, until it becomes as natural and as unforced as your breathing. When you approach your practice in this spirit, it inevitably acquires an element of ritual, a ceremonial atmosphere. And that is what transforms the practice of art into something sacred. That's what lifts it above the mundane and into the transcendental. So now, tell me, what did you feel when you saw me performing my Buddhist ritual?"

"Wow … I'm not sure how to describe it … It was a bit strange at first, but very dignified somehow, very quieting … I guess I would say that I felt transported. Like I was in a Buddhist temple somewhere watching the priest contemplate the mysteries of existence."

Elijah let out a soft, almost inaudible laugh. "I couldn't have said it better myself. The sole purpose of the ritual is to make us aware of the mystery that surrounds us. Now if you can approach your practice session in the same spirit, then you will discover music's power to transport you out of yourself and into something greater, out of your small mind and into big mind. I don't mean that you should burn incense or bow five times to Mecca before you pick up your instrument. Those are just props for people who need them. What I mean is that you should be aware of the true purpose of your practice. It will make a world of difference, brother. I can promise you that."

In the weeks to come Elijah would fine-tune each segment of my daily practice: breathing exercises, listening exercises, tone, scales, arpeggios, patterns, and finally structured solos followed by the unrestrained joy of free-form blowing, the same routine that I'd heard from my apartment window the morning I moved in and which I would continue to hear at the same hour any day thereafter that I happened to be at home. It did indeed become a ritual, one that gave a welcome sense of order to an increasingly disordered life. Elijah's regimen was specifically designed to train me to gain mastery of my instrument, and through my instrument, mastery of myself. Though it took me a while to begin thinking in those terms, I could feel the effect of that discipline almost immediately, and the effect only grew stronger with time. For the first time ever, I felt like I was starting to catch hold of the reins of my life. Just in time, as it turned out. It was a very unbohemian approach to jazz, of course, and that would introduce a discordant note into my days, but discord is the soul of jazz and this was a healthy discord. As the chaos grew and I became increasingly swept up in the fervor of the San Francisco cultural revolution, the rising swell of late-fifties bohemia that would give birth to the flower children of the sixties, it was Elijah's discipline with its sacred overtones that kept me grounded. Who knows where I would have been without it.

6

MY FRIENDSHIP WITH DIANA dates from the following weekend, but it wasn't the first time our paths had crossed. I'd run into her twice before, and from those two brief encounters I had already formed an image of her as the prototypical bohemian poet, which was a quasi-mythological figure in the Bay Area of those days. The first time was in October at The Place on Grant Street. I was still new to the area, but I was already under the spell of the flourishing bohemian counterculture that was so unlike anything I'd been exposed to in Southern California, and The Place was one of those cultural hot spots where the avant-garde used to congregate. If you hung out there long enough on any given night, you were bound to see some of the luminaries of what was already beginning to be called the "beat movement," huddled over their beers and debating the state of the world in conversations that would one day be immortalized in print. Wednesday night was Blabbermouth Night. There was a small loft at the back, affectionately known as the "blabber box." They would set out a yellow soapbox on the railing with the words "soap for cultural sanity" inscribed on it, and anybody who wanted could stand behind it in the blabber box and compete for the grand prize: a bottle of champagne. There were always poets in attendance who would try out their latest verses, and an occasional stand-up comic, but by and large it was just what the soapbox implied: an open venue for political harangues and all-around venting — North Beach-style. In other words, the more outrageous the better, like the time Barney Google launched a campaign to wall off North Beach and charge admission fees for nonbohemians. The crowd would really get into it, hooting and hollering and egging on the speakers, shouting out questions or comments, and even in some cases hooting them from the stage. But the moment Diana mounted the steps to the blabber box, a hush fell over the crowd and people started snapping their fingers, something they had begun doing during poetry readings in North Beach. They seemed to know who she was but I didn't, and yet, even if I had been talking, the sight of her would have shut me up. She wasn't pretty—at least I didn't think so at first—but she was striking: black velvet slacks cut off just below the knees with the straps of her sandals rising up to meet them, a handwoven purple sash wrapped around her waist, long copper earrings, and a sheer black blouse that was barely but tantalizingly visible behind a wild mop of sandy-brown hair that fell over her shoulders and breasts, making her seem like some grinning Italian Medusa daring you to look her in the eyes. She was bobbing her head to the finger snapping, still not saying anything yet, and I found myself pushing to get closer on a night that was so crowded the lone waitress had trouble getting through to bring people their drinks. By the time she started reciting her poem, the room was silent except for the finger snaps, a perfect blend of hushed anticipation and bohemian groove. I don't remember what she read, just my reaction, which veered very close to astonishment. The poem was very radical, very clever, and rather raunchy—liberally sprinkled with the kind of public obscenities that could get you arrested in those days—and she had a hip, infectious energy that made the language seem to jump out and grab you by the throat. And in other parts of your anatomy as well. I was astounded because I was still in many ways an uptight kid from the Valley and I don't think I had ever seen a person less affected by convention. She couldn't have opened herself up more if she had taken her clothes off right there on that makeshift stage. I was also astounded because I hadn't realized how close poetry could come to jazz. She was snapping her fingers with everyone else, keeping time with her body like a dancer and inflecting her voice and playing with the sounds and rhythms of the words like a jazz singer scatting over changes. I hadn't thought she was pretty at first, but after ten minutes of staring into that Medusa-like face and falling under the spell of words and rhythms that seemed the match of a good jazz solo, I was convinced she was the most attractive girl on the California coast. And the most talented as well. I would have given anything to talk to her after she stepped down to a sea swell of applause and congratulatory caterwauling, but I didn't have the courage, and anyhow she was quickly swallowed up by a crowd of admirers far more hip than myself. The best I could do was to turn her name over on my tongue and dream about the day she would hear me play and fall under the very same spell.

That next time turned out to be December, and to my astonishment my dreams were surprisingly prescient. By then I had gotten over some of my congenital shyness and was starting to feel at home in the city that had been the principle reason for my emigration from the Valley. It was common in those days to come upon small impromptu jam sessions at some of the coffee houses and bars of North Beach, and I began bringing my saxophone with me on weekends when I would head over the bridge. Any lack of confidence I had generally disappeared when I had an instrument in my hands, so whenever I got the chance I started sitting in, usually on the sax but sometimes on piano, if there was one. My first real gig came the week before finals when the owner of the Coffee Gallery, Leo Riegler, agreed to let me and a couple of classmates play a short warm-up set on a Friday night before Pony Poindexter came on—Leo had heard me sit in once or twice in afternoon jam sessions and figured it was worth a few free beers for me and my buddies. We were about halfway through our little set when Diana walked in with a couple of female friends and took a table uncomfortably close to where we were playing. The Coffee Gallery had an old Kimball upright, but I was playing the sax in our little trio—piano, bass, and alto—and that gave me a chance to look Diana's way without being conspicuous about it. She seemed to enjoy the music—all three of them did—and she even seemed to have a special smile for my solos, the same electric smile I remembered from the reading.

When we finished our set she came up to me without a second glance for my buddies. "That was really cool, man. I really dug it. I gotta go but I'll see you around, okay?" Her friends were waiting for her at the door so that was the extent of our conversation, but I went home that night sure that the interest wasn't entirely one-sided.

I ran into Diana again at Bop City in the Fillmore, the weekend after my second lesson with Elijah. Bop City was officially a waffle house—the owner, Jimbo Edwards, didn't have a liquor license—but once the 2 AM curfew rolled around, it became *the* after-hours club in San Francisco, what Minton's Playhouse was to New York in the forties. The list of those who had jammed there would have made up a who's who of modern jazz: Bird, Dexter Gordon, Billie Holiday—even Louis Armstrong had dropped by once to listen to Bird. The musicians would start appearing as soon as their paying gigs let out, and the jam session would still be going strong at dawn. Black or white, it didn't matter. Anybody could sit in as long as they could hold their own on the bandstand without getting cut too badly. For the hepcats in the music department at Berkeley it was *the* place to be in the wee hours of the weekend. You could always find some of us there, grooving to the music and hoping for a chance to sit in. I was at a table in the back that night, munching on peanuts and listening to Frank Foster trade choruses with Sonny Stitt, who was in town with Billy Eckstine's band. Flip Nuñez was on piano—Jimbo had a Baldwin baby grand in excellent condition—but I don't remember who else was sitting in. I mostly remember Diana. She showed up about a half hour after I did and came straight to my table, flashing the same smile that I had been dreaming about since before the Christmas break.

"You gonna sit in?" she asked as she pulled up a chair and sat down beside me, leaning over so she wouldn't have to raise her voice.

I shook my head, startled by this sudden apparition. "I don't think so," I said, making an effort not to sound surprised. "Flip looks like he's going to be going strong for a while."

"Flip Nuñez? But he's a piano player. You're a saxophonist."

"I am actually more of a pianist. I wouldn't dare get up there with my sax, not with those guys."

"Okay. Cool. By the way, do you remember me?" She leaned back and turned her head in profile, first one way then the other, and amped up her smile, which was about as coquettish as Diana ever got.

"Sure, I remember," I said, unable to stifle a laugh. "You were at the Coffee Gallery last month during our gig. Actually, I'd seen you before, you just didn't know it. It was at The Place a few months ago, on Blabbermouth Night. Diana, right?"

Maybe it was the setting, maybe the music, maybe it was Diana and her freewheeling ways, but I felt surprisingly unselfconscious. We sat there until four, trading comments and snapping our fingers and whistling or cheering after a particularly hot passage, but mostly just listening, absorbing the energy of some excellent musicians in the best of settings. They weren't playing for the crowd at Bop City, they were playing for themselves, challenging each other, seeing if they could break new ground, the kind of setting that has produced some of the most memorable moments in jazz, moments that never made it to vinyl, though the ideas that were spawned in those late night sessions would provide source material for some of the most famous recorded solos in the jazz archives.

During the applause after a fifteen-minute rendition of "Body and Soul," Diana squeezed my arm and told me she had to head back. I offered her a ride and a few minutes later we were out on Post, wrapping our scarves around our necks and zipping up our jackets. The fog was moving in, advancing up the street from the bay like a stalker on the prowl, and I told her in my most gallant manner that a lady shouldn't have to walk in this fog. I took her the eight blocks to Fillmore, where she was staying, and when I jumped out to open the car door for her—something I had always wanted to do, having been raised on the movies of the forties and fifties (she got out before I could actually open the door)—she asked me to come up. The apartment belonged to a friend of hers, the artist Joan Brown. It was a building full of artists, in fact, that some people took to calling "Painterland." Wally Hedrick and Jay DaFeo lived downstairs in the same apartment where DaFeo would later spent eight years painting her masterpiece, *The Rose*. There were more painters in the upstairs apartments, and Joan Brown was always putting up other artists in her spacious flat—in those days San Francisco was as much a mecca for painters and visual artists as it was for poets. Diana had a room to herself at the time, and once she opened the door to the apartment she grabbed my hand and led me straight there. "There's no point in you going all the way back to Berkeley at this hour," she said. "You can sleep here." No preliminaries, no romantic prelude. She was out of her clothes and helping me out of mine before I had time to close the bedroom door. I'd had a couple of near misses with a pair of Berkeley girls during my first semester, and the usual awkward petting attempts in high school with girls even shyer than myself, but until that morning I was probably the oldest virgin still walking the streets of San Francisco—or Berkeley, for that matter. Once again I was astounded, but it turned out to be nothing like I had imagined. Diana ushered me into the mysteries of sex in a way so natural, so down-to-earth, so matter-of-fact, that I wondered why I had wasted so much time and energy in the whole adolescent buildup—or why anybody else did. She put her wealth of experience to excellent use, as near as I could tell, but I got the impression, as we lay back sprawled out on her bed with our heads propped up on a huge pair of downy pillows, watching the dawn grow rosy outside her bedroom window, that she enjoyed the conversation afterward even more than the sex. And once my excitement simmered down, I think I felt the same.

I had grown up swapping ideas with my brother and a few close friends, and sometimes engaging in long debates about the merits of this musician or that movie, but I had never met a conversationalist like Diana. She had something unique to say about everything, and she was even more curious to hear what you had to say. The most innocuous remark on my part could spark her off, sending her on some wild, unexpected tangent, and at times I found the same thing happening to me, almost as if her fecund inventiveness was a communicable disease—which probably explained why the sex seemed like foreplay: it could never live up to the conversation that followed. No wonder she turned out to be such a prolific and original poet: her mind was fertile ground and she never let a day go by without cultivating the soil.

We spent that first night swapping coming-to-age tales from opposite coasts. I drew the curtain back on the ultra-conventional fantasyland of the San Fernando Valley—which for some inexplicable reason she found endlessly fascinating—and she regaled me with stories of growing up in ultra-hip New York: cutting class with a friend at Hunter High to go hang out in Union Square, where they would debate for hours with an eclectic blend of anarchists, communists, and fascists, the combatants pelting each other with vegetables to show their fury with one another's political ideas; roaming the all-hours coffee shops of the Village, where the city's poets, amped up on espresso, would congregate to talk about their work and scribble in their notebooks; discovering Garbo, Dietrich, and Jean Cocteau in the Museum of Modern Art film series and stumbling along the way into a lifelong love of Picasso and the other giants of modern art; wandering into the Actors Studio and having Lee Strasberg use one of her monologues for an afternoon student exercise; moving into a cold-water flat after dropping out of Brooklyn College and having to rip up the floorboards on a January night to burn in the stove so she could keep from freezing to death; the string of kooky lovers that seemed to come with the apartment, mostly women, some men, a lot of them openly gay, but all artists of one kind or another; and my favorite: meeting Bird outside a Manhattan tavern where he was handing out fliers for his next gig, striking up a flirtatious conversation with the surprisingly garrulous jazzman, and then catching him and Dizzy that night at the Open Door and dozens of other times after that, along with most of the other jazz musicians whom I had idolized while growing up—Miles at the Café Bohemia, Monk at the Five Spot, venues that had achieved sacred status in my imagination.

We had just finished comparing our first impressions of *Rebel Without a Cause,* surprised to find out that we had been in the same theater on opening night, when James Dean reminded her of Jack Kerouac passing around a gallon jug of wine during the Six Gallery reading, and of her other New York friends who had come out to San Francisco bringing the revolution with them, iconic characters like Corso and Ginsberg, who was in the Northwest at the moment but expected back in a few weeks.

"So that's why you came out here," I said. "You were following them."

"Not them, featherbrain," she said, knocking me on the head with a throw pillow. "The muse. I came out here to rescue her. Men have been holding her hostage since the ancient Greeks and I intend to break her loose."

"You don't say. And then what? You're going to bring her back to New York?"

"You're damn straight."

I had never heard the expression before—some kind of New York slang, I assumed—but I could guess what it meant. "And what if the muse likes it out here?" I said. "Did you ever think of that?"

"Sure, I thought of it. But there's a big difference between taking a vacation and settling down for good. She belongs in Olympus and Olympus is that way—east about three thousand miles. You'll know you're there when you see the Statue of Liberty. If the gods ever take up full-time residence in California, then cool, she can move out here and settle down, and I'll be right behind her. But for now New York is the land of poets and that's not going to change anytime soon. Look at it this way: You're a jazzbo. Where did Bird go to make a name for himself? Where did Miles go, Dizzy, Lady Day?"

"New York."

"Right. And none of them were New Yorkers. They had to go to Olympus if they wanted to live with the other gods of jazz. It's the same way with poets. You guys have your muse and we have ours. And they both live in New York."

"So once you find your muse and break her free you'll be heading back?"

"Don't worry, Blondie. It won't be for a while yet. I have to complete your education first." She added a wicked smile that sent a thrill through me.

Diana was only three years older than me, but it felt more like twenty. She had hitchhiked to the Coast in September with twelve dollars in her pocket, following the trail of poets who had temporarily defected from Olympus, in a time when a woman hitchhiking alone was practically unheard of. Half the people who picked her up only did so so they could lecture her on why no decent young woman should be hitchhiking. Being Diana, she lectured them right back and probably turned some heads with her charm. Even in those days Diana had very strong ideas about the second-class status of women in American society, and she was determined to do something about it. The male poets were almost as bad as bankers in this respect, she told me. They treated their women like groupies, food for their appetites and material for their muse — or worse, like secretaries. But they wouldn't put down a good poem when they heard one, whatever its sex of origin, and that was the battlefield on which she had chosen to wage her one-woman war.

"These guys think they are going to change the world," she said. "And they just might do it. But if they do, they're not going to do it without me. Somebody's got to show Emperor Macho that he's not wearing any clothes. It might as well be me. What about you? Where do you stand? What would you say, for instance, to a woman saxophonist or pianist who wanted to play bebop? Would you hand her a microphone and tell her to stick to singing?"

That made me hesitate for a long moment. We had some great scat singers like Ella Fitzgerald that could hold their own with an improvised line, and the pure genius of Billie Holiday, who could turn any tune into a masterpiece, but in those days there were no female jazz instrumentalists that I knew of. Their place *was* behind the microphone, at least that was the way it had always been. But I could see Diana's condemnation bearing down on me, and that was enough to make me admit that there was no real reason why it had to be that way. I may have hesitated but when I did speak, it was with a newfound conviction.

"I say if she can blow like Bird, then why not? Black or white, female, male, or Martian, it's the music that counts."

"Right answer, Blondie."

"So I passed the test?"

"You passed."

That took us into a long discussion about women in the arts that eventually ended in sleep.

I woke up at noon with Diana still asleep in the bed beside me. I was a little dizzy from the late hour and the residual buzz from our long conversation, so I sat up and did my breathing and listening exercises, familiarizing myself with the San Francisco street sounds in a way I had never done before. Diana was awake and propped up on a pillow when I opened my eyes.

"You a Buddhist?" she asked.

"A Buddhist? No. But my sax teacher is. At least I think he is. I never actually asked him. I was just doing some breathing and listening exercises he taught me. I've only been at it a couple of weeks but they're really helping my playing."

"What kind of breathing and listening exercises?"

I started telling her what Elijah had taught me, even a bit about my experience at the marina.

"So you're meditating."

"Meditating?" I said, truly puzzled.

"Of course. What do you think those exercises are?"

"Breathing and listening exercises."

Diana snorted in delight. "Dan the man. You really are from the suburbs, aren't you? That's meditation you're doing, guy. Zazen. You're a gone bhikkhu and you don't even know it."

"A what?"

"You'll find out when you meet Jack and Gary and the rest of the Bodhisattvas. Better you ask them. I don't know Zen from Xanadu. But I know enough to know that that's meditation you're doing. Which actually seems to be more than you know. So who is this guy, this sax teacher of yours?"

I told her about Elijah and his garden, how we had met and some of the things he had said, and she got a curious look on her face.

"Is he a real big guy, talks with some kind of southern accent?"

"Yeah. You know him?"

"Sounds like the guy they call Preacher."

"That's him, Preacher."

"I never met him but my friend Gary knows him. Gary's one of the poets I told you about that read at the Six Gallery. Gary calls him "the jazz master." He says he used to be some sort of Zen monk. Even lived in a temple in Japan and all that. Probably took a vow to enlighten all the sentient beings of the world before slipping off to nirvana and having a grand old time for the rest of eternity. That's the way they talk, all of them: Kerouac, Snyder, Watts, Whalen,

Dalenberg, the whole gone gang of them. Not me though. You won't catch me in a kimono contemplating my navel. So you're not a Buddhist?"

"No, I'm a musician."

"Okay, but just wait till Gary and Jack get hold of you, once they hear who you're taking sax lessons from. Prepare to be fattened up and sacrificed at the altar of pointless conversation. Jack will stuff you so full of the void they'll have to tie a string to you to keep you from floating away, and Gary will have you scribbling ideograms and squinting your eyes like a proper Oriental. Better beat than Buddhist, I tell them, but they seem to think the two fit together like yin and yang."

And that was how I learned that I had begun meditating. I had a vague idea that Buddhists practiced meditation, not that I had any real notion what meditation was, but for some reason I hadn't connected the dots until that day on Diana's bed. It was a little disconcerting, but there was nothing I could do other than wait to ask Elijah about it when I met him for my next lesson.

It was a curious footnote to my friendship with Diana. She was the one who first pointed out to me the path I was on, and later I would be the one to point out the path to her.

7

It was raining when I showed up at Elijah's cottage on Tuesday. The gusting wind drove the rain onto the porch so we stayed indoors. As usual Elijah wanted to know how my practice had gone, and that gave me a chance to bring up Diana's comments.

"I was with a friend of mine over the weekend, and she told me that the breathing exercise you taught me is actually Buddhist meditation."

"Is that so?"

"That's what she said."

Elijah shrugged his shoulders. "Okay, then call it meditation. Now let's start with our breathing."

I found his indifference unsettling. He didn't seem to see the point of my observation, almost as if it were a complete non sequitur, but after a few minutes counting my breaths I decided it didn't really matter. So I was meditating. That didn't make me a Buddhist. Or did it? I really wasn't sure how these things worked. I had grown up as a Methodist but religion hadn't played much of a role in our house. As far as I could see, the main reason we went to church on Sundays was so that the other families in our social circle would see us there. If you weren't at church, people would talk and nobody wanted that. So you went to church and listened to a few homilies, and when it was over you said hello to your friends and shook hands with the pastor. That was the extent of it until another Sunday rolled around, at least in our house. So if going to church on Sundays made me a Methodist, a practice I abandoned without a second thought the moment I left home, did practicing Buddhist meditation somehow turn me into a Buddhist? Or was it like the classical piano module that was required for music majors? It was good for my technique but it didn't make me a classical musician. That seemed to make sense to me, so I put the thought on the back burner and returned to counting my breaths, letting the question of religion blend in with the other mental distractions that I was becoming increasingly aware of every time I sat.

For the last part of the lesson Elijah broke out his tenor sax and played a walking bass line in the low register while I practiced soloing over changes, doing my best to play without thinking, as he had been drumming into me since the first time we'd met. I thought I was blowing pretty well but Elijah obviously thought otherwise.

"Relax!" he barked, putting down his horn. It wasn't exactly a reprimand but it wasn't a pat on the back either.

"But I thought I was sounding pretty good," I answered. Wrong answer. Elijah's voice dropped in volume but increased in severity.

"There is a sign by the door when you come in. Go out and read it. Then come back and tell me what it says."

I knew very well what the sign said. I remained where I was, glued to my cushion, burning from the chagrin that I had no doubt was mirrored on my face.

"Well?"

"It says, Leave your ego at the door."

"And did you leave yours at the door when you came in? Is that what made you so proud of your playing?"

I didn't say anything. I just shook my head.

"I could hear the mental noise in every note, brother, which is why there was nothing fresh in what you played, nothing spontaneous. It was all recycled ideas. As long as you insist on thinking while you play, your music will be earthbound. Is that what you want? Or do you want to use your horn to fly?"

I wanted to fly, of course, the way he was able to do, and he knew that.

Elijah picked up his sax again. He had been kneeling, but now he bound his legs in the lotus posture with the barrel of his horn resting on the floor and his eyes closed. "Listen," he said. For at least a minute he didn't play, though his lips were brushing the reed. The silence kept growing until it seemed enormous. Then he started blowing, the purest, most beautiful stream of notes I had ever heard, like the transparent waters of a mountain stream, the sound of the world itself, majestic and indecipherable. When he stopped several minutes later I had tears in my eyes.

"If you want to play like this, you have to play the same way that water falls." His exact words and the exact image that had been in my mind. "Without thought, without conscious design. You must exist as music in the same way that falling water exists as falling water. In Japan the word for meditation is *zazen*—sitting Zen. There is also walking Zen, standing Zen, laughing Zen. This is *jazuzen*, jazz Zen, the music of no-mind. All truly spontaneous artistic creations are born in a state of emptiness in which there is no striving, no expectation, no clinging, no purposefulness—only awareness. It is that emptiness that gives you wings. What was the first thing I taught you?"

"How to breathe."

"And how do we begin each practice session?"

"With breathing practice."

"We begin by cultivating the presence of mind that is a prerequisite for the creation of great art. We begin by trying to empty ourselves of the ego. It's that state of emptiness that makes the impossible possible. Everything we practice on the horn has one purpose and one purpose only: to smooth the way to this state of mind. If you stumble over the elements of music, or if your technique gets in the way, then you'll start thinking again and your mind will muck everything up. So you practice the elements of the music until they become automatic. Then you can relax and *be* the music. When you meditate you cultivate this presence of mind, and when you play your instrument you do the same. There is no difference. Okay? Now play again. And this time, brother, relax. All you are doing is watching your breath, watching your breath become sound. That's all. Don't worry about the notes. Just relax."

Jazz Zen. So that was what he was teaching me. I knew the first half of the equation but not the second, so when the lesson was over I asked Elijah if he had any books on Zen he could lend me.

"You want a book?"

"If you have one. I've heard about Zen but I don't really know what it is. If I'm going to be practicing jazz Zen it would be kind of nice to know something about the Zen part of it."

I don't think I sounded too confident, but Elijah went to his bookshelf and pulled out a thin book protected by a book cover that looked to be recycled from a brown paper bag. It was a collection of forty-eight koans entitled *The Gateless Gate*, each koan accompanied by a commentary and a short verse by the Chinese Zen master Mumon—Ekai in Japanese—and as I learned in the introduction, it was a fundamental text in the Rinzai school of Zen Buddhism. I had no idea what a koan was, and the short introduction did little to clear up my ignorance, but these seemingly insoluble riddles and puzzling commentaries so incited my curiosity that I read the entire book that night and again the next day when instead of taking a practice room during my two-hour midday break, I bought a carton of milk from a dispenser and ate my sandwich under a tree in front of the music building with *The Gateless Gate* propped up on my knees. I found it almost as baffling the second time through as I skipped around to the sections that had most caught my attention the night before, racking my brain trying to extract some hidden logic from what seemed a brilliant exercise in illogical wisdom. My favorite was number twenty-nine, perhaps because it was the one that seemed most intelligible:

> Two monks were arguing about a flag. One said the flag was moving; the other said the wind was moving. The sixth patriarch, Huineng, who happened to be passing by, said, "Not the wind, not the flag; mind is moving."
>
> This was followed by Mumon's comment: The sixth patriarch said, "The wind is not moving, the flag is not moving; mind is moving." What did he mean? If you truly understand this, you will see the two monks there trying to buy iron and gaining gold. The sixth patriarch could not bear to see those two dullards, so he made such a bargain.

> *Wind, flag, mind moves.*
> *The same understanding.*
> *When the mouth opens*
> *All are wrong.*

I had asked Elijah the previous day if he would be willing to give me lessons twice a week, and to my surprise he had agreed without the slightest hesitation—Tuesdays and Thursdays, my two free weekday afternoons. We hadn't discussed payment yet, but I had the money and I was so enamored of his teaching that I would have paid whatever price he named. So on Thursday, when I arrived for my lesson, I returned *The Gateless Gate*, which I had read a third time the previous evening, finding it even more baffling and more intriguing on the third read.

"And?" he asked when I handed him the book.

"To be honest, I don't know if I understood a single word," I said, shrugging my shoulders, "but I loved it. There was something about it that just made me feel good, sort of like listening to Bird but a lot harder to understand."

This produced a belly laugh from Elijah, a startling rumble that escaped into the afternoon air like a series of thunderclaps. "Not a single word!" he said when the air settled. "Ekai would have liked that answer."

"My favorite story was the one where two monks are arguing if the flag is moving or the wind is moving and the master passes by and tells them that it's the mind that's moving."

The weather had cleared up since Tuesday and we were sitting on the porch. Elijah disappeared into the cottage for a minute and came back with another thin volume bearing an identical brown-paper book cover. "If you liked Huineng then you might as well have a look at the *Platform Sutra*. You won't find Zen in books but maybe it will find you."

Much like *The Gateless Gate*, the *Platform Sutra* baffled me in a way I found oddly compelling. The unfamiliar ideas seemed to leap from the unexpected and the confounding to the even more unexpected and confounding in ways I could only compare to the best jazz solos that I had grown up admiring and trying to emulate. Only this was an improvisation in the realm of the human spirit, composed of leaps of wisdom that confounded my rational mind and left me thirsting to experience the uncanny wisdom that seemed to be contained in those indecipherable pages. Once I puzzled my way through the *Platform Sutra*, I paid a rare visit to the university library and emerged with a satchel full of books on Zen. That was the day I discovered the writings of D. T. Suzuki, beginning with his *Essays on Zen*, which I devoured over the weekend to a background of Stravinsky's *The Rite of Spring* and the usual diet of bebop.

Elijah, as I would soon discover, was not a great proponent of "book learning," as he called it, when it came to Zen, though he was surprisingly well-read for a man who liked to scoff at the idea that anything really important could be learned from the printed page. "Life," he cautioned me, "is the only real teacher," but from that day on I started devouring books on Zen as fast as I could lay my hands on them. My lessons with Elijah awoke a craving in me, and the only place I could go to satisfy that craving outside of those lessons was the printed page. Whether it helped or hindered is difficult to say, but twenty-two years and several books of my own later, I can say with conviction that it was certainly comforting and remains so till this day. Whenever life gets too bizarre or too challenging, as it is wont to do, no matter how much zazen or jazuzen we have under our belts, I can always unearth a Zen story from my memory to shed light on my predicament—or at the very least, to make me laugh and take myself less seriously, a very Zen-like quality. And most of those stories were planted in my mind by the books I read, beginning with *The Gateless Gate* and the mind that moves in the shape of a wind-blown flag.

8

I met up with Diana again on Saturday afternoon at the Co-ex-istence Bagel Shop with my head full of D. T. Suzuki and my heart upping its tempo at the prospect of hanging out again with the girl who had taken my virginity and made it seem like the most natural thing in the world. She had a corner table with her back to one of the bay windows, and when I tapped her on the shoulder she looked up from her book and beamed a great Medusa smile that chased all thoughts of enlightenment straight out of my head.

"Just in time. Have you had breakfast yet?"

"It's three o'clock."

"You must still be on San Fernando Valley time. Don't worry, I'll get you up to speed. I've got your education to think of."

It took no time at all for us to pick up where we had left off the previous weekend, careening from one subject to another while Diana steadily worked her way through two orders of bagels and cream cheese and several cups of steaming black coffee: global and local politics, the turmoil in Southeast Asia, the connection between jazz and poetry, what modern dance had that ballet didn't, the dif-ference between New York and San Francisco, and why California took a back seat to the elder coast in everything that didn't depend on being out of doors. We were somewhere between the medieval Italian love poetry she was thinking of translating and the symbol-ism to the title track of Mingus's *Pithecanthropus Erectus*, when a short, wiry black guy came up to the window and tapped on it to get Diana's attention. He was wearing a blue T-shirt and jeans in fifty-degree weather and had crosses made of Band-Aid strips stuck to his hair and face. He had been out there for a while, going up to the cars stopped at the light and babbling into their windows—I knew this because I had been watching him out of the corner of my eye while Diana talked, taking him for one of those wandering lunatics that seemed to be cultural fixtures on the streets of North Beach, where they were far better tolerated than their counterparts in LA. When Diana turned around, her face lit up and she waved for him to come in.

"Do you know Bob?" she asked after he saluted and ambled toward the door.

I shook my head.

"Then it's time you did. There are poets and there are poets. Bob's one of a kind, a true street bard, blowing poetry into people's ears when they least expect it. They're all uptight because they're stuck in traffic, and then they get blindsided by his street-corner wisdom and their world is never the same. I call him the bard of North Beach, poet laureate of the San Francisco streets."

Moments later Bob Kaufman was seated at our table and Diana was introducing us.

"Bob, this is my friend Dan, jazzman extraordinaire from the lily white streets of Northridge, down LA way, come to enliven our nights with his music and drink in our bohemian chatter."

"Cool, man. I can dig it. What's your ax?"

"Sax and piano."

"Right on. Double trouble."

"So what you up to, Bob?" Diana asked.

"Educating the yokels in their abomunist rights. You have the right to reject everything except snowmen. You have the right to join nothing except your arms and legs. And if the men in blue insist on hassling you for no good reason, you have the right to prove your patriotic worth by standing up and drinking yourself to death for your country."

"Do I detect another run-in with San Francisco's finest?

"Second time this month. Vagrancy. I gave them an earful of poetry and they let me off with a warning.

"And the yokels in the cars, did they understand their abomunist rights?"

"Indubitably."

"How could you tell?"

"Because they drove off, exercising their abomunist right to rejection. Everything is symbol, Diana. Fuck Carlos Williams. No things but in ideas. Maybe I should add that to the abomunist credo. What do you think?"

"You see?" Diana said, turning to me. "He's very Buddhist but he won't admit it."

"I'm a black Catholic Jew," Bob said, clasping me on the shoulder. "Buddhism is for crazy white people and sane Orientals. But don't tell anyone I said that, especially the crazy white people."

Diana raised a warning finger. "Be careful, Bob. Dan here is thinking about becoming one of those crazy white people. He's been hanging out with that Preacher guy, navel gazing and whatever else they do."

The waitress, a wan brunette in a plaid knit skirt, a light-blue blouse, and a short white apron, saddled up with a third cup and refills for Diana and me. She had a warm smile for Bob, whom she seemed to regard as a kind of underground celebrity.

"Elijah's been teaching me jazuzen," I said, after we had our cups filled. "That's Japanese for jazz Zen. Very cool stuff. I guess you could say he's my mentor."

Bob raised his cup with a flourish. "To mentors and jazzmen. To mentors who *are* jazzmen. This deserves an improvisation, for jazzmen everywhere and their mentors. Diana, will you do the honors or shall I?"

"The floor is yours, Bob."

Bob rose to his feet, rapping on the cup with his spoon, and turned to face the nine or ten unsuspecting members of his audience who were scattered at the different tables nursing coffees and pastries, some of them with a newspaper or a book in their hand, others carrying on a lazy conversation with the person at their side. I saw the waitress break into a grin, which made me think that this wasn't the first time Bob Kaufman had entertained the Bagel Shop crowd on the spur of the moment.

"To jazzmen everywhere, mentors with a horn, an improvisation in the key of G minor."

Bob raised his arms as he raised his voice, like a country preacher embracing the crowd, infecting them with his energy. A young couple who had their arms draped over each other disentangled themselves and clapped in anticipation.

> Beat prophets with kinky hair and ancient eyes,
> projecting shadows on the walls of memory,
> dance, say the shadows, say the talking notes, say the laugh-
> ing eyes,
> dance until your feet come home to roost in soul memories
> escaped from unknown heavens,
> caught in a horn and spilled earthward for your ears to
> drink and drown.
>
> Telling time with the beat, they scratch on parchments of air
> testaments of timelessness.
> The Fillmore is their Harvard, their cave of shadows, their
> *sanctum sanctorum,*
> and we, their faithful acolytes, in sacred t-shirts and divine
> dungarees,
> gather in high bagel noon
> with mouths open and ears rent wide
> to reap their daring and let it light the way.

He finished with a dramatic bow that was met with the enthusiastic applause of listeners who seemed to recognize their singular fortune. I certainly did. For five months I had been working my way into San Francisco's bohemian culture, cautiously at first and now full bore with Diana's assistance, and I had begun to catch a glimpse of the huge historical shadow that kept the city in perpetual shade. But it was only then, when Bob Kaufman rapped out his bit of improvisational magic, that I realized with a visceral primacy that I had landed in the middle of something entirely new and consequential, perhaps even epoch-making. A wheel was turning and I was caught in its spokes, rolling toward an unforeseen destiny of monumental importance.

When the applause faded, Bob drained the last bit of his coffee and set the cup down on our table. "Okay," he said, flashing a mischievous smile, "the minstrel has had his refreshment and supplied the customary entertainment. I thank you for the invitation, but now I must get back to the trenches. There is a battle being waged and my comrades await."

Held fast by the feeling that I had stumbled into a web of historic significance, I asked Diana about the battle Bob was returning to.

"Materialism, racism, sexism, cultural imperialism and spiritual solipsism, all manner of closed doors and the alienation it creates. An end to all isms — that's the essence of his abomunist credo. Bob is a crusader and poetry is both his sword and shield. He's convinced that if he can turn up the rant loud enough, then there'll come a time when they won't be able to tune it out. That's when the change will come. He's like Johnny Appleseed. He goes on sowing the seeds of resistance, convinced that one day those seeds will take over the forest."

"Is he really a black Catholic Jew?"

"He is. Black Catholic mother, white Jewish father, and educated in the streets. Who better to speak for everyman?"

An end to all isms. Diana had hit it right on the nose. While we sat there nursing what was left of our coffee and talking poetry and social change, Bob was back on the streets beating against those closed doors with his naked fist. If there is a center to the wheel of history, then I'm convinced that by the mid-nineteen-fifties it had shifted its locus operandi to San Francisco, where it would remain until the sixties flamed out in a smoke-filled blaze of glory.

9

"Look here, brother, you have to understand the difference between practice and playing. If you play Charlie Parker riffs when you solo then you're just practicing. You're not playing. When it comes time to improvise you have to leave Bird behind."

We were sitting on Elijah's porch after the lesson, nursing a hot cup of tea on what was a blustery, chilly afternoon. I had been trying to improvise without thinking, but the more I tried to relax and let the notes choose themselves, the more my favorite riffs, many of them borrowed from Charlie Parker solos, came sliding out of my horn, causing Elijah to shake his head while he held down the bass line.

"I wasn't consciously trying to play those riffs, Elijah. They just came out. I mean, what else do I have? They're all I know."

"Real improvisation, brother, is when you play what you don't know. Anybody can play what they know. There's no great art in that. But playing what you don't know, ah ... now that's the real thing. Not just anybody can do that. For that you have to dive into big mind, where all things are possible. That's where the magic lies, brother. That's where the great ones hang out. You just have to be quiet enough on the inside to let your Buddha nature blow. You hear what I'm saying?"

"I hear you, Elijah, I just don't know how to get there. It's hard enough playing what I know. But playing what I don't know — well that's a whole nother story."

"Of course it is. That's where the discipline comes in, all the work you put in expanding your vocabulary and refining your technique. You train until the music *is* your nature, until it's running through your veins and riding on your breath, so that when it comes time to pick up your horn and blow, you can do it without thinking. So you can leave it all behind and fix your gaze on the horizon. Because if you don't, you'll never be able to step out into the unknown."

I loved listening to Elijah talk. He sounded like a preacher from the Deep South, or what I imagined such a preacher would sound like: stretching out his vowels, adding hills and valleys to his voice, filling the blustery air with fire and metaphor. But I was still frustrated with what I thought of as the triteness of my playing, and I'm sure it showed on my face.

"Okay," he said, "maybe I can find a better way to explain this. Old Tokusan would give you thirty blows but I don't think that's going to work here…When you learned to read, did you use the Dick and Jane books? Dick sees Jane; run, Spot, run? Did they have those in California?"

"Sure, I remember those books. From first grade."

"Okay. So you learned to read and write the same way you learned to talk. You create simple sentences that work, and then you gradually add new vocabulary and more complex grammatical structures that allow you to express more complex ideas. You start by mastering the raw material of the language, and eventually you end up with pure, unimpeded communication—or rather, impeded only by your ability to think. Music works the same way. We begin with the physical mechanics of the instrument—fingerings, embouchure, breath control. A child doesn't have to be trained how to use their vocal cords, but we're not born with a reed in our mouth, so we have to work on our technique until it's as automatic as speaking; and at the same time we learn how to put musical sentences together, simple sentences at first and then gradually more complex ones. We start out playing a C scale over a diatonic C major progression or an F7 arpeggio over an F7 chord, and eventually we learn how much cooler it is to play a G triad over that F7, or an altered scale, and along the way we build up our vocabulary. A child builds their vocabulary by reading storybooks and listening to their elders. Musicians get their musical ideas in the same way: from other musicians, preferably from the great ones. So you start copping Bird solos and learning Ellington tunes, and if you're smart you'll learn some Ravel and some Beethoven, maybe some oriental folk tunes. And those ideas go into your brain and from your brain into your fingers, and eventually you start imitating those ideas, like you might try writing poetry after you've read some, and it comes out sounding like a poor imitation of what you've read—or if you're especially talented, maybe a good imitation. That's how a person begins to develop their musical voice: it starts out as an echo of all the musical voices they've absorbed over the years, and when they reach their musical maturity—*if* they reach musical maturity—then they use that voice to express their own ideas. Most people just skate by repeating what they've heard other people say. They don't have any real ideas of their own. It doesn't matter if they're speaking English, jazz, or Japanese. But a mature human being looks at the world and tells us what *he* thinks. Not what other people think—what *he* thinks. Whether he says it through music or through painting or through spoken language. Are you with me this far, Brother Dan?"

"I'm with you."

"Okay. Now that's as far as your small mind can take you, whether you're up on the bandstand or standing at the pulpit or just kicking back with your friends, shooting the breeze. If you have something worthwhile to say, people will listen. But what about the truly great poets in their best moments, the Miltons, the Shakespeares, those cats? Where did that kind of genius come from? Why did Mozart claim that he didn't compose anything, he just heard this music sounding in his head and wrote it down? Where did that music come from if he didn't compose it? People say they were inspired, that the divine breath blew through them. Okay. But where did that divine inspiration come from?"

Elijah paused, waiting for me to answer, but I shook my head.

"It came from big mind, brother. That's where all great art comes from, the kind that lifts you out of yourself and makes you realize that life is so much huger than you thought. If you want to create that kind of music you have to cross over into big mind, and you can only do that if you leave your ego behind and everything it's learned. The ego can only play what it knows, which is almost nothing, but beyond the ego is a world without limits. That's where you go to play a big-mind solo. Look around you, brother." Elijah made a sweeping motion with his arms. "Do you see it? Do you see how amazing it is, how far beyond anything our small mind can create? Do you think any painter could paint that? Can any poet describe it? This world is the spontaneous expression of Buddha nature. It's a fountain of endless creativity—magnificent, mind-blowing, perfect in every way, even in its imperfections. The trick, my dear brother, is to open your horn to that Buddha nature. Only it's not a trick—it's a discipline." Elijah stretched out the vowels in "discipline" as far as they could go. "It's a practice—a practice that brings you to the edge of the endless lake of Buddha mind. From there all you have to do is dive in. No more thought, no more playing music. Take the ego out of the equation and the music plays itself. It takes time, brother, I know, but you will get there, I promise you that. We are prisoners of hope for a reason. Because there's reason for hope."

I was feeling better now, not because I understood where I had gone wrong or because I was encouraged by Elijah's assurances—though I was—but mostly because we were sitting together on his porch talking about art and about life. Before that Saturday afternoon in the Coffee Gallery, I had never referred to Elijah as my mentor. The word had just popped out, but it only took me a moment to recognize its true significance. When Bob Kaufman raised his coffee cup to toast mentors with a horn the world over, his eyes ablaze with a kind of sacred street respect, I raised mine to Elijah, realizing at that moment that the word couldn't have been better chosen. Elijah wasn't just my sax teacher—he was my mentor, in life as well as music, and whatever my failings as a musician, I felt fortunate to be sitting on his porch watching the twilight slowly folding the world around us into silence.

To mentors come students with their questions and I had many, but at the moment I was still thinking of Bird and his big-mind soloing. "Did you ever get a chance to hear Bird play?" I asked. "In person, I mean?"

"Bird? Sure. I played with Bird."

"You played with Bird! You're kidding!"

"Oh yes, I played with Bird. Let's see, the first time was at Minton's. Then we did a gig together at the Five Spot, then a couple of weeks at Birdland. A few other gigs here and there. And when we weren't playing together I used to go listen to him whenever I could. Oh yes, I knew Bird, for better and for worse."

"Wow! How long ago was that?"

"Five, six years ago, before I came out west."

"That must have been amazing. What was it like, playing with Bird?"

"Playing with Bird was cool. He was the baddest mother to ever pick up a horn. I used to shake my head at the ideas he came up with. You couldn't see them coming. You thought you knew where he was going, but then he'd surprise you, leave you with your mouth hanging wide open. When Bird invited you to play with him, it was a big deal. Made you want to play your ass off to keep up. Dealing with Bird off the bandstand—well, that was a different story."

"What do you mean?"

Elijah gave me a curious, sideways glance, as if he were checking to see if I was as innocent as I sounded.

"You know Bird was a junkie, right?"

"Yeah, I know."

"I don't imagine you've been around any junkies, clean-cut suburban kid like you."

"Not personally."

Elijah laughed. "Is there any other way? Look, brother, Bird was a certified genius. Smartest guy I ever met. He told me once that he never forgot a single thing he'd ever read—and he was a well-read guy. Tolstoy, Einstein, Kant, that kind of stuff. He could talk about anything—nuclear physics, philosophy, literature, you name it—and do it better than most professors who teach it for a living. People like him don't come around very often. If he had been a writer, he would have won a Pulitzer or two. Music was just the way he did his thinking. But offstage he was a load. Always trying to con you, trying to get money out of you for his next fix, telling you he needed it to get his horn out of hock—I won't even tell you how many times I fell for that one. Don't get me wrong, I loved the brother, but his appetites were bigger than he was—heroin, alcohol, sex—that's the way it is with junkies sometimes. When he wasn't playing he was prowling the streets for money to support his habit or downing a fifth of whiskey with a girl on his lap. Just imagine if he had put all that energy into his music. But he didn't. Everything came down to his next fix. I tried to help but he was a strong-willed guy. We used to talk about Zen sometimes, really get into it, but when it came to discipline, forget it. It wasn't his thing. Too bad, because that brother was connected. He could be falling down blind drunk and then he'd step on the bandstand and blow the most mind-blowing shit anybody's ever heard. He was a kind of Buddha, just not the kind of Buddha you want to hang out with. He knew about big mind, and he could get there sometimes on his horn, or pretty close—that's why his music was so great—but he couldn't stay there. His appetites wouldn't let him. Big appetites and no discipline—that's a lethal combination, and in the end it killed him. He destroyed his body with the drugs and the dissipation. Greatest musical genius of our time and he couldn't even make it to his thirty-fifth birthday."

"Like Mozart."

"No, not like Mozart. Not like Mozart at all. Mozart died of natural causes. He was sick and poor and couldn't afford a proper doctor. Bird brought it on himself, plain and simple.

I had heard some of this the year before in my last semester of high school. It was all over the papers when the news broke, how Bird's lifestyle had killed him. But nothing so raw as the stories Elijah told me. He had been there. He had loaned Bird money, had let him crash in his room at the Claremont Hotel, had seen him shoot up in person and ridden with him on the subway afterward, trying to help him make it home to his wife. It was hard to reconcile those stories with the image of the musical genius that had such a prominent place in my mind. This got us talking about great artists and their demons, whether those demons took the form of heroin or depression or madness. The van Goghs, the Rimbauds, the Charlie Parkers, a long list of extraordinary artists who had careened over the edge at an early age, and it made me wonder if there wasn't something about artistic genius that could lead a person down the road to madness. But Elijah didn't see it that way.

"One man's genius is another man's madness. Great artists are visionaries. They see things other people don't, and sometimes what they see can drive them to despair. Most people are asleep, brother, asleep and blind. They're asleep to their own spiritual nature and they're blind to the hypocrisy and ignorance in the world around them. When an artist opens his eyes to the truth, it can shake him to his bones. And if he speaks the truth it's a dangerous business. Society has never been very fond of the truth and it's never been very tolerant of genius. They'll call you mad and use it as an excuse to shut you up so they don't have to hear what they don't want to hear. Madness, heresy, whatever excuse is handiest. It wasn't always that way, though. In the villages in Africa they still believe that a person who sees visions has been graced by God. They don't call them crazy, no sir. They bring them presents and hope that some of that divine luster will rub off. For them, artists are divine messengers sent to testify of the other world, the spiritual world. It was the same way in all ancient cultures—India, China, even right here on our own continent, before the white people came and started slaughtering our Indian brothers and sisters. For the ancients, art was a gateway to the infinite, a mystical practice. There was no such thing as secular art or music or poetry in those days. All art was sacred art. Nowadays we've lost that sense of the sacred; we've sacrificed it on the altar of commerce and fame. It's all about the ego now, but that's not the way it used to be, and it's not the way it should be. Real art is very close to religion. The deeper you go, the closer you get to the land beyond the ego, whether you call it Buddha nature or the holy spirit, like they do in the black churches where I grew up. Remember that, the next time you pick up your horn. Bird knew. There was no madness in him; he just couldn't control his appetites. As far as I know, Bird never made it to Africa, but if he had they would have treated him like a god—not because he was famous but because of where he could take them with his music. People have it ass-backwards in America, brother, especially white people. They glorify whoever has the most money, mostly people who make a living off of exploiting others, when they should be paying attention to the saints and the artists. That's the real madness, if you ask me. This is a sad society to be a genius in."

I had been a practicing churchgoer in the church of jazz for some years now, but I had never thought about music or art in those terms before, and that got me thinking about what Gary Snyder had told Diana.

"My friend Diana heard that you were a Zen monk in Japan. Is that true?"

"More or less. I wasn't ordained but I lived in a Zen monastery for two and a half years."

"Is that why you wear a kimono?"

"I wear a *yukata* because it's a lot more comfortable than pants and a shirt. It's the indoor version of the kimono. Even businessmen in Japan change into a *yukata* when they get home. It's more practical, that's all. Anyhow, being a Zen monk is not like being a Christian monk. If you want to live in a temple and study Zen, then you have to be a monk while you're there, but for most people it's a temporary gig, like going to college. Parents send their kids to the temple so they can get some discipline and learn some Zen. Once they get some training, they go back home and continue on with their lives. There's no stigma attached to leaving, like there is in Christianity."

"So how did you end up in a Zen monastery?"

"I was with the occupation army in Japan. When my tour of duty was over I didn't feel like re-upping, but I wasn't ready to go back to the States, either. I knew something about Zen by then and it seemed like a good idea. By that time most of the guys were just into having a good time. My regiment was a little better than some of the others—we still had some pride in ourselves, unlike the guys in the white units—but the boys still spent most of their time running after *panpan*s and that got old pretty quick. So I took my discharge and checked into a monastery."

"What's a panpan?"

"A panpan? That, Brother Dan, is your Japanese woman of the night, not to be confused with your normal American streetwalker. They were recruited by the Japanese government to serve as 'comfort women' for us GIs. To preserve the chastity of the country's women—that was the official explanation."

"Preserve their chastity? By prostitution?"

"It's not as strange as it sounds, brother, not if you look at it from their point of view. They were used to their own soldiers in Manchuria and China raping every woman in sight. They just assumed we would do the same if they didn't take care of our needs, so they advertised for young unmarried women to step forward and sacrifice themselves for their country. Thousands of women applied and hardly any of them were professional prostitutes. Mostly they were young girls who wanted to do their patriotic duty—to save Japanese womanhood from the depredations of the conquerors. They were already organized and waiting for us when we got there—the RAA, they called it, the Recreation and Amusement Association. There were RAA centers all over the country where a GI could just walk in and ask for a woman—fifteen yen a throw, about a dollar. MacArthur closed them down after eight or nine months, when syphilis and gonorrhea started getting out of hand, but it didn't change anything. They just moved out of the government buildings and into the red-light districts. By then most of the girls had decided that they were better off being panpans. The only Japanese who had it better in those days were the black marketeers and the bankers. Most people were lucky if they didn't starve to death, that's how bad things were after the war. There was no work, no money, no housing, very little food, and MacArthur had a strict hands-off policy when it came to the economy. Regular Japanese had a hell of a time getting by, but if you were a panpan you had it made. Even better if you were a panpan for a black unit. Some panpans, you see, were assigned to us black soldiers and some to the white units. They started comparing notes and found out that we treated them a whole lot better than the white boys did, so pretty soon most of the panpans wanted to hang with us. We would empty out the PXs and give it all to them. It was the guys' way of helping out the locals. Things were so bad, it was hard not to feel sorry for them."

"I had no idea."

"Of course you didn't. You think they were going to let the rest of the world know what was going on, much less America? Hell no. Nothing got published in that country without going through the CCD, the censorship detachment. Every scrap of newsprint, every photo. You couldn't even mention the bomb. It was like it never happened. People dying of starvation? Couldn't talk about it. That implied criticism of occupation policy and that wasn't allowed. Any mention of the devastation and it wouldn't pass the censors. That's just the way it was, whether you were Japanese or American, didn't matter. It was a closed ship. I saw this documentary in '46 by a Japanese filmmaker, Kamei. He spliced together footage from the Japanese government's own propaganda newsreels and used it to expose how the ruling classes had manipulated Japan into a war of aggression, exactly the kind of film you would think American officials would love. A couple of weeks after it hit the theaters the CCD banned it and confiscated all copies. You want to know why? Because there is a scene in the film where it dissolves from a shot of Hirohito during the war in his military uniform to a shot of him in civilian dress after the surrender, looking like an ordinary citizen. The CCD decided that this was an implied criticism of MacArthur's decision to absolve Hirohito of any blame for the war. And that was the end of the film. They killed it."

"Wow. So what got you interested in Zen?"

"I was with the 24th infantry. When the fighting ended we were stationed in Okinawa and after a while they sent us to Gifu, about sixty miles from Kyoto. Kyoto is Japan's religious center, like Rome is for Catholics or Jerusalem for Jews. If you want to learn Zen, Kyoto's the place. I knew nothing about Zen when I got there, but I had this friend, Sam Jenkins, from Mississippi. We had been together since Fort Benning, six years in the same platoon. He was big into philosophy and religion, and when we got to Gifu he started buying books on Buddhism and going into Kyoto when he was off duty to visit the temples. Thing was, he didn't speak Japanese so he couldn't really talk to the monks. But I did. I had been working on it for two years and I had gotten pretty good at it by then. So one day he asked me to come with him and translate. We spent the weekend in the guesthouse at Shokokuji—that's a famous temple in Kyoto—and I translated for him while he talked with the monks. Those conversations were what sparked my interest at first. I had never been exposed to anything like it, the whole Zen approach to life. It was fascinating. But it was the sense of stillness that really did it. After nearly six years in the army, I had forgotten what it was like to feel a real sense of peace, but at Shokokuji you could feel the stillness the moment you walked in. It was like the outside world with all of its misery and its craziness couldn't get past those temple gates. I had been through three years of fighting after Fort Benning—Guadalcanal, Saipan, Tinian, the Kerama islands, nasty stuff—and two more years with the occupation in a country where I saw almost as much suffering on a daily basis as I had seen during the war. Maybe more. Shokokuji was a shock after all that—the good kind, the kind that wakes you up. On the second day we got an interview with the *roshi*—a roshi's like an abbot—and he had this aura, like a perfectly still lake. No wind, no waves, absolute stillness. You felt good just sitting near him. That's when I realized that it wasn't the place, it was the people. The place was quiet and beautiful and all, the gardens, the grounds, the architecture, the whole Japanese aesthetic, but the stillness was coming from the monks. Once I realized that, a light went on. I grew up in the church. My grandmother raised me and she was a Baptist preacher, Southern Baptist, so I had been around goodhearted, God-loving people my whole life, but I had never been around anyone with that kind of stillness inside them. You could almost reach out and touch it. So after that I started going back, sometimes with Sam, sometimes on my own, and it never got old. Every time I went the pull got a little stronger. So when it came time for my discharge, instead of catching the next troop ship to Pearl, I thought, why not give it a try? Why not see if I could develop some of that same stillness in me? Two days after they handed me my papers, I showed up at the gate at Myoshinji with my sax and a duffel bag. As far as I know, I was the first black American ever to be accepted as a student in a Zen monastery. Hell, the first black of any kind. Not that they cared what color I was."

"They took you in just like that, even though you were a GI?"

"Hell no. First you have to pass the test, brother, and they don't make it easy, GI or no GI. But I was prepared. Sam knew a boatload about Zen by then, and he told me what to expect; otherwise, I might have given up. He was the one who recommended Myoshinji—it's the biggest temple complex in Japan and the monastery with the most students. He thought I'd have a better chance of getting accepted there."

"What was the test like?"

"Pretty simple. Basically, they send you away and if you won't go, no matter what, then you're in. But I knew that, so I was ready for it. Of course, Sam didn't tell me everything. When I got to the gate there was this huge bell hanging from the arch. Beautiful bell, a real work of art. I figured it was some kind of doorbell, so I rang it to let someone know I was there. Only it wasn't a doorbell. It was a ceremonial bell that they only rang during certain special rituals—and my arriving at Myoshinji wasn't one of them. A couple of minutes later a monk showed up at the gate, a short stocky guy in his forties. I could see right away that he wasn't happy. I didn't find out why until later, but I knew it wasn't an auspicious start. So when he opened the gate I bowed as respectfully as I knew how. In Japan most people bow really quickly. It's like a handshake over here; they don't even think about it. But not the monks. With them it's serious business, very deep, very formal. So I made this really deep bow and explained that I wanted to join the monastery and study Zen. That surprised him, I could tell, though he hid it really well. He just shook his head and said, 'Sorry, the roshi is not accepting any more students. Perhaps you can try some other temple.' Kind of surly, like he was making an effort to be polite but really couldn't wait to get rid of the black barbarian. I figured it was a gambit, so I asked him to please ask the roshi anyhow. He told me the roshi was busy at the moment and he didn't know when he would be free, so I bowed again, nice and deep and formal, and I sat down in front of the gate to wait. He didn't like that, but he didn't say anything. He just scowled and turned around and closed the gate. This was maybe seven or eight in the morning. After two or three hours he came back and told me that he had talked to the roshi, and so sorry, the roshi wasn't accepting any more students. 'I'll wait,' I said. 'Perhaps tomorrow he will change his mind.' It was October and it was getting pretty nippy, but I had an army-issue blanket and I was ready to wait it out. So I sat back down and at sunset he came back with the same scowl and told me that according to temple policy they could allow me to stay the night, but in the morning I would have to leave. And that was day one. He escorted me to the visitors' guesthouse where there was a meal waiting for me and a mat to sleep on, and bright and early the next morning he brought me back to the gate. After that it was like a ritual. When we reached the gate I would bow to him and then sit down to wait. I didn't know how to meditate yet, but I did my best to make it look like I was meditating. Sometimes I would play my sax, mostly Japanese folk tunes, nothing that would have seemed out of place. At meal times he would show up at the gate and bring me to the dining hall and then escort me back, and after dinner he would bring me to the guesthouse to sleep. Finally, on the fourth day, he brought me to Zuigan-roshi. Roshi was sitting on a mat in his cottage, studying a manuscript. He was nearly seventy then but very spry and healthy, with a pure Buddha smile that started in his eyes and stayed there even when he was scolding you. As soon as he looked up I could feel the attraction. He had that same stillness that I had felt in Shokokuji, but with him it was even stronger.

"He asked me to sit down, then got straight to the point. 'I hear you have been waiting at our gate for several days now. Why?'

"'I have come to study Zen.'

"'I am so sorry. You must have been misinformed. We don't teach anything here.'

"'Even so, you have students. I would like to live with them and practice with them.' The exact script Sam had given me.

"'I see. You are with the army?'

"'I was, until a few days ago. I was just discharged.'

"'But you do not want to go back to America?'

"'No, I want to study Zen.'

"'I see. Unfortunately, we are too poor to take you in, but I wish you well. Perhaps you will have better luck at another temple.'

"I had money but I knew it wasn't about that, so I just bowed and went back to the gate and went right on waiting. The next day at dusk a different monk came and brought me to see the roshi.

"'I hear you are still waiting at the gate,' he says. 'Why is that?'

"'I have come to practice Zen.'

"'I see. You may stay for one month then, but no longer.'

"And that was that. They gave me some robes, assigned a young monk to teach me the routine, and I started living in the monks' quarters. A month went by and nobody asked me to leave so I stayed on. I kept waiting for somebody to say something, but nobody ever did. I was just another monk to them, bigger and blacker but otherwise the same as anyone else. That was October 1947 and I stayed in Myoshinji until March 1950."

"That was some test."

"If you go by tradition, it was nothing. Supposedly, when Bodhidharma brought Buddhism to China he made his first disciple, Huike, wait for several weeks in the snow, and Huike ended up cutting off his arm to prove his sincerity before Bodhidharma accepted him as his disciple. You might say I got off easy."

"Okay. So what was it like, living there?"

"That was some serious discipline, brother. Reveille at 3:30 every morning, Zen-style, 364 days a year—you get one day off. You wake up, splash some water in your face, and go straight to the meditation hall for two and a half hours of practice, then a quick breakfast, then work detail—I was assigned to the gardens and eventually I became the chief gardener's number one assistant—then back to the meditation hall for practice, then lunch, and on it goes right up until bedtime. It was like spiritual boot camp but harder. I had never meditated before and sitting six hours a day was murder on my body and even harder on my mind, but once I was able to sit without my legs catching fire it became my favorite part of the day. And eventually I got what I came for. When I walked out of Myoshinji I wasn't the same person who had walked in. I had gained some real peace of mind—not anything like Zuigan-roshi, of course, or the senior monks, but for me it was a real achievement, worth every bit of the struggle it took to get there. But I would never have gotten there on my own. It was the enforced discipline, the company of the other monks, and Roshi's guidance that made it possible. And along the way I learned jazuzen."

"They taught jazuzen in the temple?"

"No. I discovered that on my own, though I had help later on. Whenever I had free time I would go to the gardens to play my sax.

Myoshinji is a huge place. There are a lot of different gardens, and you can always find someplace where you won't disturb anyone. I didn't have much free time, a half hour here, forty-five minutes there, but it was enough, especially in that environment. The thing about living in a Zen monastery is that eventually everything becomes practice. Whether you're working in the gardens, like I did, or in the kitchen, it doesn't matter; you're supposed to be concentrating the whole time on your koan, or whatever particular practice the roshi's given you. So when I played my sax I approached it in the same way, first as a form of zazen and later, when I started koan practice, as a means to solve my koan. After a while one of the monks told the roshi about my playing and he called me to his room. When I told him what I was doing he was pleased. He told me about a fifteenth-century Zen monk who attained satori while playing his flute, Ikkyu. Ikkyu was also a great poet, a great calligrapher and painter, and one of the true characters in Japanese history. Then Roshi gave me some instruction: 'You should not think that you are playing,' he said. 'There is no you. There is only the garden, the sax, and the blowing.' That's how I discovered jazuzen. It's not that it didn't already exist. It's just that I had to discover it on my own, like Ikkyu did. Later Roshi sent me to study with a *suizen* master one afternoon a week. *Suizen* means 'blowing meditation.' It turned out that there was a whole Zen school dedicated to attaining enlightenment through music, specifically through playing the shakuhachi, the Japanese bamboo flute. I learned to play a little shakuhachi, but my teacher let me play the sax during my *suizen* lessons. *Suizen*, jazuzen — it's really the same thing. The idiom is different but the spirit is the same. The Buddha plays and you're the instrument."

After that day I started thinking of Elijah as a kind of American Bodhidharma. Bodhidharma crossed the Himalayas on foot to bring Buddhism to China, a long and arduous journey that is said to have lasted three years, and Elijah braved the battles of the Pacific Theater to bring jazuzen to California, fighting his way from Guadalcanal to Okinawa in a journey that also lasted three years. History wouldn't remember Elijah like it remembered Bodhidharma, but he was just as important to me, though I wouldn't have given my left arm to become his student like Huike did. Before I left Elijah's porch that afternoon, he quoted a verse that I remember to this day:

> *At the Gateless Gate, I play the old tunes on my bamboo flute*
> *It's cold at night and everybody weeps to hear the ancient songs*
> *Yet this Zen is beyond sentiment*

To me that is jazuzen at its very best, the way it was when Elijah played. An empty reed that shakes you to your core until only the emptiness remains.

10

I WAS A FEW MONTHS from my eighth birthday when they dropped the bomb on Hiroshima. My father came home from work that day with the *LA Times* in his hand and a look on his face that seemed to vacillate between shock and jubilation. "This could end it," he told my mother, with a noticeable tremor in his voice, laying the paper down on the kitchen table and sliding it toward her as she wiped her hands on her apron and sat down to read. I had no idea what he was talking about, but the sight of my mother sitting down to read the newspaper in the midst of her dinner preparations caught my attention. I don't think I had ever seen her sit at that hour, not until dinner was served and we were all at the table. "Do you really think so, Frank?" she said, her face the mirror of her husband's. "We may be talking about days, Maureen. They don't have any choice. If they don't surrender now, there won't be anything left of them. No one could do that to their own people, not even those bastards." His voice was steadier now, but I could sense that he was still having trouble containing his emotions. I remember looking at Jack, both of us realizing at the same instant that they were talking about the war. We were just children but the elation that swept over us while we watched our parents sitting at the kitchen table, sharing their jubilation in subdued silence, was very real. We might not have fully understood what it meant, but we knew how we felt, how everyone around us felt in those days of tragedy and celebration.

Similar scenes were being enacted that day all over the country, perhaps all over the world, an outbreak of jubilation tempered in most quarters — though not all — by the shock of just how mercilessly the war was being brought to its swift conclusion. I could not remember a time when war hadn't been a part of my daily consciousness, when there had not been an enemy on the other side of the ocean, whichever ocean it was, to incite my fear and serve as a target for my hatred. The picture I had formed of the Krauts and the Nips, the twin demons who had terrorized my childhood dreams and fallen to defeat hundreds of times in backyard games with my friends, was the same picture most Americans had—more simplistic and childish, of course, but the same black-and-white line drawing that the American propaganda machine had sketched out in print. While there was still room in some people's minds for good Germans ruthlessly subjugated by the evil gangsters who ruled their country, half-insane with their visions of the master race, the Japanese were either mindless automatons, herded by their leaders like sheep toward their evil ends, or sadistic savages, fanatical "monkey-men" who were barely recognizable as human beings. I don't remember if I was particularly shocked when I learned after dinner that upward of ninety thousand Japanese civilians had been vaporized by a single blinding flash above their heads. I do remember wondering if they had had time to look up before they were gone. And I remember being gripped by a guilty paroxysm of vindication—finally they had gotten what was coming to them for their evil deeds. Or perhaps it was just my child's version of what my parents felt that evening.

My parents' emotions finally got the better of them two weeks later when Japan surrendered. We had already experienced one Victory Day celebration, but it had been muted by comparison, knowing that the war still raged in the Pacific—especially in California, where thousands of interned Japanese-Americans were one of the few visible features of a mostly imagined and greatly reviled enemy who stared out at us from across our very own ocean. RCA sent everyone home when the news broke, and my father took us into the city in his Packard where we drove around for hours, waving the American flag from the window of the car and drinking in the delirium while confetti rained from the windows of the buildings we passed. When we finally parked and walked to a restaurant for dinner and dessert, we were as giddy as I can ever remember being, an emotion we shared with everyone we saw that day. It was as if the city had exhaled a collective sigh of relief that had been held in for nearly four years.

Elijah was the first person I'd met who had actually been to Hiroshima, and the first to speak the untarnished, unromantic truth about the desolation and suffering that singular act of destruction had occasioned. For Elijah, Hiroshima was a crime against humanity, a conviction he held because he had seen with his own eyes what I had failed to see at the dinner table that evening: that the hundreds of thousands of Japanese civilians who were vaporized in Hiroshima and Nagasaki, or who died painful, lingering deaths from radiation poisoning in the weeks and months and years that followed, and the hundreds of thousands more who had died during the carpet bombing of Japanese cities by American B-29s in the months preceding Hiroshima, were human beings—most of them poor and hungry, as much victims of the war as the hundreds of thousands of Chinese and other Asian civilians that their own soldiers had brutalized and killed. A crime made even more heinous by the knowledge that there was no need whatsoever to use the bomb, a fact the American authorities who authorized the flight of the *Enola Gay* were fully aware of.

"But Elijah, it would have cost hundreds of thousands of American lives had we invaded the islands. They would have fought to the death."

I wasn't ready for Elijah's glare and I can still remember its fierceness. "Propaganda, brother. Pure bullshit propaganda. They couldn't have lasted more than a few days at that point, a few weeks at most, bomb or no bomb. I saw it with my own eyes. Hell, I knew it the whole time we were fighting our way up Okinawa. We all did. They were done for. The whole country was starving. You try fighting when you haven't eaten for a week. The only thing you will fight for is a potato. The bomb might have made the politicians' job easier, but it didn't save American lives. They were bombs of convenience, that's all. Convenient for the politicians and the generals, for the plutocrats and oligarchs, but pretty damn inconvenient for the people on the ground."

Elijah's face was a mask of displeasure, though I realized after a few uncomfortable minutes that his disapproval wasn't really directed at me. I was just repeating what I had been taught in school, what most people in America believed because they had read it in the papers, and he knew that. Nowadays, after Vietnam and Watergate, most people with half a brain are mistrustful of the American government and its congenital duplicity, but it wasn't like that in the fifties. Elijah's open disdain of the wartime authorities was a first for me.

"I don't suppose you saw any pictures of Japanese cities after the war? Of course not. Well let me tell you how it was. It was a wasteland: mile after mile after mile of rubble, everywhere you went. Here and there a few scarred buildings sticking up, a bathhouse chimney, an iron safe, that sort of thing. It made me sick to my stomach, and I had a pretty strong stomach after three years in jungles and swamps trading bullets with Jap soldiers. People sleeping in subway stations, makeshift shacks, tents, craters, the hallways of any building left standing. I don't know how MacArthur managed it, or why, but the poor caught the brunt of it. I remember when we entered Tokyo for the first time, riding up from Yokohama. It was a wasteland until you got to the wealthy neighborhoods and the financial district, where MacArthur made his headquarters. They were virtually untouched while the rest of the city was leveled. You can't convince me that wasn't on purpose. Before they sent us to Gifu we spent a month in Hiroshima. You know how a piece of scorched earth looks, like if you dump some gasoline on the ground and set it on fire? That was the city center. It was incinerated. From what I heard, ninety thousand people died in the blast and another ninety thousand from radiation poisoning in the next few weeks. First they started vomiting, then their hair started falling out, then their skin began dropping off in clumps. And then they died. My platoon policed the hospitals while we were there. This was months after the bomb and I saw people dying every day from the aftereffects.

"I told you about the CCD. No mention of the bomb, radiation poisoning, or anything of that sort could get past MacArthur's censors. That's my definition of a guilty conscience. Don't talk about it, don't let anyone else talk about it, and it all goes away. Only it doesn't go away. I'll have those pictures burned into my memory for the rest of my life. And I'll always be glad I do. Some things should never be forgotten. When people die like that, they have a right to our memories, especially when it was for no good reason, not that there can ever be a good reason for such a thing."

"But they started it, Elijah. They attacked Pearl Harbor. And China before that."

"The people I saw starving in subway stations didn't have anything to do with Pearl Harbor. Or China. Or Manchuria. The people who started the war from Tokyo are the same people who ended it in Washington: the politicians and the generals, the plutocrats and the autocrats. People for whom power is a game. Did you have anything to do with dropping the bomb? Did your father or mother?"

"No."

"Well the people I saw sifting through the rubble, looking for food or a place to sleep, didn't have anything to do with Manchuria or Pearl Harbor either. They might've been brainwashed into supporting their government during the war, but that just made them victims twice over. Just like you were brainwashed into thinking it was necessary to drop the bomb and kill hundreds of thousands of innocent people. You want to know why they dropped the bomb? Because they could. Because they had this powerful, shiny new toy, and after Alamogordo they were drunk on what it could do. I saw it happen on the ground, hundreds of times—on a lesser scale but in the end it's the same thing. They put this powerful weapon in your hand and the urge to use it gets the better of you. And second, because they had spent four billion dollars to develop it and they were afraid of the reaction they would get if they didn't use it. And last but not least, because they wanted to frighten the Soviets. Lot of good that did. Scared them so much they went right out and made their own bomb. It had nothing to do with defeating Japan. Japan was already defeated. And it had nothing to do with the Japanese people. They were just numbers they threw around in the war room when they were deciding which city to drop the bomb on. A few more, a few less, it didn't matter to them. Well it sure as hell mattered to the Japanese. And I haven't even mentioned Nagasaki. How do you justify Nagasaki?"

I didn't know what to say. It had always seemed strange to me that the president and his brass hadn't given them a few more days to make up their mind—the ruthlessness of that act was hard to negate—but I had never really given it much thought. I guess I had just accepted the party line: they had to be bullied into surrendering; it was unfortunate but necessary. But a second bomb only three days later? A second city vaporized? Suddenly the explanation I had been fed didn't seem plausible. And yet I had never heard anyone seriously question the bombing of Nagasaki.

"Once you go down that road there's no turning back, brother. You have to build more bombs to protect the first bomb, and they have to be more powerful than the other guy's. That's how you get a cold war and a society of concealment. Because you're Americans, a blessed people, you have to justify what you do. And since there is no way to justify genocide, you invent a story and you feed it to the public. It's called brainwashing, brother, and we're all victims, whether it's Hiroshima or slavery. We're fed a whole lot of hogwash from the cradle to the grave."

"By the government, you mean?"

"Government, teachers, preachers, parents. It's a society of ignorance, brother. You might as well say it's hereditary. The politicians, the generals, the oligarchs—they're the worst offenders, but we all do our part to keep it going. If there's one thing my grandmother taught me, it's that there's no one among us without sin. We are all brothers and sisters in the mud, and it begins with the politicians and plutocrats on both sides of the ocean. The Japanese weren't our enemy and we weren't theirs. The real enemy is human ignorance. That's why the Buddhas and the Bodhisattvas of the world are the real heroes, not the generals or the guys in the trenches. Because of how much they've done to remove our ignorance. The war against ignorance is the real war and they're our advance guard, whether you realize it or not. Practice what *they* preach, brother, and you just might wash your brain clean."

Social activism and mistrust of the government were breeding fast in the Bay Area in those days. I had been soaking it up by osmosis since I'd arrived at Berkeley, but Elijah's indignation was markedly different than the usual well-meaning rant. It was wiser, gentler, more grounded in the practical realities of what he had seen and experienced. In his eyes, we were all victims of social conditioning. Some were recovering victims while others were still unaware of how much their consciousness was infected by imposed ideas of dubious value, but for Elijah we were all on the same journey, even the most egregious offenders against human dignity. This was one area where he considered it a distinct advantage to be black. Because of the brutal discrimination that had plagued the black community for centuries, especially in the Deep South, Elijah had been brought up with a keen mistrust of government promises and government propaganda—as opposed to us "white boys," who swallowed the hook and line without a struggle and chewed on it proudly until they lowered us into a box. Most black soldiers were aware that they were fighting for a government that wasn't theirs, not in the real sense of the word, for a government that would just as soon roast them on a spit once they got back from the war, as they had been doing for the past four hundred years. Those who enlisted, as Elijah did at sixteen, lying about his age, had different reasons for doing so. Some did it for pay, some for adventure, others because it just seemed like the right thing to do with the world going up in flames, but none because they felt they owed their government their blood and their bones. There wasn't a black man alive, none that he had ever met, at any rate, who didn't know how little value their government placed on their Negro blood and bones, who didn't have a lynching somewhere in his black bloodlines to remind him of that fact. But the color of a man's skin was no barrier to being buried under the weight of social conditioning or social injustice. It just made it a little easier to see where you stood.

Slowly but surely, being around Elijah forced me to question the way I had been raised and the ideas and values I had come to think of as my own. His were not the only radical ideas that my young mind was soaking up at the time, and I probably paid less attention to him than I should have whenever our conversations strayed outside the ambit of music or Zen. But untended seeds have a way of sprouting if conditions permit, and the Bay Area in the late fifties and sixties was a radical gardener's dream. Long after Elijah left on his quest, his words and his example kept throwing out shoots and branches. To whatever extent I've been able to undo the unplanned, unconscious social engineering that is so much a part of our human burden, I owe much of it to Elijah and the hidden goad he left under my skin.

11

I DIDN'T HAVE A TELEPHONE at that time and neither did Joan Brown, but the telephone in the apartment one flight up—another painter's pad—served as the message center for many of the artists who camped out in the building. I would usually call Diana from a pay phone at school and leave a message, but sometimes, if I was lucky, whoever picked up the phone would shout down the stairs and Diana would come bounding up to take my call. One day in mid-February I managed to get her on the line and we arranged to meet up on Saturday at a new café that had just opened its doors—the Caffé Trieste, with its shiny new espresso machine and lacquered-wood tables and chairs. I had a gig that evening that required her presence and she had someone she wanted to introduce me to, so we met up for a late lunch where we were serenaded by the owners singing Italian arias, an unscheduled performance that I enjoyed a good deal less than Diana, who had grown up listening to those same songs on her grandparents' record player—my idea of a good aria at the time was any ballad sung by Billie Holiday.

Diana's companion that afternoon was the poet Gary Snyder, whom she had described to me as a cross between a Canadian woodsman, an Indian shaman, and a wandering Chinese Buddha, a description that still fits, more than twenty years later. He was a short, wiry fellow in his late twenties whose burnished skin seemed to be drawn taut over a loom of well-toned muscles, and he had a kind of clipped, deliberate way of speaking that gave me the impression of a man sorting through the rubbish bin of banal conversation for the uncut gems the rest of us had missed. Or perhaps it was his eyes more than his speech that gave me that impression. They were a pure blue haze, like two pools reflecting an unclouded sky, and they always seemed to be in perfect earnest, probing the world for its secrets even when he was laughing or reeling from a half-emptied flask of wine. He was always watching—watching you, watching the world, watching himself watch the world—and that, I believe, was the key to his art. For Gary the world was a theater and he, its audience—a truly Buddhist sensibility. You can see it even in those early poems, the ones he was writing at the time, which later found their way into *Riprap*.

Gary had just returned from a trip to the Pacific Northwest, and I was surprised to learn that until recently he had been living in a cottage on Hillegass, only a few minutes by bike from my garage loft—he had been enrolled at Berkeley studying Asian languages and culture. He was also, I learned, one of Elijah's regular visitors, having pedaled by my place many times on his way to visit the man he considered the purist bhikkhu of them all.

When I told him what Elijah was teaching me, his face lit up. "I'm planning on following in Preacher's footsteps, you know. If everything works out I'll be going to Kyoto in a few months to live in a Zen temple. Not the same temple—he was in Myoshinji and I'm going to Shokokuji—but it's the same school of Buddhism, the Rinzai school. Same environment, same routine, pretty much, minus the saxophone. He's been helping me get ready."

"Won't it be difficult to communicate?" I asked. "Elijah told me that hardly anyone speaks English in Japan, especially in the temples."

Gary grinned like he had been waiting for the question. He pulled a book out of his satchel and showed it to me: an English-Japanese primer. "Preacher's been helping me with my Japanese and I've been taking classes. *Ohayo gozaimasu. Watashi-wa Gary-san desu. Anata no namae wa nani desu ka?*"

I had to admit that he sounded pretty authentic. A lot better than I could do with my two years of high-school French.

"So Diana tells me that Preacher is turning you into a regular Bodhisattva, a Pure Land jazzman?"

"I suppose that's the idea, though I'm still not entirely clear on what a Bodhisattva is."

"A Bodhisattva is a great wise being, a lunatic angel who takes a vow not to accept liberation until all sentient beings are liberated.

He's the true apostle of hip in a woefully unhip world. A kind of assistant Buddha, you could say. We screw up and the Bodhisattva cleans up our mess. Until we get it right. Isn't that so, Diana?"

"If you say so, Gary. I'm still waiting to see an actual Bodhisattva. But if you say they're out there..."

"Oh, they're out there. The streets are full of Bodhisattvas running around doing great wise deeds, saying great wise sayings. Bodhisattvas for a moment or two, before getting swallowed up again by the illusion. But a moment or two is all it takes. You're one of them, you just don't know it yet."

Diana did look like a kind of Italian Bodhisattva with her porcelain skin and smiling face framed by that wild shock of hair, but it was Gary's words that made the image come to life. The more he talked the more his exuberance seemed to cast a spell over us. Thimblefuls of espresso stirred by slim silver spoons became tiny Tibetan prayer bowls filling the air around us with ethereal overtones, adding an enchanted aura to the murmur of voices and the intermittent whir of the espresso machine: magical sounds in a magical world where Bodhisattvas roamed the streets and anything was possible — at least as long as Gary's poetic imagination spun them into being, giving a pedestrian reality wings to lift itself up above the bay.

"Do you know what Bodhidharma did after he left China?" Gary asked.

Diana and I shook our heads.

"He came to San Francisco. I saw him riding up the street this morning on a bicycle. God's honest truth. Made me proud to be a Californian."

"He wasn't a big black guy wearing a kimono, by any chance?" I asked.

Gary let out a short explosive laugh. "Didn't look like it, not from where I was standing, but you never can tell. It's not easy to see through the disguise. That's the problem with these modern Bodhidharmas. They're always going around in disguise. Keep that in mind the next time you go to Preacher's for a lesson. You never know who's sitting in front of you. He could be anybody. Could be the Buddha himself in blackface, putting you to the test."

That was Gary, the gonest of all the gone poets I met that year—the year of my baptism, as I sometimes call it. Escorted to the edge by virtue of his tenacious trafficking in the ways of Zen. He had to leave after lunch, but he invited me to drop by his cabin in Mill Valley anytime I liked, and in recent years I have been a frequent visitor to his ranch in the Sierra Nevada, just as he usually drops by my place whenever he is passing near Los Altos. Since his apprenticeship in Japan his approach to Zen has become much more formal, but if you look closely enough you can see the same lighthearted, playful bhikkhu that I first met that February afternoon in North Beach.

After Gary took off, Diana and I made the rounds until it was time to head to The Place for my gig—or rather, our gig, though she didn't know that, the first of many we would do together over the next few years. I had sold the managers, a pair of renegade painters who had studied with Willem de Kooning at Black Mountain College, on the idea of Diana and I performing a set of poetry and jazz, and since I hadn't had a chance to run it by her beforehand I had decided to make it a surprise. It seemed like a good idea at the time but I wasn't yet acquainted with Diana's rather sizable temper. I waited until we got inside the door to tell her and she rounded on me like a female Corleone, informing me after a string of well-chosen epithets and a brandished finger that her family in New York was "connected." Diana might have been playing the mafia card for comic effect, but she was genuinely angry. It wasn't so much that I had arranged the gig without her approval as it was the fact that I had sprung it on her at the last moment without giving her time to get her poems. All she had with her was the notebook she always carried around that contained sketches of the pieces she was working on and odd scraps of verse that she snatched out of the air while riding on buses or ruminating under the dimmed-out lights of a cinema hall. I guess I'd just assumed she knew her poems by heart and the rest she could extemporize, like a jazz musician with his repertoire of standards and originals that serve as a platform for improvisation, but that just showed how little I knew about poetry and poets at the time. Once she cooled down and took stock of the contagious energy of a crowd that was filled to overflowing, Diana fell victim to the challenge. She decided that she would make do with her sketchbook and those few poems she had memorized, and extract her pound of flesh from me later.

There was something unique about the crowds in North Beach in those days, a kind of electricity that crackled in the air of any local bar or café whenever there was a live performance. It's not like that anymore. Nowadays it's the name that draws people in and sets the anticipation flowing in their veins, but in those days it didn't really matter who was performing. There was an unspoken assumption that anyone brave enough to stand up in front of a North Beach crowd was sure to have something worthwhile to say, whatever medium they used to do their talking. It was the height of what people were already calling the San Francisco Renaissance, and those who weren't artists themselves (in those days you could usually count on half your audience being artists or would-be artists) took it as gospel that whoever mounted the stage — even if the stage was only a cramped corner in a dimly lit bar — would be somebody they would be telling their grandchildren about in the years to come. Most of the dancers, musicians, painters, and writers in the audience that night knew Diana, but for the most part the rest of the crowd didn't. And yet, it didn't matter. She was a poet, and that was all they needed to know. If there was any kind of hierarchy in the pantheistic world of Bay Area artists at that time, poets occupied the topmost rung. They were the archivists of the movement, the voice of a generation, sworn to record that unique moment in time, the bearded and clean-shaven prophets who enjoined us to remember that history itself was unfolding around us, and history could only be ignored at the peril of your life. You could see it in their faces the moment Diana opened her notebook, the unmistakable earnestness, almost Zen-like in quality, as they prepared to open their ears and minds to the voice of an oracle.

The Place didn't have a stage, as such. It had an open space in the back, just under the loft, with an upright piano and reasonable acoustics despite the long rectangular layout, and it regularly hosted both local musicians and poetry readings. Anyone who really wanted to hear the performance made sure they got a table up close or lounged against the wall with a drink in their hand, while those who were just there for the ambience or to while away the time sat closer to the entrance, where the sounds of the performers reached them like tidewater lapping the edges of their table.

I'd never played with a poet before, but I had attended a couple of such recitals since coming to the Bay Area—they were just becoming popular at the time—and I felt sure I could hold my own. It didn't seem much different than accompanying a singer (not that I had done much of that): you stayed out of their way when they were singing and then filled up the spaces, taking care not to stray too far from the melody. But as I soon discovered, accompanying a poet was closer to playing free jazz with another instrumentalist. There was no harmonic structure to attend to—you could play whatever chords or melodic ideas seemed to fit the mood. Chords, after all, are nothing more than color, the difference between taking a walk in the park in a hot pink T-shirt or a navy blue. Same melody, completely different feeling. And that was the key: to make the music fit the mood of the poem.

Diana's first pieces were straight out of her sketchbook, those drafts she considered fit for public consumption. She would call for something upbeat or sorrowful or laid back and wistful, and I would lay down a chord or two to set the mood and then try to divine where the poem was heading as she leaped from one idea to another, leading me through constantly shifting landscapes that I translated into the language of the piano, following a logic I had never encountered in any musical composition. For the most part I followed her lead, letting the poems shape the music, and as happens sometimes with singers, Diana guided me with her eyes or with her body as she swayed to the pulse, providing me with a subliminal push in the right direction. I had already gotten a sense for how nuanced the rhythms of poetry could be, especially with a poet as accomplished and as spontaneous as Diana, and as the night progressed we started playing off each other with more and more aplomb, each of us syncopating the beat in different ways until we found the one certain groove that the poem reveled in, an act of spontaneous combustion that the crowd helped to ignite with their finger snaps, thigh slaps, and whistles. On a couple of occasions we even stumbled into some unexpected polyrhythms that seemed to spring out of the air of their own volition and dance above our heads like living creatures born of the mysterious alchemy of her words and my music.

We ended the performance with a couple of long poems that Diana had performed on previous occasions. She was more sure of herself by then, and the interplay between us became so tight that it almost felt as if I were playing from a written score. Her smile had grown as the night wore on, and when the applause died down after a short encore she wrapped me in an Italian bear hug that served as a welcome preamble to an equally welcome night of carnal rumble and tumble. My pound of flesh was safe and all sins forgiven.

I had experienced the highs of a live gig before, starting with my grade-school band concerts, but I had never experienced anything quite like this. Nor had Diana. The electricity we tossed back and forth that night was my first direct experience of how chemistry can ignite between performers and spur them to creative outpourings they could not have summoned without the catalyst of interhuman combustion. It was also my first real gig as the sole instrumental-ist—the closest I had come till then was accompanying singers in the annual high-school talent show—and I found the freedom intoxicating. Diana influenced what I played, certainly, but I was free to let my musical imagination roam in a way that I wasn't when I played with other musicians. It wasn't free jazz exactly, not the kind Ornette Coleman would approve of, but it was free in spirit. To this day, I find that there is something about solo piano that feels closer to the spirit of Zen. A veil seems to drop down when I sit alone at the piano, separating me from the outside world and transporting me to Gary's Pure Land jazz paradise where big mind is the only light that shines and the pianist cannot be separated from the piano. Just ask Keith Jarrett. I haven't talked to him about it, but I'm sure he would agree. Or better yet, listen to his music.

12

I met Allen Ginsberg for the first time in Elijah's garden a few days later. I had just finished my afternoon lesson when he and Gary Snyder came walking up the path, kindred souls in very disparate bodies. Allen was tall, gangly, slightly myopic, and visibly Jewish, while Gary was a diminutive version of the hardy colonial woodsman, of Scots-Irish and English parentage, as Anglo as they came. But both were keen observers of the world, which they funneled into their poetry, and while Allen was not yet the evangelical Buddhist meditator that he would later become, he saw the world, as Gary did, through spiritually tinted lenses, thanks to a series of mystic visions at Columbia in the summer of 1948, a dip into the waters of satori that came to him without effort, without meditation, without any kind of conceptual preparation other than the poems of William Blake that he'd been reading when the doors of perception swung open, removing the veil that ordinarily cloaks our eyes.

Elijah arranged the benches so we could sit facing each other, and the four of us soon settled into a conversation that was very different than what I was used to on Elijah's porch. As comfortable as I felt around him, I was always aware that he was the teacher and I, the student. I was also in awe of his prowess as a musician and the life he had led, from his war experiences to his years as a Zen monk to his time onstage at Minton's and other New York jazz clubs, jamming alongside Charlie Parker, Dizzy Gillespie, and other icons of the jazz world. He was also ten years older than me with the aura of a man older and wiser than his years, while I was acutely conscious of having led a sheltered and uneventful life. But Allen was the same age as Elijah and Gary only four years younger, and they had both soaked up a wealth of experience that gave them a worldliness and a self-assurance that I could only dream about. They were also spiritual hipsters and serious artists at the beginning of long, illustrious careers who looked upon Elijah as a comrade rather than a teacher.

Elijah asked them about their travels — they had recently returned from a hitchhiking trip to the Pacific Northwest — and after a colorful description of the Seattle streets, Allen pulled a mimeographed flier from his satchel and handed it to Elijah.

"We are going to be giving a reading in three weeks at the Berkeley Town Hall Theater. Myself, Gary, Whalen, and McClure. Rexroth is going to MC. We'd really like you to come. Everybody's going to be there."

Elijah broke into a jovial smile that had been absent during our lesson. "Everybody who's anybody, right? These days I'm more interested in being nobody, but I suppose there's no harm in having a nobody or two in the crowd."

"Is that why you don't perform?" Gary asked. "Because it will get in the way of being nobody?"

It was a question I had been wanting to ask Elijah for some time. There was little doubt that he was the best tenor saxophonist in the Bay Area — and there were some pretty good ones, beginning with Pony Poindexter. Why then didn't he play around town, at least from time to time? Why didn't he share his mind-altering music with more of the world than just the plants in his garden and an occasional neighbor who happened to leave his window open? I knew that late night gigs in the jazz clubs didn't mesh with his reclusive Zen lifestyle, but there were other venues and other time slots: afternoon concerts in the park, the laid-back atmosphere of the North Beach cafés, recording sessions where a sideman of his talent and experience would always be in demand. Those kinds of gigs seemed perfectly compatible to me, but not to Elijah, for reasons he quickly made clear.

"That's exactly it, brother," he answered. "There is nothing that inflates the ego more than adulation, and adulation is something you can't escape when you perform, not if you're any good. People are always letting you know how great they think you are, always reminding you that you're somebody. 'God, you're amazing. I just love the way you blow.' And that's on top of the applause, the reviews, the women chasing after you, people recognizing you on the street and asking for your autograph. It's a round-the-clock banquet for the ego. I did my best not to take it seriously back in the day, but that kind of attention is insidious. It's hard not to start believing all those sweet-sounding words, especially deep down in your subconscious. It got to the point that I was spending most of my zazen time trying to undo the damage. I just decided one day it wasn't worth it, so I packed my bags and came out west. Fame is a drug I can do without."

"What about recording gigs?" I asked. "You don't have to deal with that in the studio, right?"

"As long as your name is on the jacket, there's no escape, brother. They'll track you down wherever you are and make you believe you're somebody. And even if no one sees the record, you'll see it, and there's something about seeing your name on a record jacket that gets to you. It's the illusion of permanence, a beachhead for the ego. Pacific Jazz has been pestering me to do a solo album but that would leave footprints, and once you start leaving footprints you're too easy to track. They still check in from time to time, to see if I've changed my mind, but I don't see that happening."

"The path of the enlightened one leaves no track," Gary intoned. "It is like the path of birds in the sky."

"Well said, Brother Gary. The Dhammapada. 'Those for whom there is no more acquisition, whose dwelling place is an empty and imageless release — the way of such people is hard to follow, like the path of birds through the sky.' It's hard to be a Buddha if you go chasing chimeras in the dark. Hard enough even if you don't."

"Is that the reason for the sign?" Allen asked.

"That's it, brother. It's a reminder to myself to leave the ego outside where it belongs."

Allen leaned forward on the bench with an earnest expression on his face, his black-rimmed glasses and receding hairline adding a scholarly touch to his boyish good looks. "But aren't the chimeras necessary? The self-deception, the whole veil of maya thing? Without their masks people wouldn't be able to get on with their daily lives.

If the towers of Babylon collapsed, the grocery stores would collapse with them, and then where would we get our food? How do you ride your bike or take a bus or give change if you're zonked out on the eternal? The way I see it, it's a cosmic self-correcting mechanism: a few tormented souls get to climb the walls and tell everyone else what it's like on the other side. That's what artists are for. Artists and saints. But if everyone escaped from the menagerie it would be chaos. Saints have to eat also, you know. Someone has to mind the store. For most people too much mysticism is as dangerous as heroin. They get enough of it through their dreams, but in controlled doses, no more than they can handle. If it spills over into their daily life, most people get overwhelmed. The wheels grind to a halt."

"Are you saying that from personal experience?"

"As personal as it gets. I had a mystical experience of my own about eight years ago when I was studying at Columbia. I know firsthand just how much it shook me up and how difficult it was to adjust afterward. But it's not just that. My mother went through the same thing. She was in and out of asylums when I was young, and I had to take care of her when she was home. I wasn't even a teenager yet, so I didn't fully understand what was going on, but I learned to see a side of her that other people couldn't. She'd be going off the deep end, but then she'd make these lucid observations that were more insightful than anything anyone else in my family had to offer. Like an oracle, almost. Most people just thought she was crazy and that was all there was to her, but I knew better. Later I spent eight months in the same hospital my mother had been in, the Rockland State Psychiatric Institute. June 1949 to February 1950. I was in a legal mess over some stolen property that some junkie friends of mine had been stashing in my apartment and it was either that or jail. I don't regret it, either. I made a lot of friends in Rockland, and it was obvious that many of them had had a vision of a reality beyond the one we can see with our eyes, the socially agreed-upon reality. They just couldn't handle it. They couldn't make the adjustment, couldn't reconcile one world with the other. They were diagnosed as schizophrenics but what does that actually mean? I had to see a psychiatrist every week, like everyone else, and we really got into it.

I challenged them as much as they challenged me, and one thing I learned from those conversations was that they had no real idea what was going on inside their patients' heads. They analyzed their behavior and their speech and hung a scientific-sounding label on them, but it was just educated guesswork. They tried to do the same with me but I was able to catch them at their game. The biggest farce of all is that they claim to be experts on reality. I didn't catch the slightest whiff of enlightenment from the staff psychiatrists in Rockland. There was a stink, but it wasn't the stink of enlightenment."

"I hear you, brother. I've met some so-called crazies who were more tuned in to spiritual realities than the doctors who wanted to put them away. You see it in the army sometimes. But that doesn't mean too much mysticism is dangerous or that it's going to create chaos in society. Just the opposite, in my opinion. I've never met anyone more grounded or more capable than the Zen masters I hung out with in Japan. A true Zen master can boil rice like a New York chef and dwell in emptiness at the same time. Being a master doesn't just mean that you have access to a deeper reality: it means that you're a master of life — and life includes all realities, from the mundane to the transcendental. You'll see what I'm talking about when you get to Shokokuji, Brother Gary. What impressed me most about the monks in Myoshinji was how self-assured and self-aware they were, especially the senior monks. And it had nothing to do with being Japanese. Ordinary Japanese are just as screwed up as ordinary Americans, if not more. But not in Myoshinji. It was a whole different class of human being. The way they walked, the way they talked, the way they went about their work — they had a kind of quietness and sure-footedness you just don't see. Somebody had taught them how to live like a real human being while the rest of us are just floundering in the dark. And where did they get it from? From gradually waking up out of the illusion. It all depends on how you go about it. The people you're talking about just stumbled into something without any preparation. They weren't following any kind of spiritual discipline. They didn't have a teacher or the dharma to guide them. Dropping the veil, even a little, is a powerful experience — as you discovered, brother. If you're not prepared for it, then sure, it can knock you off your senses and make it difficult to adjust to the regular world. But if you're prepared for it, if you've been working your way toward it, step by step, then it's perfectly natural, no big deal. It's like the difference between being pushed out of a plane and jumping out with a parachute after going through paratrooper training. The first guy's scared out of his wits and then he gets his brains scrambled, while the other guy is blown away by the beauty of gliding through the air at twelve thousand feet. Then he lands as light as a feather, folds up his parachute, climbs into a jeep, and drives away, like it's a regular day. And after you've done it a few times it *is* a regular day. You do what you do at twelve thousand feet and then you do what you do at sea level. No big deal. You see what I'm saying? All kinds of people have spiritual or mystical experiences at one time or another, in or out of their dreams, but if you want to explore the territory then you have to know where you're going. If you haven't been there before, you need a good guide or at least a good map. Hell, it's the same no matter what you do. Try working in a machine shop with no training, no manuals, and no one to show you how to work the equipment. Likely as not, you'll lose a hand before the day is out. Life can be dangerous if you don't know what you're doing, whether it's spiritual life or mundane life. But that's on you. Don't blame the Buddha if you go it on your own."

"Allen's coming around," Gary said, with a ring of satisfaction in his voice. "He doesn't admit to being a Buddhist yet, but he's been dreaming of Bodhisattva angels jumping from planet to planet. You can see it in his work. It's only a matter of time."

"My poetry is my method," Allen countered, "and William Blake is my teacher. William Blake and Walt Whitman."

Allen was being perfectly serious when he said that poetry was his method. For him it was an *upaya*, a *sadhana*, as much as music was for Elijah. He wouldn't begin his daily meditation practice until thirteen years later, first with Swami Muktananda and then with Chögyam Trungpa, who thereafter became his spiritual guide, but even in his early poems you can see how deeply his spiritual sensibilities were tied in to his artistic quest. Like some of the great poets who preceded him, he was able to pry open the doors to a deeper level of reality through the pursuit of his craft, gaining access to a universal vision that was at the core of all higher human experience. I can't help but think, however, that his willingness to go it alone, without an established practice or an experienced teacher, opened him up to certain torments of the soul that he might have otherwise avoided. But then perhaps we wouldn't have gotten that stupendous poetry that so resonated with the torments that most of us were feeling in those days of social and spiritual constriction. Perhaps it was an unconscious sacrifice he made to be the poet of his generation, the voice in the wilderness of one who was as lost as the rest of us but infinitely more able to give meaning and a shape to our longings.

"So did William Blake teach you to separate the spiritual from the mundane?" Elijah asked.

That drew a wry smile from Allen. "Not really," he said. "I think I did that on my own."

"He was actually very Zen, William Blake," Gary said. "'Think in the morning. Act in the noon. Eat in the evening. Sleep in the night.' That's from one of his poems."

The little I knew of William Blake consisted in a vague recollection from high-school English, but I could see why his words had Elijah nodding in appreciation. "That sounds like something a Zen master would say," he said. "They don't have much patience for metaphysical claptrap. Chop wood, carry water. The spirit of Zen in four words. Do you remember any other good lines?"

"Sure. 'If the doors of perception were cleansed everything would appear to man as it is: infinite. For man has closed himself up, till he sees all things thru chinks of his cavern.'"

"That one I'm familiar with. Have you heard of Indra's net?" he asked, glancing at each of us.

I shook my head along with Gary and Allen, glad to be on even footing for once in a conversation that was mostly above my head.

"It's an old Buddhist metaphor from the *Avatamsaka Sutra*. It compares the universe to a vast net with a jewel at each node. In each jewel you can see the reflection of every other jewel. And each of those reflections reflects all the other images, and on and on to infinity. In other words, the entire universe is reflected in every particle of the creation. It's the Buddhist way of saying that everything depends on everything else. It's called the 'doctrine of mutual interdependence.' The universe depends on you and you depend on the universe. There are no disconnected events. So from the Buddhist point of view there is really no such thing as spiritual or material. There's only one reality seen through different lenses. No matter how much our small minds chop it up and label it as this or that, it remains one interdependent reality. The rest is just our mind playing tricks on us."

Gary nodded vigorously. "But if you can cleanse the doors of perception," he said, "then you see it all for what it really is: infinite."

"Exactly. You see Indra's net."

"If that's true," Allen said, "then nothing is insignificant. A hobo riding a freight train or scrounging in the city dump is just as important to the big picture as some politician in Washington handing out a multi-million-dollar construction contract to his golfing buddy. That seems right to me. Blake has another saying: 'Eternity is in love with the productions of time.' What does eternity care if a man is a homo or straight, a hobo or a king. We're all jewels, right? Each reflected in the other?"

"That's right, as far as eternity is concerned, but human beings don't usually see it that way. That's why you get the blind beating up on the blind."

"But doesn't that happen for a reason?" Gary said. "If everything is karma and mutually interdependent, then the greedy politicians and the bigots and the religious fanatics are just as necessary as the Bodhisattvas singing their Pure Land mantras. One depends on the other."

"Of course. But that doesn't mean you have to like it." Elijah's smile seemed to be coming out of the shadows now like a lantern in the twilight. "When you take a dump, open a window and light some incense. If you don't like something, then do something about it. That's what a natural man does. If you just pinch your nose in disgust, then you deserve a good thwack upside the head. And any self-respecting Zen Buddhist will be happy to give you one."

"A lot of self-respecting poets also," Allen added. "As far as I'm concerned, that's one of the main purposes of poetry: to give as many people as possible a good thwack upside the head. See if we can't wake them up a little, or at least shake them up a little."

"And is it working?"

"I don't know. You come to the reading and tell me."

"I'll come. But I'm curious to hear what you think, brother. You're writing poems and giving readings around town, both of you. Is it having some effect? I sure hope so."

Gary and Allen looked at each other for a moment or two before Gary answered. "I think it is, especially since the Six Gallery reading. That made some waves. We didn't plan it that way. It was just supposed to be a small reading for our friends, but it had a major impact. Since then people have been paying attention. They come to the readings, they discuss the poems, the ideas get passed along. Allen read a long poem called 'Howl' at the Six Gallery, and in a few other places since then, and I've been hearing snatches of it on the street, people sitting around and talking about it. Just mention the word 'Moloch' and people know exactly what you mean, though no one had ever even heard the word before 'Howl.' The tyranny, the bigotry, the intolerance, the greed, the insanity — it's all there in the poem and that one word conjures it up. 'Howl' has become a kind of symbol, an extension of our everyday language. It exposes the madness and makes people want to do something about it. That's what we're all trying to do with our poetry, but Allen's leading the way."

Allen shook his head. "I wouldn't say that," he said. "It's work by committee. When people listen to your poems they feel more connected to the land, more contemplative, more grounded. You have that Buddhist thing going, that spaciousness, that sense of balance. Whalen has it also. McClure is really tuned into environmental issues, Sartori gives us the female point of view. Everybody has their own niche, their own sensibility, a different piece of the puzzle, but when you put it all together it makes for a powerful voice. I read this quote the other day in the *Chronicle*, from Margaret Mead: 'Never doubt that a small group of committed citizens can change the world; it's the only thing that ever has.' So why not us?"

"Exactly," Gary said. "Why not?" He turned to Elijah. "Ferlinghetti is going to publish Allen's work. You're still planning on calling it *Howl and Other Poems*, right, Allen?"

"That's right. Short and simple."

"That's what the world needs, Preacher. Somebody to let out a good powerful scream that everyone can hear. We need somebody to stand up and howl."

"Ain't it the truth, brother. There's a lot of ignorance out there and a lot of good ordinary people suffering for it. Ignorance, not money, that's what keeps the oligarchs and plutocrats in power. That's what really brings people to their knees. If you can throw some light in a dark place, everybody benefits, even those brothers and sisters who are cashing in on other people's misery. They won't like it. They may even come after you. But in the end they benefit just the same as everyone else. So go for it. Shout it from the rooftops. That's what the great ones have always done. No better way to spend your life. Be a truth teller and a witness bearer. Remember the scars but don't let the scars have the last word."

The conversation continued until dusk enveloped us, with Elijah serving as a spiritual sounding board for Gary and Allen. A black jazz saxophonist, ex-WWII vet from Alabama serving as a spiritual compass for a couple of anti-establishment white intellectuals. I was certainly a long way from Northridge. But they weren't the only ones. As I would soon discover, most of the local artists with Buddhist inclinations found their way to Elijah at one point or another. At the time he was the closest thing we had to an authentic American Zen monk. He wasn't a philosopher per se, but he could riff on spiritual ideas almost as fluently as he played the sax. I remember one late night conversation with Alan Watts in Mill Valley where Elijah blew him away like Bird schooling a greenhorn on the bandstand. By the end of their exchange Watts had absolutely nothing to say—and that was a first for a man who had never met a conversation in which he wasn't cast in the lead role. But even speechless, he had a smile on his face. Just about everybody did after talking with Elijah. It wasn't much different than listening to him play, the same voice but without the horn. The voice of a truth teller and witness bearer who made sure the Buddha had the last word.

13

A few days later I got a chance to ask Elijah what he thought of Allen and Gary's aspirations to change the world through their poetry. He was silent for a minute or two, as he sometimes was after my questions, looking out on the garden and nodding his head very slowly as if he were searching for the answer somewhere out there among the plants.

"I guess it depends on how good they are," he said at last, "or how good they will be if they keep at it. The better they are, the better it will be for all of us. Most people don't look to Zen masters or saints or spiritual philosophy to make sense of their lives, brother. They get that from the arts, from music and movies and novels and paintings and dance and on down the line. That's where they get their inspiration. The world is in a sorry state right now, and part of the reason why we keep spinning our wheels in the mud is that the artists people take their cues from are just recreating the dark. They're not trying to wake people up — they're trying to make a buck. Most of them. You were luckier than most. You grew up listening to Bird, not Eydie Gorme."

"Allen and Gary aren't in it for the money, Elijah, that's for sure. Neither is my friend Diana. Or you."

Elijah smiled. "You're right there. They have their heads in the right place, and from the looks of it they're willing to take the criticism and the backlash, which they'll have to if they want to do something worthwhile in a world as screwed up as ours. It's more a question of how clear their vision is and how strong their language. How far can they understand where we've gone wrong and can they inspire us to move down a better and wiser path? In other words, can they become real sages and speak their wisdom through their poetry in a language we can relate to, in a way that grabs us deep down inside, in our emotional core, and won't let us go? That's the real test. And once they grab us, can they help us find a way out of the mud? It won't be easy, brother, especially if they succeed."

"Why is that?"

"Because if they are wise enough to see the truth and brave enough to tell it, then they're going to have to step in the ring and go toe to toe with ignorance. And ignorance never goes down without a fight. The oligarchs and plutocrats and the politicians they keep in their pocket have too much at stake. Their money and power are riding on the status quo, and the status quo depends on the hypocrisy and the selfishness and the intolerance and the greed and all the dogma to keep itself propped up. That's where cheap entertainment comes in, brother. Popular art nowadays is in the business of putting us to sleep. Its whole purpose is to perpetuate the illusion, to keep us stuck in the mud. I have no patience for it anymore. Just put on a pop record or pick up a bestseller from the newsstand or go to just about any movie. It's all about *moha* and maya, infatuation and illusion. They sell you on romance, patriotism, glamor, the lifestyles of the rich and famous, the unending bliss of consumer heaven — anything but taking a good hard look at why our lives and our society are such a mess and inspiring us to do something about it, which is what real art is all about. They sell us a dream that just increases our suffering and we cling to it like it was the only thing keeping us from the abyss. Reality is just not very palatable when compared to the illusion, which is why most people get extremely uncomfortable when an authentic artist comes along and forces us to look in the mirror. Do that and you open yourself up to criticism, ridicule, and worse. When Bird and those guys started playing bebop, they were blasted by the mainstream press and shunned by the musical establishment. Their music was too chaotic, too angry, too complicated. Well, brother, they were just being real. The world is full of chaos and anger, and it's getting more complicated by the minute. What you heard in their music was what they were living on the street, not some lullaby from yesteryear. But out of the chaos and the anger and the complexity they created something beautiful, something that didn't exist before, a musical voice that speaks to us like the music of earlier eras can't—because it resonates with our times, because it was born out of our struggles. Beethoven's music is beautiful, don't get me wrong. It's amazing what he did, but his music doesn't speak to the world we live in the way Bird's does. Bird brought beauty out of the chaos, and that's what we need to do with our lives. We need to make sense of what is going on and find our way to higher ground. That's why his music had such a powerful effect on people. It gave meaning to the chaos."

"I haven't heard Allen or Gary's poems yet, but from the way they were talking that sounds like what they're trying to do."

"It certainly does, and I hope they make it. We need a *kavi* or two in this country to get us heading in the right direction."

"What's a *kavi*?"

"It's the Sanskrit word for 'poet,' but actually *kavi* means 'seer' or 'visionary.' The idea is that a great poet or a great artist can decipher the currents of the past and the present and see where they're taking us. There are all these forces at work—economic forces, political forces, cultural forces, contemporary beliefs and values—and they're all leading us in a certain direction, the present pushing toward the future, but most people can't decipher the currents. They can't see what's up ahead. That's where the *kavi*s come in. They are not only able to articulate those forces so that the culture begins to wake up and understand its experience, but because they can see where we are going they are able to steer the boat. You know what a vector is, right? You must have studied it in school."

"Yeah, sure. I wasn't great in math but I know what a vector is."

"The thing about a vector, brother, is that if you alter its direction just a fraction, say an nth of one degree, you won't notice any effect right away. Compare it to its original trajectory and you won't see any noticeable difference. But the farther it goes the more noticeable it becomes. Take that same vector far into the future and the difference becomes enormous. That's what a great artist can do through his art. If he can change the direction of people's thinking, even slightly, then eventually—maybe one, two, three, four, five generations into the future—the effect of that change becomes monumental. The course of history is altered. A Buddhist philosopher would say that an artist doesn't actually do anything—it's Buddha mind expressing itself through that artist that brings about the change, and that's true, but he's still the instrument of Buddha mind, he's still the instrument of history. I don't know if Allen or Gary are going to be instruments of whatever changes lie up ahead but it's entirely possible. Maybe this poem 'Howl' that Gary was talking about will be part of that. I haven't heard it yet but who knows, it could tip the balance, push the vector ever so slightly. It wouldn't shock me. There is a writer or two out there somewhere who is going to push the vector. That much I'm sure of. Bird did it with his music. Somebody is going to do it with literature. Why not one of them? We'll have a better idea when we go to the reading."

"What about jazuzen? Could that also push the vector?"

"Of course. Anything Zen can push the vector, brother. It's like Kool-Aid in water. Add it to the music or the poetry and it colors every drop. Japan's greatest artists were Zen practitioners. Basho, Ikkyu, Sesshu. They've been dead for hundreds of years now but people still remember them, still look to their poems and songs and paintings for inspiration and guidance. There were famous artists in Japan who had no feeling for Zen, or for any kind of spiritual endeavor, but no one remembers them anymore. Basho, on the other hand, lived four hundred years ago and every Japanese child knows his poems. And they'll still be reciting them hundreds of years from now and learning how to see the world through his eyes, the eyes of wisdom. That's the power of Zen. He put his Zen into his poems, and it was the Zen that made them immortal."

I hadn't heard of Basho, but I was fascinated by the idea of a Zen monk wandering the hills of Japan reciting poems.

"It seems like half the artists in North Beach are into Zen in one fashion or another," I mused. "Like you said, it's in the water. Maybe some of them will be like Basho."

Elijah raised an eyebrow. "Let's not get carried away now, brother. Basho was a Zen monk who spent most of his life practicing Zen, not talking about it. His poems were born out of satori; they weren't the droppings of his monkey mind. Last I looked, I didn't notice any

Zen monks wandering the streets of North Beach reciting poems. There are a few serious practitioners around, I'll give you that, and more on the way, but most of what the Zen crowd around here practices is talking Zen, and that's no Zen at all. Real Zen is found on the seat of your pants. You can think about it and talk about it all you want, but if you want to know what real Zen is, then you have to stop thinking, stop talking, and just sit. Sit and wrestle with your monkey mind until it stops jumping around. Until you can make your mind quit its chatter, you don't know what Zen is. You just think you do. And that's half the problem right there."

I didn't say anything but that didn't mean I was quiet. Didn't you have to understand what Zen was before you could practice it, I thought? What about all the philosophy I was reading, the sutras, the dharma? What was that if not talking Zen? There was no doubt in my mind that the Zen-inspired North Beach crowd was light years ahead of where most of America was hanging out. Wasn't that something to be proud of?

I could tell from the look Elijah gave me that he was aware of the tumult in my mind. "Okay, out with it," he said. "If you are going to think like a banshee you might as well shriek like one."

That got me going. In my own inarticulate way I stood up in defense of the talking Zen that was making the rounds in North Beach alongside the radical political consciousness that Elijah clearly shared. There was a cultural revolution going on in the Bay Area, I insisted, and Zen teachings were playing a big part in it, maybe bigger than he knew, locked away as he was in his private temple. Elijah listened patiently to my disjointed ramble, his attentive silence making me all the more aware of my muddled thinking. I think it was the first time I had ever spoken at any length with any real conviction in front of him. Normally I just asked questions and listened. But he seemed to like it, and that made it easier for me to complete my thoughts.

"Is that what you believe?" he asked, when I finally ran out of steam.

"Yes, it is."

"Okay. Fair enough. I don't disagree with much of what you said. It's been a terrible half century, and maybe that's what it takes to get people to start waking up. There is no denying that people learn more from their mistakes than they do from their successes, and the last fifty years seems like one huge mistake after another. But how much better it's going to be five years from now or ten years—if it's better at all—well, that's going to depend on how much wisdom we've gained, and I don't see a whole lot of wisdom in the San Francisco crowd, not yet at least. There's one thing you need to understand about Zen if you are going to be a wise being yourself one day. You can't gain wisdom by thinking; you can only gain it by not thinking. Wisdom is what is left when the delusions of the mind no longer cloud your sight. Wisdom means clarity of mind, and clarity only comes when the storm settles. The storm within. You hear what I'm saying?"

"But what about the philosophy, Elijah, the sutras? Don't they teach us how to understand the world?"

"They do, and that has its place, but I'm going to let you in on a little secret: philosophy is for convincing others—or for convincing ourselves if we're still not convinced. Convincing us of what? Convincing us that the path to wisdom is learning how to empty our minds. To let the world settle until we see it as it really is. That's all you need to understand. That's why intellectuals are at a distinct disadvantage. They think too much and all that thinking just gets in the way. Let me tell you a little story. Once a monk went to the Buddha and threatened to give up his spiritual practices unless the Buddha answered his question: is there life after death? The Buddha told him that if a man who has been wounded by a poisoned arrow tells the surgeon that he won't allow him to remove the arrow and treat the wound unless he can first tell him whether the archer belonged to the Brahmin caste or the warrior caste, whether he was tall or short, dark or fair, from the country or the city, then he will die before he gets his questions answered. The poison is ignorance, brother, and unless you accept the treatment and reach enlightenment then you are a lost cause. No amount of questions and answers can cure you. The treatment is to bring your body and mind into harmony through Zen practice. You hear what I'm saying?"

"So studying Zen is just an obstacle?"

"I didn't say that. There's a place for talking Zen also. There's a place for everything. But there's a danger as well, and the danger is that your mind will convince you that you know Zen, that you understand it, when actually you don't know Zen until you experience the egoless state. That's why I told you that you learn Zen on the seat of your pants. The fifth patriarch had five hundred elevated monastic disciples who were all well versed in Zen doctrine, but he made an illiterate lay disciple his successor, a firewood peddler. When they asked him why, he told them, 'Because he is the one disciple who doesn't understand Buddhism; he only knows the Way.' Have you been sitting?"

"Every morning and every night, just like you taught me."

"Good. That's the main thing. Go ahead with your talking Zen. There's no harm as long as you sit. It has its place. There's walking Zen, working Zen, why not talking Zen?"

"And jazz Zen."

"Of course. But just remember: the whole purpose of talking Zen is to get you to sit. If you do, then the rest is just window dressing. That's where Zen begins and ends—on your cushion."

We were quiet for a while but I still had questions, and after a few minutes I tried a different tack.

"Even if we don't have any Bashos yet, don't you think that the artists who are practicing Zen—even if it's mostly talking Zen and only partly sitting Zen—don't you think that's going to have some effect on their work? I know Gary sits every day. I'm sure it shows up in his poems. I know it does in your music. I've heard you play. Even a little Zen must leave its mark. Like Kool-Aid in water, right? Isn't that what you said? You said you wouldn't be surprised if Gary or Allen pushed the vector."

"You might also one day if you learn to play from your *hara* and not from your monkey mind; otherwise, I wouldn't be spending my time teaching you. It's certainly not for the money."

That much was obvious. Elijah had yet to accept a single dime for my lessons. I had offered several times but he kept putting me off.

"I'm not a pessimist, brother," he continued, "but I saw what happened in Japan. Japanese culture is steeped in Zen, but they still invaded China, got in bed with the Nazis, and bombed Pearl Harbor. Eight centuries of a living Zen tradition and it didn't stop them from kowtowing to an imperialist military regime. I don't know, I'm still trying to figure out how a country with so much traditional wisdom and so many elevated Zen monks could fall in with the fascists and try to conquer half the world. The only thing I've been able to come up with is that the monastic orders became isolated from society. They shut themselves up in their monasteries and hid behind their begging bowls and stopped being of any real relevance in people's lives. They let the ordinary temple priests take care of people's spiritual education, and the temple priests in Japan don't do zazen. They lead the rituals and conduct the ceremonies, that's all. They have no spiritual experience of their own. I suspect that's why Japanese society lost the true spirit of Zen. Real spiritual experience makes you feel a bond with all of life that precludes self-centered behavior. There's a moral core at the heart of Zen, and it comes directly from that experience. I saw it in Zuigan-roshi and in the other senior monks. If that spirit had still been alive in the people they would have never let their leaders push them into war. If it had been alive in the artists they would have raised an outcry from Kyushu to Hokkaido that the emperor wouldn't have been able to ignore. I couldn't read much Japanese when I got to Myoshinji, but I got pretty good at it while I was there, mostly by studying the sutras, and as far as I can tell none of the influential twentieth-century artists were serious practitioners. They were Sunday Buddhists like everyone else, in the same way that most Americans are Sunday Christians. They lit incense in front of the Buddha's image when they went to the temple, but they didn't practice zazen. There were no Bashos or Ikkyus around. Too bad. If there had been some real Zen artists to keep the spirit of Zen alive among the people, they might have been able to prevent the country from committing collective hara-kiri. Or else artists don't have as much influence on society as I like to think."

Elijah didn't seem to be talking with me as much as he was sifting through his thoughts. His gaze was fixed on the drifting clouds of early March, and when he talked about Japan there was a wistful tone in his voice that made me aware how strong his ties still were to that distant culture. It made me think that his Japanese garden and private temple were a way of keeping his link alive to the islands that had led him to the spiritual path.

Elijah fell silent as the twilight deepened, and the silence continued as the shadows thickened into darkness. I started shifting uncomfortably on the bench, thinking that it was time for me to leave. But then he picked up the conversation where he had left off, as if he had paused on the bridge between one thought and another to watch the water flowing by, a pause that lasted close to half an hour but which didn't in any way disturb the continuity of his thoughts.

"Most of the monks didn't support the war, but some did. They weren't like the thousands of bishops and priests in Germany and occupied Europe that openly supported the Nazis, but there were some open militarists, like Yasutani-roshi. What's worse, they gave spiritual training to the Japanese military. That's where the kamikazes got their inspiration. Yasutani and a few others taught them Zen techniques and distorted the philosophy of egolessness so that they would sacrifice their lives for their country without questioning what they were doing. In the meantime, the real Zen practitioners, the ones that understood the true spirit of Zen, did nothing about it. They locked themselves up in their monasteries and they locked the real Zen up with them. That has to stop. The war is proof of that. Enlightened souls can't remain shut up in monasteries if the world is going to change. They have to get their hands dirty and be willing to be leaders. Not political leaders but cultural and spiritual leaders. People need guidance, and you can't expect them to come to you in your monastery or your mountaintop—the only people you'll see there are other spiritual seekers. You have to go to them."

"But you never leave your cottage and you don't play in public anymore. Isn't that the same as those monks shutting themselves up in their monasteries?"

Elijah appeared startled to hear my voice, as if he had forgotten I was there. Then his eyes crinkled and he let out a generous laugh.

"That's different. Just because I don't want to perform doesn't mean I'm going to stay in this cottage forever. First you have to gain some wisdom before you can share it. And the best way to do that, brother, is to sit. That's why I'm here. Which reminds me, it's time for my evening practice. Would you like to join me?"

His offer took me entirely by surprise. I had never sat with Elijah outside of our twice-weekly lessons, and I had never imagined that I would. Delighted by the invitation, I followed him into the cottage where I got my first look at the inside of what he called the *zendo*: the back room that he used for sleeping and meditation. It was an eight-by-twelve cubicle with a bedroll in one corner and several cushions in the other, divided off from the main room by a slatted partition and sliding door fitted with the same opaque paper that was ubiquitous in traditional Japanese dwellings. There was a tiny altar under the lone window with a small golden Buddha, an incense burner, and a picture of an elderly shaven-head monk sitting on a mat and smiling at the camera, whom I later discovered was Zuigan-roshi.

I had only been meditating for a couple of months, and Elijah's practice was far more rigorous than I was used to: forty minutes zazen followed by ten minutes *kinhin*, walking meditation in the garden with our eyes lowered and our attention on our breathing, followed by forty minutes zazen, ten minutes *kinhin*, and one final forty-minute sitting in the zendo with my legs aching and my mind clinging to my breath like the proverbial Zen monk hanging by his fingernails from the edge of a cliff. By the time I headed home I was mentally and physically exhausted. But I was also convinced that Elijah was right: Zen had to be learned on the seat of your pants. My mind was a tempest and no amount of philosophy or clever conversation was going to calm those raging winds. If I was going to do it, I would have to do it the same way that Zen practitioners had done it since Buddha's day: I was going to have to stare down my mind and bring it to heel. And I was just beginning to realize how difficult that would be.

14

ELIJAH EXTENDED ME AN open invitation to join him for morning and evening meditation, and I took advantage of the offer as often as I could. Mornings were difficult — Elijah got up at 3:30, a holdover from his days at Myoshinji, and after a quick trip to the bathroom he sat on his cushion until 6:30, alternating between sitting practice and short rounds of *kinhin* — though once or twice a week I would get up early enough to splash some water in my face and join him for the last half of his practice. But on weekday evenings I was almost always there, as if I were a lay brother sitting with the monks in a Zen monastery after work. And really, it wasn't that far from the truth. For all intents and purposes, Elijah had recreated his life as a Zen monk in his Berkeley cottage, right down to the Zen garden that he worked in each morning like he used to do in Myoshinji, sequestered from the rest of civilization. He got up, seven days a week, at the time most jazz musicians with a gig were going to bed — earlier than those who joined in the after-hours jam sessions like the one at Bop City where I would usually find myself in the wee hours of the morning when the weekend rolled around. But that was just logistics. Once I started joining Elijah for meditation, I started feeling that I was breathing the atmosphere of two very different and seemingly incompatible worlds. The contrast was never more striking than when I went straight from an evening in the clubs to morning zazen in the zendo. It was like transiting from an interstellar carnival, full of flashing lights and incomprehensible chatter, to a medieval Asian oasis steeped in silence — the same universe, perhaps, but opposite poles. Elijah never discouraged me from my midnight rambles. Sometimes over breakfast — either rice gruel and pickled vegetables or miso soup and boiled rice — he would ask me who I had seen play that night and what I thought of their music. And I would try to describe the scene through bleary Zen eyes that had yet to go to bed. He knew that my dream was to get up onstage one day and transport an audience to the unseen worlds where the gods of jazz dwelled, and every time I entered his garden for a lesson he took me one step closer. It wasn't his dream any longer, but it had been for years, so he knew where I was coming from, perhaps better than I did myself. He had realized that dream in the jazz mecca of New York City, only to discover that his years of sitting in the zendo at 3:30 in the morning, trying to put down the disorderly insurgency of the monkey mind, had made him too acutely aware of the dance of delusion to remain willingly under its spell. But I would have to earn that realization for myself, and he knew that.

As the weeks and months went by, images of his life would float up like flotsam to the surface of our conversations, but many of the details I only filled in later, when I went to New York to research my first book and took advantage of the opportunity to run down the tracks that Elijah had left in the jazz sky. Many of the musicians I interviewed knew him from his brief sojourn in the city, and they were happy to talk at length of what they remembered of a supremely talented saxophonist who had defied convention by dropping out just when his star was ascending on the horizon.

I learned that Elijah had found the kind of success in New York that most jazz musicians only dream of. Less than six weeks after his arrival in the spring of 1950, with his soldier's savings and the same tenor sax that he had lugged from island to island through three years of fighting in the swamps and jungles of Southeast Asia, but still unable to land a gig, he climbed onto the bandstand at Minton's with Charlie Yardbird Parker and played two choruses of a Zen-inflected, Alabama-born spring lament over the changes to "Laura" that brought him instant admission into the holy academy of righteous blowing. He was twenty-four years old and no one had ever heard a horn played quite that way. I wasn't there but I had heard Elijah play enough to know exactly what froze those musicians in their seats that night and had them lift their eyes to heaven to discover the source of those uncanny sounds. How many times had

I closed my eyes and opened my ears to his horn and found myself wandering by the living waters of a mountain stream, suffused in a melancholy so sweet it made my insides ache? I imagine that whatever conversations those musicians who were not on the bandstand were having were hushed by the first notes from Elijah's horn, replaced by the recognition that this hulking young Negro—whose only credentials for being allowed to sit in were his imposing size, his army-issue khakis, and the battle scars in his eyes—was the real deal: a jazz genie who had just been let out of his bottle. I can just see Bird squinting for a few moments as he scrutinized this young interloper who was bigger than anyone else in the room, then smiling as his ears drank in the one libation he preferred above all others, above the triple-malt scotch and uncut heroin that helped to make a difficult life bearable: a pure improvised solo whose melodies came straight from life itself—unrehearsed, unmediated, inimitable.

It was a tradition at Minton's that newcomers were to be tested, thrown into the deep end to either sink or swim, which in bebop meant playing through challenging changes at lightning speeds without losing your way—and if you sank, to be shooed off the stage with no condolences, never to be invited up again. At least not until you had proved yourself under the lesser lights of other gigs. Elijah remained on the bandstand for the next tune, a right he had earned by silencing an audience that included some of the best jazz musicians on the planet. Bird called for "Ornithology," one of the most challenging tunes in the bebop repertoire. As I heard it described by a pair of musicians who were in the audience that night, Bird tapped out a tempo a full twenty beats per minute faster than the tempo at which he had recorded the tune. And Elijah nailed it. Perhaps it was the birds of Japan that he evoked with his horn, perhaps the mist around Mount Fuji, I don't know, but after that the offers started flying in at all hours. Over the next year and a half he played several engagements with Bird, went on tour with Miles, and did a three-month stint with Fletcher Henderson. Monk had lost his cabaret card by then and wasn't allowed to play within a fifty-mile radius of the city, but he went to hear Elijah play and started inviting him to his apartment for jam sessions that would have become even more legendary than they already are had Monk bothered to record them. But that was Monk to a tee. The only voice he listened to was the voice inside his head, a voice that was half genius, half extraterrestrial. It's easy to see the affinity between the two. Monk could have been wildly successful had he been willing to play outside New York—and he had plenty of offers—but he refused and instead spent six years holed up in his apartment, revolutionizing the world of jazz without anyone but Elijah and a handful of others knowing about it. Elijah was even more extreme. He could have easily become just as famous as Monk would later become, but one day in late 1951 he packed up his sax and boarded a train for San Francisco without so much as saying goodbye or letting anyone know where he was going. He never came straight out and said it, but as I understand it, he had a kind of gradual counter-satori. He realized that for all the great music he and his fellow musicians were creating, music that sometimes bordered on genius, he was living in the den of Mara, in a world propped up by the kinds of delusions that the Buddha had described as the enemy of the enlightened being, and he knew that if he was ever going to clear his mind of those delusions, then he was going to have to alter the course of his life.

He played a few sporadic gigs once he arrived in San Francisco, more out of habit than for the money, but by the time I got to know him he was a confirmed recluse who had no interest whatsoever in seeing the inside or outside of a jazz club. He hadn't disappeared. Musicians in town knew who he was—that kind of reputation doesn't go away—but they also knew that it was futile asking him to play a gig or sit in for a recording session. By and large they left him in peace, especially since whenever they came around to talk music he would talk Zen and send them running politely for the San Francisco hills.

I was sitting with him on his porch one day before our evening practice when Sol Weiss, the owner of Fantasy Records, a bifocaled, aging hipster with a high-pitched laugh, dropped by to try to convince him to do an album of sax music for Zen meditation. He had been trying to sign Elijah to a recording deal for the past three years, and I guess he thought that if he could make it look like the record was somehow connected with Zen, then he might be able to convince him to sign with his label. Elijah was amused by his pitch but that was as far as it went.

"Think about it, Preacher. This is your chance to bring Zen to the masses. Just think what will happen when young people get hold of this record. It'll make them want to sit down and meditate, you can count on it. We'll put a Buddha on the cover and some liner notes about how the music was composed to help you calm your mind and attain inner peace. The minute they put the record on they'll feel the vibration, and it's only one step from there to the nearest meditation cushion. People who are already meditating will put it on to get them in the mood and clear their mind of distractions, and those who aren't will start thinking that maybe they should. Especially if it can inspire music like this. Zen is already catching on on the West Coast. This record will put it right over the top. It will bring Zen into people's living rooms. Everybody will want to be able to experience the kind of tranquility they hear in the music. And between the liner notes and the cover, they'll discover that meditation's the answer, Zen's the answer. And you won't have to tour or play in clubs or even promote the album. We'll take care of everything. You just show up at the studio for a few days, and after that the only thing you'll need to do is deposit your royalty checks. If it catches on, you'll never have to play another gig. You'll be able to live off the royalties. So what do you say? Is it time to bring Zen into the living rooms of this country?"

I was convinced. It was the greatest idea I'd heard since I'd arrived in the Bay Area. Fantasy Records was a big-time player in the jazz world — it was Dave Brubeck's label — and Elijah was the most unique jazz soloist I had ever heard. I would have been the first to buy the record and I would have worn it out learning his lines. But Elijah was a hard sell. While I was convinced that such a record would induce more than a few people to try meditating — at the very least it would have brought some joy and some serenity into the lives of those who listened to it — Elijah's only reaction to Sol's pitch was an amused smile and a gentle shake of the head.

"I appreciate the offer, Brother Sol. Somebody should do an album of music for Zen meditation, and sooner or later somebody will. It may even do what you say it'll do. But I'm not your man, at least not for now. For now I'm just trying to stay in the moment, you hear."

"Just think about it, okay?" Sol said, unable to keep the disappointment from his voice. "You don't have to decide today. Just promise me you'll give it some thought."

Elijah's smile widened. "Well, I don't know if I can promise you that, brother. Like I said, right now I'm just hanging out in the moment. Let's just say that the future's not in my plans. But check back in a few months. Like I said, it's a good idea. Who knows, I might wake up one morning and find out that it's time to record an album. If that happens, there's no one I'd rather record with. And not because you're just over the bridge. I appreciate what you're doing at Fantasy. You've made some good albums over there. If I do decide to record, you'll be the first to know about it. Straight up."

Later I asked Elijah why he didn't take this chance to push the vector, footprints or no footprints. What Sol Weiss had said made sense. If Elijah believed that great art could change the world, then why didn't he take this chance to put his imprint on the world of jazz, knowing that there was no telling how far the ripples would extend?

"You can't let your ego decide these things, brother, not if you want to walk the enlightened path. We're instruments, that's all. Make the mirror empty and let the Buddha decide. When the world needs a jazz album for Zen meditation, it will get one. You can be sure of that. The time just isn't ripe yet. And you know how I know that the time's not ripe?"

"No, how?"

"Because if it was, I would have said yes."

Eight years later Tony Scott recorded *Music for Zen Meditation* in a temple in Kyoto, and I reviewed it for the *San Jose Mercury*. In my review I dusted off some of Elijah's old ideas about the role of art in society and predicted that the album would push the vector in the direction of a more enlightened, more spiritual approach to jazz improvisation. Fourteen years later I can safely say that this was an accurate prediction. Scott's album sent ripples through the jazz community — calming, consciousness-deepening ripples. He was a big influence on Paul Winter, Ralph Towner, and other musicians who are in the process of revolutionizing the world of jazz, forging a spiritual context for the music that has become America's classical music and one of the true jewels of our culture. But I couldn't help wondering then, as I still do now, what would have happened to the music if it had been Elijah who had recorded that album. No disrespect to Tony Scott — he was only doing what the Buddha asked of him, and there is no doubt that he was playing from his *hara* when he recorded that album. But Tony Scott is no Elijah. I've never seen anyone with Elijah's blend of improvisational originality and single-minded devotion to the work of cleaning the mirror of the mind. I'm convinced that had he taken up Sol's offer and recorded that album, he would have pushed the vector much further than Tony or anyone else could have done, and the world would have been a better place for it, a more compassionate, more enlightened place. But this is all idle speculation. The world got the album it needed, and Elijah was able to hang on to his cherished obscurity. No amount of wishful thinking on my part will change that. But the future has yet to be written, and I still hope that Elijah will emerge one day to play a prominent role — or rather, that he will be one of the instruments that the Buddha picks up when it comes time for him to play the music of the coming years.

15

THE WEEKEND OF THE Berkeley poetry reading was a watershed weekend for me in many ways. You might even say it was that weekend that I finally left behind the cautious, conservative, borderline robotic insularity that seemed to be part of the genetic makeup of middle-class America at that time—nowhere more so than in the San Fernando Valley, where neighborhoods like the one I grew up in served as poster images of the American dream. I met up with Diana in Washington Square after my last class on Friday and spent the rest of the weekend perambulating with her and an ever-changing cast of characters from one ebullient summit to another in cafés and bars and apartments and parks, a delirious, high-spirited odyssey with no acknowledged destination and no overt purpose other than enjoying the camaraderie of kindred souls. Wherever we went, there was music and poetry, street theater and art, but the glue that held it all together was the ongoing conversation that kept to its course though the different participants came and went. The world was the central theme—where it was at and where it was going—and running through the dialogue was an incurable optimism that despite the repressive conditions in which we lived, despite the gaping jaws of runaway capitalism and the maniacs in the White House and the Pentagon, the future belonged to us. And we were going to make sure that it wouldn't be anything like what our fathers had imagined. The world was changing. It was perched on the edge of a precipice, and we were the ones with our hands on its surface, getting ready to push it over—us and thousands more like us scattered across the wastelands of the world. The poets among us supplied most of the words—Ginsberg, Sartori, McClure, Snyder, Corso, Whalen, and others—but they plucked their words from the same air we all breathed. They were the voice of the era, but the spirit was a collective creation, a rising tsunami carrying us toward the floodgates of consciousness that would burst open in the unforgettable sixties.

For me that weekend was the confirmation of something I had been feeling for some time but had yet to articulate: the feeling that I was home, that for better or for worse these were my people and this was where I would make my stand. In some ways I had always felt out of place in the Valley, as if I had been stranded in a foreign land. I think a lot of people feel this — there is no discounting the fact that the world can be an alienating place, wherever your destiny strands you — and not everyone reaches the point, both within and without, where they can say they truly feel at home. I was lucky. I had found my tribe, and with Elijah's help I had begun my search for life's one true mooring: the unassailable peace of a mind free from delusion.

I met Whalen for the first time that weekend and Dalenberg also, two dharma friends who have stuck with me throughout the journey, even when it got ugly, as it did for a couple of lost years in the early sixties when the "jazz life" nearly took me down. It may be a cliché but it's worth repeating that it's in hard times that true friendship shows its mettle. I wouldn't be where I am today if it wasn't for Philip and Ananda and Diana, and others who shared that carnival weekend with me. Buddha called it the sangha, the community of seekers. I think we are all seekers in the deepest sense, but most people don't realize it. Somehow we all felt it in those days, whether we were Buddhists or anarchists or artists or just young people along for the ride. It was in the air and in the water — you just couldn't help it. We were a community out to reshape the world, and as I look back, twenty-two years later, there is no doubt in my mind that we had a serious hand in how different the world looks today.

I didn't sleep much that weekend and I don't remember doing any actual meditation, but on Sunday afternoon I got in my car and headed back to Berkeley for a shower and a change of clothes before going over to Elijah's to sit. The reading was at eight and Elijah had decided to move up his evening practice so we could leave at seven-thirty. Practicing serious zazen in Elijah's zendo after the tumultuous carousel of the previous two days was like getting my head dipped repeatedly in cold water. My mind was a circus of tumbling images, but there was no escaping the cold reality of my cushion. The images danced and caroused before my half-open eyes and assaulted my inner ear with disconnected fragments of the weekend's conversations, but my breath kept pulling me back to the unforgiving starkness of the zendo. Count your breaths: one on the first exhalation, two on the second, and on up to ten, then back again to one, over and over, like a water wheel that never stops spinning, until the images and conversations start to settle like sediment to the bottom of a stream. It was almost painful at first. What I wanted more than anything was to give myself up to the delights of reverie, to throw myself into the river of images and drift downstream in easeful abandon. But the way of Zen is as unforgiving as the battlefield, an unending effort to pierce the reality of the present moment, and if I needed any reminder of why I was there, I had only to glance out of the corner of my eye at Elijah sitting ramrod straight on his cushion with his body perfectly motionless, the bare hint of a smile on his face nearly identical to the one on the Buddha in the garden. Faking it wasn't an option. Gradually the alluvium settled, and by the time we were finished I was glad I had made that forced march through the jungles of my mind.

When we got up from our cushions, shortly before seven-thirty, Elijah laid his hand on my shoulder and said, "Good poetry needs silence to be properly appreciated, brother. It doesn't matter how quiet the hall is if you don't bring the silence with you. You still won't hear anything."

It seems my restlessness did not go unnoticed.

The theater was filling up fast when we arrived and there was a festive atmosphere in the hall. People were milling about as if they were at an open-air concert, exchanging hugs and punctuating the thrumming of voices with peals of laughter. The crowd was a virtual who's who of Bay Area bohemia, an eclectic mix of artists, activists, and all-around hipsters with a few curious onlookers sprinkled in who had come to get a taste of the San Francisco scene. I spotted several classmates—I had passed out cyclostyle fliers to nearly everyone

I knew in school—as well as reporters from the *Chronicle*, the *Examiner*, and a number of lesser papers. The Six Gallery reading had become a part of local folklore, and this reprisal was a chance for those who had missed out to be able to say that they were there when a new generation of American poets stood the world on its ear.

I looked around the room until I spotted Diana standing near the stage, talking to Philip and Gary. I wanted to introduce her to Elijah while we had some time, but it took us a while to get through the crowd. People kept coming up to Elijah to say hello, surprising for a man who rarely left his cottage. But as I had begun to discover, nearly everyone in town who was into Buddhism had heard about the eccentric ex-saxophonist-turned-Zen-recluse and most had paid him a visit at one time or another. He was even better known in the jazz crowd, for whom he was a local legend, though many of them had never heard him play, and there were a number of musicians in the audience that night. But Elijah would have stood out anyhow. It wasn't just his size and the color of his skin—it was the sense of calm intensity he radiated. Elijah was locked into the moment, and there aren't many people you can say that about, even in spiritual circles. Anyone who had met him would have felt the weight of his presence, and that's not something one easily forgets.

"I'm really glad you made it, Preacher," Gary said, after Elijah folded his palms to his chest and bowed, a traditional Buddhist greeting that looked as natural coming from him as it would have from a Japanese monk, despite the jeans and corduroy jacket, a change of uniform that had taken me most of the short drive over to get used to.

"I'm glad you invited me, brother. If you remember, you promised me that this reading was going to shake up the world. I wouldn't want to miss that. From what I hear, the world could use a good shaking up."

Diana broke into an amused smile. "It doesn't sound like you get out much," she said.

"Not lately. But you don't have to get out to see what's going on, sister. You just have to open your eyes."

"Okay." Diana had a doubtful look on her face. I could see the poet's wheels spinning, turning over Elijah's words to see what was underneath. "Anyhow, you're right about one thing," she said. "The world does need a good shaking up. That's why we're here. I think I can guarantee you won't go home disappointed."

It was already eight by then and Allen called from the stage for Philip and Gary to come up. Diana had saved some seats for us in the front, and I left her and Elijah there while I went to say a quick hello to a couple of classmates. When I got back, I found the two of them in the middle of an animated conversation about—of all things—Dada. Or rather, Diana was animated. Elijah was as unruffled as ever, but I could tell from his smile that he was enjoying the exchange.

"… but that's just the point!" Diana was saying. "It wasn't about the object at all. The urinal was the perfect choice, no doubt. An inspired choice, because it was sure to invoke a whole constellation of unexamined preconceptions and dogmas: it's dirty, it's filthy, it's something no one wants to look at—as if there were something inherently ugly about the human body relieving itself. But it could have been any object. The point was to take something perfectly ordinary, something no one would imagine calling art, and create a new thought for it. You alter the context, put the urinal in an art exhibition, and suddenly you call into question not only what is art but what is a urinal. It was brilliant. It was the emperor without his clothes. What he was really putting on display was our own unexamined prejudices, our unquestioned beliefs, our centuries of moral rigidity, our denigration of the human body, which if you think about it we should be admiring as the greatest of all works of art, right down to its beautiful streams of piss, like the purest gold. Do you know what they started calling the urinal after the jurors removed it from the exhibit?"

"As a matter of fact, I do," Elijah said. "*Buddha of the Bathroom.*"

That stopped Diana cold, but only for a moment. Her look of stunned surprise was quickly replaced by something closer to elation. "That's right!" she exclaimed. "*Buddha of the Bathroom.* The great teacher in the form of a urinal, showing us the crap that's in our minds. Isn't that what you Buddhists preach? That our minds are full of delusion, and that if we want to reach nirvana then we have to clean them out? What better symbol for that than a urinal? I would have gone with a toilet myself, but I was only three years old then, and anyhow, I'm sure Duchamp thought of that before he decided to go with the urinal. And that's the essence of Dada. You change the context and throw it back on the observer. Instead of art being about the object of art, it's about the subject. It's about who's seeing the piece and what they bring to the table. How do their preconceptions color and ultimately determine what they see?"

I noticed people in the nearby seats leaning forward to listen to the conversation, which wasn't easy with the buzz of several hundred voices filling the hall. I had no idea at the time what Dada was — I had never heard of Duchamp and his famous urinal — but the conversation was riveting and I was dying to hear what Elijah would say.

"Art is not about pointing out people's hang-ups, sister, any more than Buddhism is. It's about elevating people's minds. Art elevates our minds through aesthetic pleasure and Buddhism by teaching us how to attain tranquility and harmony through mental discipline. A urinal is a urinal. It doesn't matter if it's in a New York art exhibition or in a public toilet in Grand Central Station. Stop and contemplate it all you want, it's not going to change that. Sure it's a Buddha. Everything is. Anything can enlighten you if you're ready to be enlightened. In Japan they use a stick and whack you with it when you're meditating. There are monks who became enlightened when they got hit, but it didn't make the stick a work of art. Something becomes art when it has the aesthetic power to put a spell over your mind and lead you to a deeper understanding of your existence, whether it's your social existence or your spiritual existence, like I hope the poetry we are about to hear will do. If that power is not there then it's not art. It's just entertainment. In this case, it's just a urinal. Piss in it or put it on a pedestal in a Fourth Avenue convention hall and call it *Buddha of the Bathroom*, it makes no difference. It's still a urinal. It's not going to change our lives, which is what art is all about. Whether you like it or not, sister, artists have a responsibility to society —"

I could see that Diana was chomping at the bit, waiting to jump in with her rebuttal, but the gods of Dada didn't give her a chance to defend their honor. That would have to wait. Elijah stopped in midsentence when Kenneth Rexroth stepped to the microphone to open the Celebrated Good Time Poetry Night.

Rexroth introduced the evening by talking about the San Francisco Renaissance, the wave of new poets who he claimed were in the vanguard of the cultural upheaval that was preparing to sweep across the country. It was a term he had coined and popularized through his Friday-evening get-togethers in his spacious apartment on Scott street, a coinage that would be subsumed before the year was up by the term "beat poets" when Richard Eberhart introduced the San Francisco poetry scene to a national audience in the September issue of the *New York Times Book Review*. Kerouac would become arguably the most famous of the beat writers, but the four poets that Rexroth went on to introduce would all have significant roles to play in the changing of the cultural guard, none more so than Allen Ginsberg, who was the first poet he called to the lectern.

Allen was still clean-shaven then, still rail thin with a full shock of curling black hair and his usual black-rimmed glasses, looking more like an awkward undergraduate than the dharma lion whose poetry and panache would do as much as Kerouac's novels to remake the American consciousness. But he dispelled that image the moment he looked up from the papers in his hand and began reciting the opening stanza of "Howl" in a clear, penetrating baritone that would have carried the hall even without the mic.

> *I saw the best minds of my generation destroyed by madness, starving hysterical naked,*
> *dragging themselves through the negro streets at dawn looking for an angry fix,*
> *angelheaded hipsters burning for the ancient heavenly connection to the starry dynamo in the machinery of night,*
> *who poverty and tatters and hollow-eyed and high sat up smoking in the supernatural darkness of cold-water flats floating across the tops of cities contemplating jazz...*

To this day I can remember the tremor that ran through me as the opening lines of "Howl" echoed in the eager silence of the theater.

I had heard a lot about the poem from Diana and Gary, and from Allen himself, but I hadn't read it or heard it read until then. I'm glad now that I heard it that first time rather than read it, and even gladder that it was Allen's voice. Poetry is an auditory art form, traversing the direct conduit between the ear and the heart, but I felt "Howl" in my gut that night, even as my mind was escaping the theater to keep pace with the hallucinatory rush of images. I wasn't just lifted up, as I might have been by an especially melodic solo—I was punched in the gut and dragged through the Negro streets, terrified, laughing, crying, triumphant, and angry, with a righteous anger that was like a self-inflicted slap to the face. And then I was lifted up to gaze at the world with the euphoria and inarticulate wisdom that comes from having your eyes open to everything that goes on down below in the world you inhabit. I could hear voices in the audience encouraging Allen as his long, loping verses gathered force, the energy in the hall building toward an uncomfortable, almost menacing crescendo, but my voice wasn't among them. For most of those thirty minutes I was out of my body, seeing the world through the poet's eyes and lamenting the tragedy of our collective existence, even as I felt the indescribable exhilaration of pure seeing, of having my sight expand beyond all recognizable limits, until the poem's final exhilarating declaration—*I'm with you in Rockland / in my dreams you walk dripping from a sea-journey on the highway across America in tears to the door of my cottage in the Western night*—the poet's culminating cry of solidarity with his fellow man.

It wasn't satori, perhaps, but it was a true altering of consciousness, such as the one I experienced when I first heard Bird's solo on "Ko-Ko." Only this was far deeper, an expanded awareness that embraced the suffering of others, a sudden insight into the world and my place in that world: the anguish, the ignorance, the fearful exploitation; together with the certainty that I was ready to walk that road with the rest of humanity, whether it led to Rockland or anywhere else, that we are all in this together, that the only truly noble, truly lived life, is the life dedicated to making the lives of others better. To this day I don't know how much of what I experienced was the poem and how much was something sleeping in me waiting to be freed.

But that's the power of art, the power to wake what is deepest and best in ourselves. That understanding, as the Buddhists say, is already inside us, but it is covered up, buried beneath layers and layers of the delusion that holds the world in thrall. I had forgotten about Elijah while I was caught up in the world of the poem, but when the applause dragged me from my vision, I became aware of him clapping alongside me, a serene yet joyful expression on his face, and I knew that what I had just experienced was the spell that he had insisted to Diana was the true essence and purpose of art.

I wasn't able to recreate that state when the other poets stepped to the front of the stage, first Snyder, then Whalen, and finally McClure. But neither did my feet entirely touch the ground. All the poems they read that night were memorable, though in very different ways. Gary's were like Zen poems re-sculpted for the American frontier — the New World as it is, shorn of any mediating consciousness; Philip's were more reflective, foreshadowing the Zen monk he would later become; Michael's were more personal, grounded in his love of nature and his passionate defense of disappearing landscapes and wildlife. Each led me to places I had never been before, or made me see an old experience through new eyes, and none could be dismissed as mere entertainment.

When the reading finished and the applause finally died down, the images and feelings the four poets had evoked lingered on, charging an atmosphere that was beginning to fill up with congratulations and conversations. Nobody wanted to leave, it seemed, and for a long while few did. The poets, as you might imagine, were the center of attention as they circulated through the hall, basking in the afterglow of their artistic endeavor. I stayed close to Diana, hovering at the edges of admiring congregations, while Elijah remained sitting near the stage, conversing with a small group of jazz musicians whom I recognized from the Fillmore clubs. Eventually, however, the theater began emptying out and Elijah started making motions for us to leave. Diana asked me if I could give her a ride back to North Beach — or perhaps I suggested it — and after saying our goodbyes we got in my car and made the short drive to Elijah's cottage to drop him off.

Diana hadn't forgotten her conversation with Elijah, and despite the celebratory mood she launched back into the discussion the moment we got in the car, and it continued outside Elijah's gate under a blanket of spring stars that made me feel as if we were standing inside an enormous cathedral. She was saying something about the artist's only responsibility being to her art, that the moment an artist picks up the banner of social responsibility her art invariably becomes corrupted in one way or another. Instead of being true to herself, of allowing her art to flourish on its own terms and according to its own designs, she bends it to a set of beliefs and imposed ideas about what society needs that in the end often prove more pernicious than helpful. In short, she cheapens her art and risks robbing it of whatever vitality and honesty it might have had. She even cited examples from German artists on both sides of the Nazi fence, those who used their art to support the regime and those who used it to try to bring it down. "Art for Art's Sake," an idea that predated Dada by a century, was the only way, she insisted, to protect the integrity of art and keep it from being co-opted by the powers-that-be.

It wasn't exactly a diatribe but it was certainly a partisan manifesto. Unlike Diana, however, Elijah didn't belong to any party and he had nothing to defend. He just described what he saw; and what he saw, he saw with a Buddhist clarity that cut like an incisor.

He waited until Diana ran out of gas, until the only punctuation in the silence of that late night suburban Berkeley street was the slow nodding of his head, and then he stepped into the void.

"There is one law from which none of us can escape, sister: the law of cause and effect. Throw a pebble into a pond and it generates ripples, and those ripples can't be taken back. Once the pebble leaves your hand, you have no control over the reaction to your action. What you have set in motion continues in motion. The only thing you can control is your action. Do you throw the pebble or do you not? And if you throw it, then how hard and how far and what size pebble do you use? Art doesn't exist in a vacuum, sister. Never has, never will. You write what you write so that other people can read it. That's what makes you an artist. And the moment someone reads it, it has an effect. If it's a strong poem it'll have a strong effect, if it's a weak poem, a weak effect, but it has an effect, and you have no control over that effect once you've thrown the poem into the pond. But the law of cause and effect holds you responsible for the consequences. You are responsible for everything you do in this life, everything that affects others. You can't slap somebody in the face and hide behind the slogan "A Slap for Slap's Sake." You're responsible for your actions and the ripples they make, whether you like it or not. The Buddha called it karma. Every action generates a reaction, and those reactions determine our future, for better or for worse — yours, mine, everyone's. An ethical human being recognizes this and acts accordingly. He uses his actions to alleviate the suffering of others, and by helping them he also helps himself, because it is his actions in the present that determine his future. Every single poem you write is going to have an effect on this world, sister, however large or small, and if you don't use your words to help enlighten the consciousness of the people who read them, or to lighten their burden in some way, then you cheat them and you also cheat yourself. You're better than that, sister, I'm sure of it, no matter how fond you are of all these intellectual ideas. Don't prove me wrong, okay? But now I must excuse myself. It's been a truly interesting conversation and a fascinating night. I'm really glad I got a chance to meet you, especially after listening to Brother Dan sing your praises, but I get up very early in the morning, and like all mortals I need my sleep."

"Interesting friend you've got there," Diana said in a somewhat petulant tone of voice as we were pulling away from the curb. "Exasperating but interesting. He speaks like he's the oracle of Delphi instructing a two-year-old. Almost made me want to wring his neck back there, but the thing is, he didn't seem full of himself at all. Almost the opposite, really. Maybe that's what was so exasperating. I felt like I was six years old again, getting a scolding from my grandfather."

"The one you liked so much?"

"The same. He was my hero when I was a kid. He didn't scold me often, but when he did I'd bend over backward to show him I'd learned my lesson. I'll be goddamned if your preacher didn't remind me of him. If he wasn't black and twice my size I'd have been tempted to answer him in Italian."

As we crossed the Bay Bridge into San Francisco, I told her what Elijah had said about talking Zen and Zen on the seat of your pants, how Zen Buddhists considered the intellect to be a major roadblock on the road to enlightenment.

"But what do *you* think?" she asked.

"To be honest, I'm starting to think that if Elijah says it's so then it must be so. He just tells it like he sees it, and I've never met anyone who sees as clearly as Elijah. There's no ego involved that I can tell. You haven't heard him play. If you had, you'd know what I am talking about. When he plays it's like there's no one there. There's just the music. And music like you've never heard before. It's so intoxicating you can't help but forget yourself as well. It's like the world itself stops to listen. That's the way it is when he talks about Zen. It's not his intellect talking. He's just describing his direct experience. So with the rest of it I give him the benefit of the doubt. I don't think either of us knows anyone who knows what it means to be an artist better than he does."

We were pulling up to Diana's building by then, and when I stopped the car she was looking at me as if I had just dropped in from another planet. I assumed that I had weirded her out with my talking Zen — something very hard to do with Diana, to whom weird was synonymous with interesting — but I need not have worried. She followed that look with a girlish laugh and asked me if I wanted to come up and spend the night. I had an early class the next morning but some things are more important than sleep. I doubt I got more than a couple of hours that night, but I made my class on time and counted those hours in Diana's bed as the perfect culmination to what was, up until then, the best weekend of my life.

16

THAT NIGHT IN DIANA'S bed she filled me in on Duchamp's urinal and Dada, but it was little more than a cursory glance since we had other things on our mind that had nothing to do with philosophy or art. But my curiosity was piqued—I knew next to nothing about the art avant-garde—and the next time I had a chance I asked Elijah about it. Surprisingly—or perhaps not—Elijah had learned about Dada and Bauhaus in Japan while wearing a monk's robes, thousands of miles from Western civilization. Myoshinji, like most Japanese monasteries, had a number of lay disciples attached to it, people who lived outside the temple grounds and led ordinary lives with jobs and families but who would come to the temple in their free time to meditate with the monks and study with the roshi. Shortly before Elijah joined the monastery, a forty-year-old American woman, Nancy Wilson Ross, and her husband, Charles, moved to Kyoto, where she became a regular visitor to the temple and an ardent student of Zuigan-roshi. She also became Elijah's closest friend during the two and a half years he was there, helping him with his Japanese—she spent much of her time translating Zen texts—and giving him practically his only outlet for conversation in his mother tongue. She had lived in Germany during the heyday of the Bauhaus and was friends with prominent avant-garde artists on both sides of the Atlantic, including Marcel Duchamp. She was also a true Zen fanatic, a highly educated, mystic-minded Texan who filled Elijah's mind with the philosophy and tradition that was behind the practice he had devoted himself to without knowing anything of its history or its texts.

"I started getting anemic after I moved into the monastery, so Zuigan-roshi gave me permission to go out after lunch to supplement my diet. I think he was afraid I might die on him. The food there is terrible, brother, mostly rice gruel and pickled vegetables, and that's no kind of diet for a two-hundred-and-forty-pound black man who grew up on ham hocks and bucketfuls of grits. Nancy offered to let me eat at her place — she lived a couple blocks from the temple grounds — and after that I used to go there pretty much every day to fill my belly and talk philosophy. Not only philosophy: art, science, politics, what have you — she was one brilliant woman — but Asian religions and spiritual philosophy, that was her thing. And it wasn't just talk with her. She was a serious meditator, better than most of the monks in the monastery. I remember the first *sesshin* we did together. I was just trying to make it to the end with my sanity intact, but with Nancy it was life and death, satori or bust. I tell you, that sister was every bit as serious about that sesshin as we were during the worst of Guadalcanal. But we were just trying to stay alive — she was on a mission, and there weren't many soldiers you could say that about."

"What's a sesshin?"

"A sesshin? A sesshin is like boot camp for Zen meditators. Six times a year Zuigan-roshi would close the temple grounds to the public for a week and put us through heavy duty Zen drills: twelve hours a day of zazen and *kinhin,* morning and evening *dokusan* — that's the private session with the roshi where he reviews your practice — plus sutra chanting and work. Officially you get to sleep for four hours, from eleven to three, but you're expected to spend the first half hour doing late night zazen in the garden. Lay disciples, like Nancy, could join the sesshin, but they couldn't leave the grounds until it was over. They had to sleep in the monastery and follow the same routine as everyone else."

"Jesus, that sounds hard!"

Elijah let out a hearty laugh. "Hard? Brother, it was a nightmare, especially that first sesshin. By the end of the second day my legs were on fire, and they didn't stop burning until the sesshin was over. During zazen a monk would patrol the hall with a bamboo stick. If he saw that you were getting drowsy or you weren't concentrating hard enough, he would come over and give you a thwack on the back, right between the shoulder blades. Then you had to bow, to thank him for keeping you on track. You could forget about slacking off while you were on your cushion. But that wasn't the hardest part. The hardest part was keeping focused on your koan every waking moment of the day—or whatever practice the roshi had you working on. He was like a slave driver during the sesshin. Twice a day we would line up kneeling outside his room for *dokusan*, and the head monk would send us in one by one. The moment you entered his room and finished your bow, he would jump all over you:

"'What is the sound of one hand clapping? No, that's not it. No thinking, no self-consciousness! You have to feel it in your bones! Concentrate harder! Push yourself! Don't relax, even for a single second! You must be one with your koan, while eating, sleeping, walking, working, crapping, it doesn't matter. You must become possessed, to the point that your attention is not diverted from your koan even for a single second. Pour the whole force of your being into your concentration and you will get satori in a flash. It will not take even a single second to come to you. Now go back out there and work harder. Don't let this precious opportunity to realize your existence pass you by.'

"That was a typical *dokusan*. Sometimes you could ask questions, or he would ask you questions, but mostly he would just push you as hard as he could, trying to get you to break through. Do you know the story of Suiwo and the sound of one hand?"

I shook my head.

"Suiwo was a great teacher in medieval times. Once a student came to him from the south, and Suiwo gave him the sound-of-one-hand koan. For three years the student meditated on that koan, but every time he came for *dokusan*, Suiwo told him to try harder and sent him away. Finally the student came to him in tears and told him that he had to return home. 'Stay one more week,' Suiwo told him, 'and meditate without stopping. You've already spent three years. What's one more week?' The student agreed to stay but he still couldn't solve the koan. So Suiwo asked him to stay another week and again he failed. This time he begged the master to let him go, but Suiwo told him to meditate for five more days. 'You're getting close,' he told him. 'Don't stop now.' He stayed the five days but he still couldn't solve the koan. By this time he was in despair. Then Suiwo told him to stay for three more days. 'If you fail to attain satori in these three days,' he said, 'then you had better kill yourself.' On the second day he attained satori."

"Wow."

"Exactly. Wow. But that wasn't me. The closest I ever came to that kind of single-minded attention was when I had people shooting at me. And not even then. But Nancy, she was a different story. That sister had a tenacity I'd never seen before — anywhere, anytime. She was working on the *mu* koan, and I swear to you, brother, she didn't let up for a single second. Every time I saw her I could see how hard she was concentrating. Like I said, I was just trying to get to the end of the sesshin. I almost felt like I had checked myself into a prisoner-of-war camp and was paying the Japs to torture me. For a while I was even convinced they were being extra hard on me because I was an ex-GI, getting back at me for them losing the war, but actually the guys with the stick were even harder on the Japanese disciples. Nancy was the one who helped me get over my resentment at what they were putting me through — or what I was putting myself through. I'd been through the war fighting the Japs, and a woman twenty years older than me who had probably never so much as seen a fight had more courage and perseverance than I had. Believe me, it takes a whole lot of courage to stare your mind in the face day after day without any letup. Whatever demons you're hiding, whatever fears or prejudices or ego crap you've been dragging along with you, it's going to come out during a sesshin. And if you try to look away and take refuge in some pleasant little daydream, a tiny Oriental in a black robe comes over and lashes you on the back with a bamboo stick and then bows to you just as polite as can be. Nancy showed more courage that week than I had shown in my three years of fighting for Uncle Sam. She put me to shame, brother, simple as that. So I put my resentment behind me and tried to prove to myself that I could work as hard at my Zen as she could. It might not have been the best motivation but it worked. I got serious about the whole thing because of her example. And if you're not dead serious when it comes to Zen practice, then you don't have a snowball's chance in hell of making it to the finish line. The wonderful world of Mara will eat you up in a heartbeat."

"So did you solve the koan, the sound of one hand clapping?"

"I'm still working on it, brother. Oh, I know what the answer is—intellectually. It's the soundless sound, the sound of silence, the void from which all sounds arise. But no Zen master worth his salt gives a rat's ass for what the intellect has to say, no matter how 'right' the answer is. You have to *be* the silence, brother. You have to stop the mind and enter into the void. You're the answer, not what comes out of your mouth. Until you can stand in front of the master with your mind perfectly empty, you don't know what the sound of one hand is. And when you do know, you won't have to open your mouth. He'll know it just by looking at you. You can turn and walk out of the room or grab his stick and hit him with it, it doesn't matter. If it comes from authentic experience then it will be an authentic answer and the master will know it. You can't fool him. God knows, I tried. One time I hid my sax under my robes, and when he asked me what the sound of one hand was, I whipped it out and blew the most transcendental riff I could. I got a laugh out of him but he sent me out of the room all the same. 'No, no, too intellectual. Too noisy. Meditate more.' Satori is the only answer, brother. You either experience it or you don't."

Eventually we got around to the subject of Dada and the Bauhaus and the underlying symbolism of modern art, in which Nancy Wilson Ross saw many parallels to oriental mysticism, especially the nonrational, direct apprehension of reality that was the hallmark of Zen teaching.

"If you really examine what they were trying to do—Tzara, Janco, Richter, all those guys—you can see that they recognized the limitations of the intellect and made a real effort to free their art from any kind of preconception or ideology. That's very close to the spirit of Zen. Actually, Nancy believed that all meaningful art is spiritual at its core, not just modern art, even if that spiritual urge is unconscious in the artist. You know that Buddhists believe in reincarnation, right? Of course you do. Well, Nancy believed that artistic geniuses are born with a great spiritual hunger due to their experiences in past lives, and they express that hunger through their art, even if they don't realize what's driving them. It's their way of reaching for nirvana. Their art becomes their method. She made a pretty convincing case for it, too."

"Do you think she's right?"

"Not being omniscient, I've got no way of knowing, but it makes sense. Anyhow, that's not so important from a Buddhist perspective. The Hindus make a big deal of past lives but Buddhists don't, since everything connected with the ego is illusory. When you wake up from the illusion the dream world disappears, so there's no sense wasting needless energy on it. But I don't think there is any doubt that great art is spiritually motivated. Nancy was certainly right about that. Think about the kind of pleasure you get from a great piece of music or a great poem or a great painting. That kind of aesthetic pleasure is so subtle the mind automatically becomes elevated. Great art can take you to the borderland between the mundane and the spiritual. The greater the work, the closer you get. Deep aesthetic experience is about as close as the thinking mind can come to satori. When an artist takes their mind to that level they get a vision of a spiritual reality. It's like somebody who gets close enough to the fence that they can see what's on the other side—their art is their way of expressing what they see. It's the old story of the finger pointing at the moon. Bird, Cezanne, Shakespeare, people like that, they got right up to the fence. You can feel it in their work. You can see it, you can taste it. But there are people who jump that fence and get to the other side. If Nancy is right, guys like Bird and Shakespeare were born geniuses because of their inherited spiritual hunger, but they weren't saints or Zen masters. Their work doesn't have the pure clarity of an enlightened being. Nancy and I used to argue about that sometimes. She thought that in their best moments they were able to touch the ultimate reality through their art, but I don't see it that way. Bird could get pretty high through his music but there was still some ego there. Listen closely and you can hear it. The same with Cezanne or Shakespeare. But Basho, now, he was at another level. His mature haiku have deep satori written all over them. The deeper you go into them the deeper they take you. The only limits are the ones you bring with you. It's the same way with Kabir or Rumi. They were great saints like Basho and great poets as well. There was this guy Tansen in India, a court musician and composer during the reign of Akbar. They say he would go into trance while he played, and that his music was so powerful the people in the audience could feel the divine presence filling the room. Now that's enlightened art, the kind that comes from an enlightened mind. Too bad they didn't have tape recorders in those days. Man, would I have loved to hear that cat play.

"That's what we should set our sights on, brother. Leave Bauhaus and Dada and twelve-tone music and *Finnegans Wake* to the intellectuals. It's advanced stuff, sure it is. And I have no doubt that Nancy was right when she said that it's really spiritual art in disguise. But we don't need the disguise. We've got the eightfold path and the four noble truths. If we are going to be artists, then let's be spiritual artists like Basho or Tansen. Let's learn how to create music from a mind so quiet there's no one home. Let's learn how to become an empty vessel, the pure instrument. It's like your sax. It's just an instrument. It doesn't make the music. Somebody has to blow through it. Somebody has to hear a melody and finger the keys and blow. In jazuzen you become the instrument and Buddha blows. He uses your fingers and your lungs to fill the atmosphere with sound, just like he does with the wind and the ocean and the rest of nature. But before that can happen you have to empty your mind. You have to leave your ego at the door. You see what I'm saying?"

It wasn't the first time I had heard this, of course. Elijah had been telling me more or less the same thing since the first time we'd met. But the picture in my head was becoming clearer, as if I were the canvas and each time I visited him he added a few more brush strokes. The painting wasn't finished, but it was starting to take on a recognizable shape, and that gave me a thrill even greater than the thrill I got from a great piece of music.

"I think so," I said, grasping at another piece of the puzzle. "Are you saying that we should consciously turn our art into spiritual practice?"

Elijah raised an eyebrow. "And what exactly is it you think I've been teaching you these past three months?"

It was a foolish question but I was glad I'd asked it, for Elijah came back to the canvas to add a few more brush strokes.

"Look, brother, anything can be a means to get you there — *if* you can turn it into practice. Music, or any aesthetic discipline, has a special power, because the subtler our art, the closer it brings us to the borders of spiritual experience. But it's still a practice. Chop wood, carry water, play jazz. You can do it with your ego, or you can leave your mind behind and be one with what you do. The best Zen is zazen, because when your body is balanced and motionless it ceases to be a distraction. But you can't spend the whole day sitting, and if you can't keep your Zen going when you're walking, talking, working, or playing jazz, then your Zen isn't worth much — not yet at any rate. Zen isn't about learning how to quiet your mind, brother — I mean, it is in the beginning, but in the end it's about *having* a quiet mind. It's about transforming your nature. If you can quiet your mind when you sit but not when you play jazz, then you don't have a quiet mind. Not yet. You're just able to quiet it sometimes. Even a monkey can sit quietly for a minute or two, but a monkey doesn't have a quiet nature and most human beings are just oversized, over-intellectualized monkeys. The object of Zen is to develop a quiet nature. And a supremely quiet nature is an egoless nature. So if you can turn your jazz practice into Zen practice, then it will eventually carry you beyond the borders of the ego, just like zazen. That's why I call it jazuzen. But in the end it's just practice, brother. Do you know why I push you so hard when you come for your lessons? For the same reason that Zuigan-roshi pushed me every time I entered his room for *dokusan*. To help you break through. To help you hear the sound of one hand. I'm teaching you jazz so I do it through jazz. If I was a basket weaver I'd do it through basket-weaving. I'm not a roshi, but for the time being I'm all you've got. When you come to see me, the whole point is to get you to hear the sound of one hand. And to do that, you have to leave your ego at the door, even if you do it kicking and screaming."

As far as I recall, we never made it back to the subject of Dada or the symbolism of modern art, but that didn't mean I was done with the art avant-garde or its hidden spiritual motivation. In one of those quirks of synchronicity, Nancy Wilson Ross took an apartment in San Francisco a few years back and became closely associated with Zen Center. When I first mentioned Elijah to her, her face lit up and she began reminiscing about her days in Kyoto and the time she'd spent in the company of the first black man ever to grace the inside of a Japanese monastery. We have since spent many fruitful hours together away from our meditation cushions, reprising some of the same conversations she'd had with Elijah nearly three decades earlier; and like Elijah, I have also built up a debt to Nancy for helping me to deepen my understanding of both art and the spiritual wisdom of the Orient, a subject in which she has few peers. Elijah was absolutely right: she is not only a brilliant woman but as dedicated a practitioner as you will find on this side of the Pacific.

17

ONE WEEKDAY MORNING IN mid-April I skipped out on class and drove Diana to Mill Valley to visit Gary at his cabin. Ginsberg was also there and a mutual friend who they all agreed was destined to set the literary world on its collective ear. Diana had told me a lot about Jack Kerouac, whom she knew from New York. Allen had also, so I knew more or less what to expect, but even so, I was unprepared for the irresistible charm of his talking Zen. Jack was a force of nature expressed in words, a sometimes hyper, sometimes moody hipster who sought his Zen in the free flow of ideas that emerged from his typewriter whenever he locked himself away for a private literary sesshin. He did sit from time to time, at least in those days, but he was without question a full-blown aficionado of talking Zen, exactly the kind of talking Zen that Elijah had warned me against and which I had learned to love with a passion. It may not be the true road to enlightenment, which, as Elijah says, is to be found on the seat of your pants, but it is enormously entertaining, perhaps the best form of mental recreation the world has yet produced.

Gary was sitting on a pallet when we poked our heads in the open door. He was dressed in a kimono, which by now seemed perfectly natural to me, and was surrounded by books and papers—he was working on his translation of Han Shan's Cold Mountain poems. Allen was next to him on another pallet, looking at the translations and offering suggestions, and Jack was lying on a straw mat with his knees bent and a book in his hands, his head propped up on his rolled-up jacket and a languid air of literary absorption on his face. Stendhal, *The Red and the Black*, an odd choice in that nest of poets when I think back on it, but Jack was a voracious reader who had a habit of checking out what books were on the shelves whenever he entered a room. There wasn't much else in the cabin: some pots and pans in the kitchen area, some clothes on hangers, several milk crates with books, a manual typewriter on the small kitchen table. The cabin's air of disarray made it look exactly like what it was: a den of indigent writers who couldn't have cared less about their poverty as long as they had their books and enough paper and ink to last the day.

Diana and Gary introduced me to Jack as an imminent Bodhisattva and an up-and-coming jazzman. I was neither but I was happy to accept the laurels. We were all imminent Bodhisattvas in those days and all serious artists—in their case, important ones, writers who would go on to help define the contours of America's literary aspirations in the second half of the twentieth century. But that was later. *On the Road* would not be published for more than a year yet, and part of the delight in being unknown and unencumbered by obligations or reputation was the chance it afforded to follow your predilections wherever they led, something all four beat writers were especially adept at, none more so than Jack, who had just hitchhiked across the country from the East Coast in search of his next literary Zen adventure.

I felt a little awkward about interrupting their labors but Diana had no such qualms. She planted herself on Jack's mat and launched into a discussion of misogynist writers who could get away with literary murder due to the beauty of their prose: Hemingway, Maugham, Melville, Henry Miller, even Henry James, who hid the unconscious dependency of his females behind a harlequin mask of spellbinding character development. She didn't include Stendhal in that group, but her list was long enough as it was. Jack, who clearly belonged to the group of male writers who all but ignored the existence of the female sex (you'd be hard pressed to name a single well-rounded, sympathetically depicted female character in any of his books), conceded her point but he launched into an impassioned defense of beautiful prose. To Jack beautiful prose was like an improvised solo in jazz: it couldn't be labeled or analyzed; it had to be felt. You had to shut down your thinking mind and let it carry you wherever it led. It was a very Zen thing to say but Jack didn't stop there. In fact, he was just getting going.

"None of it's real, anyhoo, so there's no point in getting worked up about it. Just enjoy the show. That's what it's there for. They were just dreaming how nice it would be if the world were an old boys' club, digging their dream through all that beautiful prose. And sure as I'm sitting here, some gals are going to come along and dream how nice it would be if the world were an old gals' club. But it's just a dream, here today, gone tomorrow. Just like you and me—here today, gone tomorrow. It's not real. None of it is. Let me tell you about a vision I had when I was hitching my way up here. One day just after sunset I come across a field of yellow poppies near the beach in Santa Barbara, and there's this big old willow right in the middle of the field, just begging me to come and meditate under the droop of her branches, like she's the Bo tree and I'm a wandering Buddha, which of course I was. So I go and sit there, just an old tree and me in the middle of this field, and a big old moon comes smiling up over the hill, looking down on me like he's trying to figure out why I'm there all alone in the middle of this field instead of out carousing in some back-alley bar with the rest of the curious, crazed humans that he sees each night. But I'm not alone, see. I've got the whole world inside my head. Everything that's ever existed is right there inside my mind. Then all of a sudden my mind stops and I see in a flash that it's all empty! The only thing that's real is the void. The rest is just a mirage, a host of disappearing suns. And that's what makes it perfect, forever and ever and ever. You see this orange crate? Where are the oranges? They're gone. How can you say they were even here at all? Before the oranges there was the void. After the oranges, the void."

Allen straightened up all of a sudden and thrust a finger into the air. "But during the oranges!" he cried. "What about during? Let's see you make the during disappear."

"Easy," Jack retorted. "They were never there at all. All that was there was your mind. If you take away your mind there never were any oranges. Without your mind they don't exist. Now show me your mind. Can you do that?"

Allen furrowed his brow, then picked up a book, Whitman's *Leaves of Grass*, and raised it like he was in a courtroom presenting evidence. "The poem reveals the contents of the mind. It's an artifact that testifies to its origin. The replica of speech but longer lasting."

"Scratchings on processed wood pulp," Jack countered. "And even if I allowed it into evidence, which I don't, the contents of the mind are not the mind. Show me the mind itself."

Gary started laughing and the contagion spread. After a few moments Allen succumbed and made a mock bow. "Your point is conceded," he said. "The mind cannot be shown."

"That's because the mind is empty," Jack continued. "Empty and awake. It's like the sutra says: emptiness is form and form is emptiness. That's perfection. How can emptiness have any blemish? So Melville is perfect and all the misogynist writers with their chauvinist choirs are perfect and the garbage dumps where their books end up are perfect and Diana trying to bring down Melville is perfect."

"A perfect fool, perhaps," Gary said, ducking moments later to avoid the magazine that Diana threw at him.

"I knew it," she said. "All this Buddhism is just another excuse to keep women tramping back and forth between the kitchen and the bedroom. But it won't work. We have typewriters also and our typewriters are perfect. So don't be surprised when the Henry Jameses and the Melvilles of the world are consigned to the second-class seats in the train of literary history."

"If they can write like Melville," Jack said, "then they belong in the first-class seats. I don't care if they are hermaphrodites with stripes and a tail. If they can write great prose or great verse then I'll read them all day long, whether they are fuddy duddy misogynists or great burly women with buck teeth or Martians or moon fairies. It's all just a disguise anyway. It's just emptiness in drag."

Listening to Jack was like listening to an extended solo by one of the giants of jazz. Gary, Allen, and Diana made up the rhythm section, with an occasional peep from me (picture a skinny kid with a cowbell that they've agreed to let on stage as long as he doesn't get in the way), but Jack was the center of gravity in that conversation, the one everyone else was playing off. They were all writers, of course, so the conversation always seemed to find its way back to the literary arts. I remember Jack at some point launching into his famous plea for unconscious writing, and to this day I consider it a very Zen way of looking at literary creation, something I'm sure Elijah would have agreed with had he been there.

"Stack up as many Korans and Bibles and sutras as you can find and I'll swear on them all: the best writing is when you're not thinking. Take the first thought that comes into your mind, put it on the page, then the next thought, and then the next. Don't stop to analyze it. Don't worry if it's good or bad or even if it makes sense. Just transcribe the words as they fall into your mind straight from the void. That's when the writing gets real. The trick is to trust the void. That's why the first thought is always the best thought. The moment you stop to analyze it or judge it or try to force it into some kind of literary form, it becomes artificial. That's how you fall into the quagmire of literary pretension. When that happens I start sounding like a cheap imitation of Melville. I'll be going along totally unconscious, no idea even what I'm writing, it's just pouring out as fast as my fingers can pound the keys. But the moment I start wondering if it's any good or not, it's like damming up a river: it gets muddy as hell. The unconscious writing, that's the real deal. It's the difference between self and no-self. The self is just an illusion. If you let it show up in your prose then all you have is illusionary prose. The true poem is empty. No you, just the poem."

It almost sounded like Elijah talking. Not the words, of course, but the spirit. Or rather, it was Jack's take on what happens to a writer when he leaves the ego behind.

Allen had known Jack since the forties, from their Columbia days, so he was familiar with Jack's ideas about unconscious writing. They had been arguing back and forth about it for at least a decade, and though Allen, like most poets, tinkered endlessly with his verse, he agreed that his best poems had sprung to life nearly fully formed from the unconscious. But nearly wasn't fully, and that's where he and Jack disagreed.

"They're different worlds, Jack, the conscious and the unconscious. The trick is how to get them to work together without colliding, and the secret is not to get their roles mixed up. It's like when I wrote 'Sunflower Sutra.' You remember, Jack, you were with me. We were walking along the railroad tracks and I saw this dead sunflower lying there. All of a sudden I was stopped cold by the beauty of it, the whole transitory, ephemeral beauty of this hulking, common, ungainly, perfect flower. Like your vision in the poppy field, a moment of pure insight. Then later that evening the whole poem just poured out in one long breath, completely involuntary, like I vomited it onto the page. It's just like you say, I wasn't really conscious. It was a kind of linguistic trance. There was just this image in my mind that had been sitting there, this feeling, this insight, and then when the moment was ripe the words just scribbled themselves onto the page in one long burst. It was like I was in a daze and then I came back to my senses. You and I were just going out so I didn't even read it. I just put it in my pocket and out we went. I didn't know what I had until I got back that night and started typing it up. That's when I realized that it was still in the language of the unconscious. It was all there but it was naked. Fine for the bedroom but not for the drawing room. For the drawing room it needed some clothes. It needed to become intelligible. That's where the conscious mind comes in. You take the raw material, the pure experience as it comes out of the unconscious, and you shape it so that other people can access it, so they can get some purchase on your experience. It's like the unconscious is a lion and the conscious mind is the lion tamer. He feeds it, he pets it, he leads it around on a leash when he goes for a walk down Main Street. The power is in the lion, the raw, beautiful, untamed power of nature. But you can't let it loose unfed and unleashed. If you do, it will eat up the audience. It's the king of the jungle but we're not in the jungle."

Jack clapped his hands. "Bravo, bravo! As fine a defense of civilized poetry as I've ever heard. But the lion is dharma, Allen. No salvation if you want to hang onto your skin. You have to be eaten up to be free. Let the lion loose. Let it feed wherever it finds food. The raw, unmediated experience—that's how we punch our ticket to paradise. Why not naked poems or naked prose?"

"Because they won't be understood."

"Understanding is overrated. In fact, it's nothing more than literary tyranny. Poems don't need to be understood. They need to be felt, like a punch to the gut. Like old Gutei cutting off his disciple's finger. Gary, what do you say? We've been going back and forth like this for years and we still haven't gotten to the bottom of the well."

Gary nodded as he picked up the kettle of tea that he had been brewing on his portable gas stove and filled five porcelain cups with the steaming liquid. They were small handleless cups engraved with Chinese characters, as enigmatic as the look on his face.

"First sip some of this," he said, handing each of us a cup. "It's good green tea." He cradled his own cup in both hands and took a long sip before answering. "At this point I subscribe to the Han Shan school of poetry. Han Shan spent thirty years on Cold Mountain, meditating and wandering from cave to cave, scribbling his poems wherever he went. Every so often he would come down to this Buddhist monastery and get some food but he wouldn't stay there, even though it was warm and there was always plenty to eat. He didn't want to be tied down by their rules and routine. And while he was wandering the mountain he wrote these almost perfect poems. So perfect, you're transported there the moment you start reading them. 'Clambering up Cold Mountain path. The long gorge choked with scree and boulders. The wide creek, the mist-blurred grass.' You can almost feel the wind in your face and hear the echo of his footsteps. Han Shan was the purest kind of poet. He spent his time meditating and communing with nature and being one with the dharma and all, and whenever a poem would appear in his mind he would write it down wherever he was — on a rock or a cave wall or a tree, it didn't matter. He left his poems scattered around Cold Mountain like little jewels that anybody who happened by could stop and admire and contemplate. That's what I'm aiming for. To make my mind perfectly quiet so that when a poem appears I can catch it and write it down. The way I see it the poem already exists. It's just waiting for someone to notice it, and with my poems I just happen to be the wandering monk who does. The poems are arti-facts of the mind that occupy the same landscape as the trees and the wind and the rain. If you are quiet enough then you can catch them and write them down, and after that everybody can see them and hear them. That's what makes the poet a visionary. He sees what others can't—and then they can."

"But don't you work on them afterward?" Allen asked. "Chisel them into shape?"

"Sometimes, but it's more about feeling. It's not the thinking mind that recognizes perfection. Sometimes something doesn't sit right. Maybe the rhythm needs to be adjusted or a word choice isn't quite right. But it's more that my hearing wasn't tuned enough when I first heard the poem, so I didn't transcribe it right. The next time I look at it, or the tenth time, I can see it more clearly. It's not like I'm actually changing the poem. It's more like the poem is already written and I'm just trying to be quiet enough to hear what I didn't hear the first time."

Jack slapped himself on the thigh. "Man, you are one crazy bhik-khu. Found poems! I'd like to find me some of the poems you missed. Might just do it too."

I wish I could remember more of what Jack said that day—or even better, that somebody had hidden a tape recorder in one of the orange crates and left it running. He was like an avatar of talking Zen spreading his doctrine among the mortals, although when he was hanging out with Gary it was more like a couple of old monks getting together and sharing notes. Too bad Jack's talking Zen never quite made the transition to sitting Zen, or at least not in a way he could sustain. If it had, I'm sure things would have ended differently. It's strange, looking back, to think that of the five of us, Jack was the one who didn't make it. Allen is up in Boulder with Chögyam Trungpa, America's most famous poet and one of the world's most recognizable Buddhists; Diana and I meet at Zen Center every week-end to meditate in front of the photo of our teacher, Suzuki-roshi; and Gary is probably the most dedicated of us all, a Zen recluse in the Sierra Nevada whose "found" poems are so admired he has already won a Pulitzer Prize. But Jack was the one who made words like "Zen" and "dharma" part of the Western lexicon. After his books became common currency among my generation, after his talking Zen and unfettered spirit invaded the American consciousness and divided the world into squares and hipsters, the great divide of the beat generation, I began thinking of him as a kind of fifties Avalokiteshvara, a true Bodhisattva whose advent on this earth was for the sole purpose of illuminating the murky souls of a benighted generation with the light of Buddha wisdom. For a few brief, hallucinatory years he was the beacon who lighted our path into the euphoric upheavals of the sixties. Pre-Beatles, pre-Stones, pre-Dylan, pre-Warhol, pre-Jerry Rubin and the Chicago Seven and the march on Washington, Jack Kerouac was arguably the foremost inspiration for young Americans looking to break out of the straitjacket their culture had bound them in. His dizzying literary output—seven seminal books written in the space of six years—did more to change the consciousness and shape the self-identity of America's youth than any artist of his time. And he had one thing that no artist of his stature or influence that I can think of, before or since, has had: a truly spiritual awareness. Other great writers and artists have made their spiritual quest an inseparable part of their art—John Cage comes to mind—but no one in our time has been able to articulate the spirit of the human being's quest for transcendence in a language powerful enough and accessible enough to capture the imagination of a generation as Jack did with his talking Zen.

Elijah only met Kerouac once that I know of—at Gary's farewell party a couple of weeks later—and I never did ask him what he thought of Jack, but I can guess, and my guess is about as close to certain as you can get. "It's just talking Zen," he would have said, "and talking Zen is no Zen at all. Real Zen is found on the seat of your pants." As proof he would have pointed to how Jack ended up: alcoholic, overweight, and paranoid. Dead from cirrhosis of the liver at forty-seven, bitter at the world and clinging in desperation to Roman Catholic dogmas that he had discarded years before. Perhaps Elijah would have been right. By the time of Jack's death, the gap between the man and his art had become an abyss that no bridge could span. But that doesn't negate the power or the visionary quality of Jack's incendiary prose, or what it did to liberate the minds of those who read it—or the minds of those who are just discovering it now or who will discover it in the future. Jack's finest moments found their way into his books, something we can all be glad of, and somewhere

the Bodhisattva who inspired those finest moments is rubbing his
rotund belly and smiling in satisfaction. Elijah would have listened
to his prose and heard the echoes of Jack's ego, and that might have
been enough for him to shake his head and turn away. But there
were flashes of satori also, even if they were only glimpses of the
light parting the clouds as seen from a vantage point far below. In
his best moments Jack was right there with Bird, whom he idolized,
and I'm sure that Nancy, if I asked her, would claim that he had
touched the truth, if only momentarily, through his art. And she
would be right. As with all great artists, it is not the man's life that
ultimately matters, but how the universe used that life to further its
evolutionary designs. Elijah believed that great art was capable of
changing human beings, and through them, of changing the world,
and there is no question in my mind that Jack's unconscious writing
and his talking Zen has left a little bhikkhu in us all.

18

I saw Gary again a couple of weeks later when he came down from Mill Valley to visit Elijah, his last trip across the bay before sailing for Japan. I only caught the tail end of their conversation, but he stayed for evening meditation and dinner, and before he left he invited us to his farewell party. Elijah assured him he would be there, which surprised me a little—I guess I still wasn't used to the monk leaving his hermitage—and that Friday I drove Elijah over to Mill Valley for the party.

It was early evening when we arrived, and a couple of dozen people were milling about outside the house of Locke McCorkle, who owned the property on which Gary had his cabin. They were stepping in and out of the shadows cast by a large bonfire or sitting on logs listening to a blond troubadour in a sleeveless T-shirt strumming a guitar and singing folk songs. The guitarist was one of the few people I didn't recognize. Ginsberg and Orlovsky were there, along with Whalen, Dalenberg, and Kerouac, who was wandering around with a bottle of wine and a huge, inebriated smile. Even Alan Watts had come with his family. He was chatting with Rexroth, both of them with drinks in their hands as if they were at a cocktail party. I remember thinking how out of place Watts looked in his suit and tie in this gathering of bohemians, but it would not be long before he grew out his hair and ditched the academic uniform for kimonos and jeans.

I looked around for Diana, and when I didn't see her I introduced Elijah to Jack and went looking for her inside the house, where I could hear the stereo playing. I found her dancing in a darkened living room with the remainder of the guests, twirling like a Dervish in a long pleated skirt and a loose-fitting blouse to the music of Cal Tjader, her eyes closed and a look of airy ecstasy on her face.

There was something so free about Diana in those days. I had grown up in confinement, like a wild animal in a zoo — cultural confinement, intellectual confinement, artistic confinement, spiritual confinement — forced into a box by the weight of conventional opinion, starting with my family and expanding outward in concentric circles to the entire cookie-cutter template of white suburban America. Diana was the epitome of everything I was not, the embodiment of this gathering of prehippies — the bohemian, beatnik precursors to the reshaping of America. She had no hang-ups that I was aware of, no constraints on her pursuit of freedom, no antediluvian voices crowding her head, whispering their cryptic warnings and recriminations — nothing but a deaf ear to the demands of the superego. While Elijah was teaching me about the ancient quest to lay aside the ego, Diana was introducing me to the pure joy of unfettered self-expression, and they seemed to my inexperienced eyes to be opposite approaches to the same destination, mirror images of a single thirst for transcendence. As I sat there and watched her whirl in place to the cascading melodies of Cal Tjader's sweet-toned vibraphone, submerged in some kind of bohemian rapture, I caught a clear, unmistakable glimpse of what I was searching for: Me. The big me, the capital M, the undiscovered creature that most of us assume to be a myth, a fantastical creation of some long-dead mystic's overactive imagination. Though it was night and the lights were dimmed to enhance the exuberant, dreamlike quality of the music, I could see Diana reaching for her uber-self as clearly as if she were illuminated by the light of a thousand suns. It was there in the center of her twirl, a shining nimbus around a ghostlike form, and I could see her racing toward it with each delirious orbit. Though I was sitting on the couch, apparently motionless, I could feel myself spinning with her, rushing in centripetal motion toward the center of my being, toward the encounter that I had been longing for since before my birth, the encounter with my original face.

When the record needle slid off the final groove, plunging the twilit room into the silence of the void, Diana opened her eyes and came out of her twirl. For a moment, she seemed startled to find herself amid a crowd of dislocated humans — some still dancing, others conversing, one unselfconscious couple necking in a corner. Then she saw me, opened her eyes wide in delight, and in two quick bounds leaped on top of me and wrapped me in a smothering embrace that seemed the confirmation of my vision — Diana, with all her exuberant energy, her joie de vivre and hunger for the moment, landing on my lap like a Hindu goddess to let me know without words, through the sheer power of human affection, that I had finally brushed the sleep out of my eyes and woken up to what it was all about. I was excited to see her, but I was even more excited by my fleeting vision. When she finally slid off my lap without letting go of her embrace, my enthusiasm bubbled over. Words were her domain, not mine. I probably could have explained myself better with a sax in my hand and a reed in my mouth, but she seemed to understand what I was saying.

"You have to write it down, Dan! Don't worry about the words, you can sort them out later. Look, I've got a notebook around here somewhere. It's in my bag. Now, if I can just find my bag ..."

Diana seemed as excited as I was. Having never kept a journal, I put up a short-lived protest. The closest I had come to discovering the alchemical magic of maintaining a written record of one's experience was when I had recorded some of my original melodies on my brother's reel-to-reel that my dad had given him as a high-school graduation present. But I succumbed in short order to her aura of beat poet and personal muse. It took her a few minutes but she found her notebook, and while I wrote down my experience as best I could she cuddled up to me and cast approving glances at my awkward scrawl. It was Diana, snuggled up to me on that couch, who started me on the road to becoming a minor writer in a circle of major writers — my preferred niche, since for me the written word has always been an adjunct to the music. A few days later she gave me a hardbound notebook into which I copied those notes and entertained me with hours of anecdotes and information about the notebooks of famous artists from Michelangelo to André Gide to Erik Satie. It took me a little while to get hooked, but she wouldn't let go until I was, and she still reminds me from time to time that she deserves the real credit for my literary career. But I was the one who finally convinced her to become a Buddhist, so the scales are balanced.

When I was done with my first-ever journal entry, we wandered outside, still talking about the search for the self and how the arts were nothing more than a creative rendering of that search. We found Elijah sitting on the ground next to the guitarist, playing bongos on a couple of overturned cans. Man, was he good! I had just been listening to Benny Velarde playing bongos and congas behind Cal Tjader, and I swear, it could have been Elijah in the studio with Cal and the band wouldn't have missed a beat. The guitarist was still strumming folksongs, but it sounded like jazz the way Elijah was syncopating the beat and overlaying all those wild polyrhythms, using his chest and head and thighs to add accents. A circle had formed around the two musicians, and outside the circle four or five women were dancing like they were in a jazz club, an open-air, star-spangled jazz cathedral. "Your jazz master gets more interesting every time I see him," Diana said, leaning into my ear, and I couldn't have agreed more. Elijah had more sides to him than any three human beings put together: the reserved Zen monk, the no-nonsense philosopher, the battle-scarred ex-GI, the jazz saxophonist who stole the stage at Minton's from Charlie Parker, and now out-beating the beats with his human-body, rusted-can bongos. Diana joined the dancers and pulled me in with her. I wasn't much of a dancer but I followed her example and threw my inhibitions to the wind, and I don't know if I've ever enjoyed dancing more than I did that night. I remember thinking, as I gave myself up to the music with the bonfire blazing beside us, that Elijah could even out-Diana Diana when he wanted to. It made me realize that I still had a long way to go before I would really understand him or the whole Zen experience.

Elijah had told me on the way up that he didn't want to stay long, which was fine by me, though if I had gone alone I probably would have stayed until the next day, as many did, eventually sharing a sleeping bag with Diana. After the guitar-and-bongo circle broke up — it was maybe ten-thirty or eleven by then — I could sense that Elijah was getting ready to say his goodbyes. He went for a short walk with Gary near the edge of the woods that ended with a parting bear hug and then came looking for me, but before we could reach the car Alan Watts intercepted him, wanting to know what he thought of the Buddhist doctrine of something or other.

It was the final bit of entertainment for the night, a kind of talking Zen duel at point-blank range. What I didn't know at the time was that Alan and Elijah knew each other quite well. Soon after Alan and Frederic Spiegelberg started the American Academy of Asian Studies in San Francisco—this was just after Elijah moved to the Bay Area from New York—Alan heard about him from one of his students, sought him out, and eventually convinced him to give some talks at the Academy about Zen practice in Japan, especially the Rinzai school, to which Myoshinji belonged. From what I gather, Elijah's talks proved hugely popular. Here was this six-foot-four jazz virtuoso ex-GI who had fought his way through the Pacific, entered Japan with the occupying army, and spent two and a half years as a Zen monk in a famous monastery studying under a renowned Rinzai master. He not only spoke fluent Japanese, he spoke fluent American hip, a guy who had played on the same bandstand with Miles Davis and Charley Parker. It's not hard to imagine the students' reaction. Whatever idea they had of Zen before meeting Elijah, he blew it up completely and then put it back together in a newer, hipper, yet undeniably more authentic form. The Academy was where Gary first met Elijah, and he later told me that Elijah made him see that Zen wasn't bound to Japanese or Chinese culture any more than jazz improvisation was bound to American culture, while at the same time impressing on him the importance of going to Japan so that he could drink from the fount of a living tradition. Zen can't be found in books or lectures, Elijah told him. It can only be found in an enlightened master, and Elijah hadn't seen any of them walking the streets of San Francisco. The closest Gary would get was the resident priest at the Soto Zen temple, Hobo Todase, who taught calligraphy at the Academy, but the difference between Todase and a true roshi like Zuigan-roshi was like the difference between Bird and a high-school music teacher. The latter could get you started but at some point you had to graduate and go off in search of the real thing.

Supposedly, Elijah and Alan got in a rather animated discussion one day about the necessity of regular sitting meditation on the road to enlightenment, and that eventually led to a parting of the ways. The way Gary tells it, Elijah had just finished lecturing on the fundamental importance of zazen practice when Alan opened the question-and-answer session like a true provocateur, asking Elijah how it was possible for the ego to overcome the ego—it being the ego, after all, who decides to meditate, out of a desire to overcome its suffering. It was like a man trying to push himself completely off the ground: it can't be done. Now, at Gary's party, it seemed like they were picking up their argument where they'd left off a couple of years earlier.

"The ego is just a fiction, Preacher. You know that as well as I do. It's a hallucination—in this case, a mass hallucination, a false hypothesis that society props up like it props up all its other institutions. We think it's real, but no matter how much you look for it, nobody has ever found the I. Take it all away, all our self-delusions and convictions, strip us down to the bone, and there's nothing there. I'm not saying that sitting Zen is a waste of time. Hell, I sit sometimes. But I don't do it because I'm trying to reach enlightenment, and I certainly don't do it every day by the clock like I was standing guard at Buckingham Palace. That's just the ego diddling around with itself. The ego's not going to participate in its own destruction. It's too smart for that. The whole search for enlightenment is just a very subtle head trip. When I sit, I just sit. I'm not trying to get anywhere or do anything. It just happens. It's spontaneous. It's no different than standing here talking to you. The only way to put the ego out of its misery is to deny its existence, and that just takes a single second, once you realize that there's nothing there. Now if zazen can help you see that, then sure, by all means, sit, but if it doesn't show you that the ego is just a figment of your imagination, then what good is it? There's just as much Zen in eating an ice cream cone or getting drunk and taking your clothes off at a party. More, if you can be completely spontaneous about it."

Allen Ginsberg and Peter Orlovsky had just stepped up to the edge of the small circle of onlookers who were listening to Alan and

Elijah go at it. They were both stark naked, as Kerouac would recount when he described the party a couple of years later in *The Dharma Bums*. I don't know how much Zen there was in their nudity, but it was undoubtedly what had sparked Alan's analogy. At some point they had stripped naked and continued to mingle with the other partygoers as if their nakedness were just a different set of clothes, no more or less interesting than the ones they'd arrived in. Elijah by this time was laughing. I think he considered Watts something of a crackpot—a mostly sincere, good-natured, intelligent, sometimes even brilliant crackpot, but still a crackpot.

"Now Alan," Elijah said, "you know you're just saying that because you're a lazy bastard who can't be bothered to practice what he preaches."

Everyone laughed—except Alan. His face turned red and he compounded his embarrassment with a short string of expletives.

"What's there to get angry about, Alan, if there's no ego?" Elijah countered. "It doesn't exist, remember? Or could it be that you forgot? And that, brother, is my whole point. It doesn't matter how well you understand that the ego is a fiction if you don't remember it in the moment of truth—as, for instance, when a big black mother calls you a lazy bastard. If you don't, then you're just as much a prisoner of the ego as a loudmouth redneck steelworker from Birmingham who's never even heard the word 'Zen' and would accuse you of being in a satanic cult if you tried to explain it to him. That's why zazen is so important. You have to train the mind to calmness; otherwise, you'll forget your Buddha nature the moment the shit hits the fan. And the shit is always hitting the fan, brother. That's the nature of the beast. Maya, samsara, whatever you want to call it. It is what it is. If you can't empty your mind, you'll never see through the mask. Somebody like me is sure to come along and throw dirt in your eyes. And the only way to empty your mind is to plant your ass on your meditation cushion day after day, month after month, year after year, with or without a clock, until the waves of the ocean settle and stay settled. Right practice is what the Buddha called it, without which right samadhi is just a pipe dream. You know I love you, Alan, but if you don't sit, you ain't shit."

Diana squeezed my hand and drew me toward her. "I'll say it again, Dan," she said. "Your jazz master gets more interesting every time I see him."

Alan wasn't upset any longer but he didn't have an answer for Elijah. He had regained his smile but it wasn't his usual confident smile, the one some would call smug. Kerouac was euphoric. He slapped Elijah on the back and muttered something about him being a black Bodhisattva, a regular Kannon, the Bodhisattva who attained enlightenment by concentrating on sound. He was also staggering a bit from all the wine, so I don't know how much he actually understood of Alan and Elijah's metaphysical duel.

Elijah took Watt's silence as his cue for exiting stage left, which was where my car was parked. I gave Diana a long hug and an unchaste kiss and agreed on a rendezvous with her for the following night in North Beach, knowing better than to try to drag her away from the party. Once we were heading down the hill, I told Elijah that I thought it was a pretty interesting way to end the night.

"Oh, I can deal up some talking Zen of my own when I have to, brother," Elijah said.

That he could. He absolutely could. But then, I had never thought otherwise.

19

Gary boarded a freighter for Kobe on May 6, and the following Friday I had my student recital, myself and four classmates playing a twenty-five-minute set of jazz standards: "Lorelei," "Night and Day," "Autumn Leaves," and my favorite, Monk's "Round Midnight." I was nervous, despite the mostly empty auditorium, for the sole reason that Elijah was in the first row and he had never seen me play the piano. But it was also his presence that spurred me to overcome my nervousness, because it forced me to concentrate on what he had taught me. I was so aware of him sitting there that it felt more like a jazuzen lesson, my first on piano, than a recital for the music faculty and students. "Concentrate. Take your ego out of the equation. Didn't you see the sign on the door when you walked in?" I could almost hear him admonishing me as I played, impelling me to mindfulness like the monk who used to whack him with a bamboo stick whenever his mind wandered during meditation. And it worked. Whether it was Elijah's presence or the cumulative effect of four months of jazuzen practice, I was as quiet-minded during those twenty-five minutes as I had ever been with an instrument in my hands. And it showed in my playing, though the moment I became aware of how good "I" sounded, the music lost its flow and I had to redouble my efforts to silence the ego and its judgments. The key was listening—not only to the music but to the silence of which the music was only an echo, as Elijah had emphasized a couple of days earlier when I sought his advice for the recital.

"You ask any jazzman," he said, "it doesn't matter who. If he knows his music he will tell you that the most important thing when you play with other people is to listen. If you don't listen to what everyone else is playing, then you're wasting your time and theirs. It doesn't matter how good you sound on your own, it will sound like crap if you don't play off each other. It's a conversation. That's what every jazzman who knows the music will tell you, and it's true, as far as it goes. But if you want to play jazuzen, brother, then you have to take it to the next level. You have to learn what to listen to and you have to learn who's listening. Now, you tell me, Brother Dan: Who's listening?"

"Ideally, no one. There's just the music. Which is the same as saying that it's the Buddha who's listening and the Buddha who's playing."

I wasn't speaking from experience, of course. I just knew the words, but without the words I wouldn't have known where I was going.

"Good. And now, tell me, what is the Buddha listening to?"

That made me stumble a bit. "To the music… and to everything else, right?"

"To the silence, brother, the silence. The music is just an echo of the silence. You drop a pebble into a pond, and the ripples spread out until they reach the shore. But the ripples are never separate from the pond. They are just a momentary distortion, a beautiful, mysterious fluctuation on the surface of the water. All there is is silence and the echoes of that silence, the void and its ripples, the universal mind and its waves. If you focus on the waves, you lose sight of the ocean; you become caught in small mind. But when you focus on the ocean, you don't lose sight of the waves. You see them for what they are: the motion of the universal mind. When an ordinary jazzman listens to the other musicians while he plays, then to a certain extent he forgets himself, and to the extent that he forgets himself his music takes off. That's when it really swings. He may even play lines he's never played before, and he can't tell you where they came from. The cats call it 'being in the zone.' Every jazzman worth his salt knows that feeling. It's what they play for, a high that horse can't come close to matching. It may only happen once a night, and it may not happen every night, but when it happens there's no mistaking it, whether you're on the bandstand or in the audience. And you can only get there by forgetting yourself, by losing yourself in the music—in other words, when your ego doesn't get in the way.

"That's what everyone is after, but it's still not Zen. It's just a giant step in the right direction. If you've got the technique and you can lose yourself in the music, then the music will take off, but that won't be enough to get you out of small mind, not all the way. So how do you break free and get into big mind? You listen to the silence. You train all your attention on the silence until you hear the nothing in which every something dwells. That's when you hear the music as it really is: ripples in the void. You see what I'm saying?"

"I think so. I don't know if I can do it, but I know what you're getting at."

"You can do it, brother. When you get up onstage just listen to the silence. It's everywhere; you can't miss it. You know the changes. You've been practicing these tunes your whole life; you don't have to think about them when you play. Just concentrate on the silence, the same as when you meditate. On the surface of that silence you'll hear the music. You'll hear what the other cats are playing and what you're playing, but don't focus on it, don't cling to it. Let it go by like you let your thoughts go by in zazen. Focus on the silence and let the echoes do their thing. Every time you find yourself grooving on what you're playing or what your buddies are playing, just go back to the silence, go back to big mind. Remember: there are no good notes, no bad notes, no listener to tell the difference. Just the waves of the universal mind rippling in the void."

So that's what I did. I sought the silence as I played and something magical happened. When it came time for my solo on "Autumn Leaves," the notes bubbled up without any conscious intent, like a fountain from an unseen source, musical ideas that were not my own, that swung and soared like nothing I had ever played, and the exhilaration that followed in their wake was so profound it was a shock to my system. But the moment I became aware of my accomplishment, the moment I forgot the silence and became enamored of the waves, the flow disappeared and I plummeted with a vertiginous whoosh into my familiar mediocrity. That sudden disappointment and Elijah's presence at the edge of my awareness pushed me to seek the silence again, and the closer I got the more the flow returned. For the rest of the recital, I felt like I was riding a bucking bronco: my small mind with its untamed passions. When small mind calmed, silence reigned and the music soared; when it bucked, I fell prisoner to my thoughts, to a circumscribed existence that could not begin to approximate the music that came from beyond its borders.

Elijah saw it, of course. He knew exactly what was happening, and I'm sure it made him smile. For everyone else it was an uneven performance with some very good moments during the last two tunes, moments my teachers took as a sign of tremendous promise. Bill Schumacher, my theory-and-composition teacher, made a beeline for me as soon as we finished our set and singled me out for praise that a few months earlier would have turned my ears red. "For a few bars there, Dan, you were playing like a pro. I doubt if even Brubeck could have done better. You keep working at it, keep practicing, gain some experience, and one day you'll be able to play at that level for an entire set. For the time being, though, you should be proud of yourself. You really impressed me up there." But I knew better. All I had actually done was to get out of the way of big mind for a few bars during my final two solos. It was only in those moments when I managed to get out of the way that something happened—or rather, as Elijah would put it, that "nothing" happened—and I couldn't take credit for the workings of big mind. But I certainly could enjoy it. Those few bars had been like gaining temporary admission to a higher world, the world of the Zen masters, a world that had captured my imagination and refused to let it go.

I was still euphoric when I caught up with Elijah, but he was quick to reacquaint me with the ground. "You can do better, brother," he told me, shaking his head and frowning as we left the auditorium and headed for the parking lot. "Your concentration was all over the place. The moment you managed to quiet your mind a little you lost it again."

"But, Elijah," I said, my excitement getting the better of me, "I got it, I really got it! I was right there in the silence! I know it was only for a few moments, but I was right there. I know what it's all about now."

"You remind me of a minnow in a teacup, brother, crowing about the waves he's made. Drop him in the ocean and he won't hardly raise a ripple. Remember what I told you. Anyone can quiet their mind for a few seconds now and then. It's not worth crowing about. You want to *have* a quiet mind, a quiet nature. You want to live in the silence, not just visit for a few seconds every once in a while. Got it? Okay. Now let's get back to the zendo and do some zazen, see if we can't clear some of that restlessness from your mind. A few seconds of concentration and your head's so swelled I can't get my arms around it."

That was Elijah's backyard discipline, and once I got through evening zazen I was able to admit that it was well deserved. My head had indeed swelled up, and it took most of my evening practice to get it back to a manageable size. What I had experienced was really just a glimpse of an oceanic silence that was still far in the distance. There was no immersion, no satori, nothing of the kind, really, but even that distant glimpse was enough to lift my playing to another level, if only momentarily. That had been the source of my exhilaration, the sudden auditory thrill of finally hearing a cascade of piano notes from the recital hall's baby grand that matched my aspirations, notes that hadn't come from me but from somewhere beyond me. The actual silence was still a good way off, but just feeling the salt mist in my face was a cause for jubilation. And it was enough for Elijah to work with.

Once I got over my premature sense of triumph, Elijah sat me down during my next lesson and dissected my performance, practically note by note — though he wasn't interested in my melodies but rather in the state of mind that had generated them, the wavering consciousness that he was intent on training.

"It wasn't anything to crow about, brother," he said, "but it was a stepping stone — *if* you can keep your footing. Remember how it felt, burn it in your memory, and each time you practice try to get back there. Try to recreate that feeling by reaching for the silence behind the music. Only next time, try not to get enamored with the notes. Stay with the silence and just let them slide on by, like birds crossing the sky of your mind. You see them go by, but it's not the birds you're after, so don't let them distract you."

Elijah picked up his tenor and played a walking bass line while I struggled for the rest of the lesson to play a single bar in which the notes jumped out of my sax of their own accord to swing and soar their way across the garden and out into the Berkeley streets. I didn't get there but in the next lesson I did—a single bar that was worth every drop of sweat that the onset of summer wrung out of me. Elijah was right: the memory of those few bars gave me something to aim at, a stepping stone that held out the promise of a path, of another stone up ahead for me to leap to, as long as I could maintain my footing. First I had to secure that one bar until I could navigate it without losing my balance, and that was what we worked on until the semester ended with its menacing shadow of summer vacation in Northridge.

20

My parents agreed to let me keep the apartment for my sophomore year as long as I came home for the summer. They sent me the three months' rent, since I wouldn't be back until mid-August, and Diana agreed to look after the place for me while I was gone. When I told Elijah about my plans for the summer, he asked me if I could drop him off in Ojai on my way down to Northridge. It was a pleasant surprise—I wasn't looking forward to going home, but at least Elijah's company would make the trip down seem more like an adventure than a forced march into exile. I was curious though. What would be important enough to convince Elijah to leave Berkeley when he hardly ever set foot outside his one-man monastery? I asked him about it the night after my last exam, joining him on his porch after evening practice to look at the stars and enjoy the balmy late May weather.

"The dream within the dream, brother," he said, in answer to my question. "Or in this case, the dream within the dream within the dream."

I shook my head, baffled by the allusion. Elijah acknowledged my confusion with a smile and a nod of his head.

"The Hindus say that the creation is a dream within the mind of Brahma, the Creator. And inside that dream the living beings dream that their existence is real, though actually we are all asleep, all except the Buddhas and the Bodhisattvas. Asleep to the true nature of reality, dreaming that our bodies and minds are real, that this bench is solid, that this cottage and those bushes are more than just mere imagination, that our lives are something other than what they really are: a conjuring of the magic wand of maya. That's the dream within the dream. Then at night, when we fall asleep, the sleep within the sleep, we dream up a whole nother existence: the dream within the dream within the dream."

"In other words, an actual dream."

"That's one way of looking at it, brother. It's not the Hindu way, but it will do."

"Does that mean you're going to Ojai because of a dream?"

"That's right."

"Really? What was the dream about?"

"That's what I'm going there to find out, brother. I've already gotten one opinion, but I was advised to get a second opinion. This time from a Hindu sage, someone who knows all about the dream within the dream. It seems like good advice to me."

Elijah had mentioned Hindu ideas from time to time, in passing, but as far as I knew he was all Buddhist, all the time. But the Buddha had been Indian, and though I hadn't yet read any Hindu texts, I knew that Buddhist tradition owed a lot to Hindu thought. How much it owed, I wouldn't find out until much later.

Intrigued, I asked Elijah who this sage was.

"Jiddu Krishnamurti. He has a spiritual community just outside of Ojai. You never heard of him?"

I shook my head.

"He's worth reading, brother. Since Yogananda died he's got to be the most influential Hindu sage this side of India."

"Who was Yogananda?"

"Why don't I tell you about my dream first, and on the way I'll tell you about Yogananda. So anyhow, I've been having this recurring dream. It started about two months ago. In the dream I'm sitting in a room in front of a wooden bed covered by a batik sheet, and gradually a figure starts to materialize on the bed, almost like a camera coming into focus. It's a man about my age, maybe a few years older, black hair, thick black glasses, olive skin, white clothes — but not Western clothes, Hindu clothes. He's sitting cross-legged on the bed and smiling at me from behind those glasses. That's all, just him looking at me and smiling. But his smile and his gaze are so captivating, so magnetic, it's like nothing I've ever experienced. I can feel myself being drawn to him like I've never been drawn to anyone. This goes on for some time and then the dream ends. Sometimes the feeling is so strong it wakes me up. I sit up on my mat and I can still feel him looking at me, still feel the pull. I didn't think that much of it the first time, just that it was very unusual. It was only a dream, right? A dream within the dream within the dream. But a couple of days later I had the same dream, and then a few days after that, and then again and again, week after week, sometimes as often as every other day. Always exactly the same: very powerful, very unsettling, to the point where I couldn't get it out of my mind—couldn't get *him* out of my mind. Finally I realized that I had to do something about it. By then, of course, I knew it wasn't an ordinary dream. There was something I had to learn from it, something I was supposed to discover. So I decided to see this psychic I know, to see if there was anything in my aura that could help me figure out what to do. John Laurence, very interesting guy. That's where the Yogananda connection comes in. But first let me tell you how I met John.

"A couple of years ago I was passing by the Unity on Bush Street, and I noticed that they were going to host a talk on auras and psychic abilities. Normally that kind of thing is frowned upon in Zen. Zen masters know all about these abilities, but they consider them distractions and they advise their disciples to steer clear of them. It's good advice, but I've always been curious about these things. Part of growing up in the South, I guess. My grandmother used to communicate with spirits and tell fortunes. Most of the time they came true, too. She was a self-made preacher, full-on Christian but not the kind of Christian you're probably used to. Black folks in the South have their own brand of Christianity. It's mixed up with spiritism and traditions that came over from Africa, kind of like a spiritual gumbo. Alabama is full of spiritual mediums and my grandmother had the gift. I could tell you some wild stories about the things I saw growing up. So when I saw the announcement on the letter board I got curious. I decided to go and see what this guy had to say and I wasn't disappointed. He turned out to be the real deal, brother, an authentic psychic who was also an ordained priest, an ex-Trappist monk, and a professional opera singer who had sung with Chaliapin at the Met. Not the kind of guy you meet every day. He told some great stories, mostly about different psychic experiences he'd had, past-life stuff, some of the aura's he'd read, how he'd helped people avoid some calamity or other, but he also explained some of the philosophy behind the phenomena, and the interesting thing was that it wasn't a spiritist explanation at all—I had heard a lot of that when I was a kid so I knew what that was about. This was a yogic explanation, not much different than how a Buddhist would explain it. At the end of the talk he went up to the blackboard and wrote, *Autobiography of a Yogi* by Paramahansa Yogananda, and said that if anyone was interested in knowing more about this sort of thing they should read this book. Now that really caught my attention. I had heard about Yogananda's autobiography but I hadn't read it, so I went up to him after the talk and that's when he told me the story of how he got initiated.

"Picture this. It's 1933 and he's walking down Sixteenth Street in DC one night after a performance, and he sees this figure dressed in orange robes and a turban walking in the opposite direction on the other side of the street. The moment he sees him he feels this magnetic pull. It's so powerful he can't resist it. He ends up crossing the street and following him from a distance. It's not a voluntary thing: the attraction is so powerful he's just being pulled along, like he's helpless to do anything about it. At that time Sixteenth Street was all brownstones with the front entrance right there on the street. So he follows him for a few blocks until the guy in the robes disappears into one of the brownstones. But he's still being drawn along, right up to the door. As soon as he reaches the landing, the door opens and a hand comes out and pulls him inside. It's Yogananda, with this huge smile on his face. 'You were following me,' Yogananda tells him. 'Now I'm going to initiate you.' So Yogananda takes him into a room and teaches him meditation, and it's what he's been waiting for his whole life, though he didn't know it up until that moment.

"Yogananda was a Hindu guru, you see, who came over from India in the twenties and eventually ended up in LA. His guru sent him to America to bring the teachings of yoga to the West, and he was very successful. Initiated thousands of disciples, opened centers all over the country. This was before there were any Buddhist or yogic masters in our part of the world. He was the first, the first to actually live in the West. He died about four years ago. Too bad. He's one guy I would have loved to have met. Anyhow, the next day I went right out and bought his autobiography, and I was blown away. You read it and you'll see what I mean. There's this scene in the book where Yogananda meets his guru. He's walking down a street in the marketplace, and he sees this guy in yogic robes standing in an alley, gazing at him. He tries to keep walking but his feet won't let him. The saint is pulling him toward him like a magnet. Exactly what I felt in my dream and what John felt when he first saw Yogananda. Which is another reason why I went to see John. That was this past Sunday in San Francisco. He lives in Sunnyvale, but he comes into the city every Sunday to give readings at the Unity."

"So what did he say?"

"First he asked me to describe the dream in as much detail as I could and then he read my aura. That's where it got interesting. He told me he saw a radiant figure at the back of my aura that matched the description from my dream. He was convinced that it was my guru; otherwise he wouldn't have been able to see him — according to John, only a *sadguru*, a perfect guru, has the power to appear in another person's aura — and from his appearance John was dead sure he was Indian. He believes it's my destiny to meet him and become his disciple."

"You're kidding! Did he say when or how?"

"No, that was all he could see. Just that I would meet him one day and that day would change my life. But he did think I would have to go to India to find him."

I don't know if my mouth actually dropped open or not, but I felt as if it did. All I was able to offer was an inarticulate "wow," but inside I was as giddy as if I were in that chair opposite John Laurence in a small basement room in the Unity Church. Go look for him? The mere mention of the possibility conjured up images from the stories I had been reading of Japanese and Chinese seekers wandering on foot in search of an enlightened master. But a master who appeared in a dream? A master whose only clue as to his whereabouts — *if* he even existed — was a psychic's belief that he was Indian? This was wilder than any of the stories, real or apocryphal, that I'd read in my books. Either that or downright crazy. It hadn't yet hit me what it would mean should Elijah believe what John Laurence had told him, that he might actually consider abandoning his seclusion to go halfway around the globe in search of a figure whom he had only seen in a dream. At that moment I was too taken with the story and its echoes of legendary spiritual adventures to think that it might mean that I could lose my own teacher.

"So why Ojai?" I asked.

"Well, I wasn't exactly thrilled with what he said. The dreams were unsettling enough, brother, but the thought of going off in search of somebody I had only seen in a dream? No idea who he was? He could see how skeptical I was. Who wouldn't be, right, especially a Zen guy like me, two feet on the ground and heavy feet at that? But he was real cool about it. No ego, not the slightest attempt to convince me. Very humble. He was just telling me what he saw in my aura and what his intuition told him. In his experience he was usually right about these things, but that didn't mean he was right this time. That's when he mentioned Krishnamurti. Since he thought the figure in my dreams was an Indian guru, why not talk to another Indian guru to see what he thought about it? Get a second opinion, so to speak. I got the impression he didn't consider Krishnamurti to be fully enlightened, just very elevated, but since he's the only authentic Indian sage within ten thousand miles, he suggested I go to Ojai and ask him about it. I remember, he said that he felt that whatever I decided to do, it would be the most important decision of my life, so I should do whatever it took to get it right. No room for regrets. That made sense to me."

I asked Elijah what he knew about Krishnamurti but it wasn't much. He had read a couple of his books and knew that he was very popular with the spiritual crowd in California, but he hadn't given much thought to the yogic tradition outside of the books he'd read and his conversations in Japan with Nancy Wilson Ross, who was as versed in Hindu thought as she was in Buddhist traditions and practice. What he remembered of Krishnamurti's books was that he was a brilliant thinker who was adept at cutting through the illusions that most people wrapped themselves in like a cloak to ward off the winter chill. If he was letting himself fall prey to some kind of mental delusion, he reasoned, Krishnamurti seemed like the perfect teacher to strip him of that delusion. Arranging a meeting with him wouldn't be easy—the guru who claimed he wasn't (a good recommendation, as far as Elijah was concerned) was surrounded by disciples who protected his privacy, and he had visitors coming everyday from all over the globe with questions of their own, hoping they might be addressed in one of his Sunday discourses—but he had nothing to lose by trying, except the uncertainty aroused by his dreams. At the very least it would be a chance to get out of the Bay Area, something he hadn't done in over two years, and on the only pretext capable of separating him from his cottage: a spiritual pilgrimage.

"Of course, there's another possible explanation," he said.

"What's that?" I asked.

"It could be a past-life memory. I could have been a yogi in a past life and he was my guru. That's what Watts thinks."

"You talked to him?"

"After I saw John, I dropped by the Academy to find out a little more about Krishnamurti and the setup down there in Ojai. Alan took a group of students there a couple of years ago to meet him, so he knows how it works. He asked me why I wanted to go, so I told him. He got quite a kick out of it. Who knows, he could even be right. There's a first time for everything."

If Watts was right—and it certainly seemed as plausible as any-thing John Laurence had said—then any possible trip to India might be in search of a body that had been burned to ashes decades or even centuries ago. And that's discounting the possibility—some-thing neither of us mentioned—that it was just a dream, a simple, ordinary dream. It didn't take long for me to realize that there was a lot more riding on this trip to Ojai than I had originally thought.

21

Three days later I handed Diana the keys to the apartment. It was my final night in Berkeley before going home for the summer, and to celebrate the occasion I took her to an upscale restaurant with what was left of the money my father had sent me. Afterward we went to one of the few Berkeley clubs that could compete with their counterparts across the bay, the Blind Lemon, where we listened to a local jazz combo that included two faculty members from the Cal music department. It was pretty much a traditional date, and I could see that Diana was amused by the ritual, especially the dining out at a fancy restaurant with waiters who wore bow ties and asked if the gentleman wanted to see the wine list, an underage gentleman with an impeccable fake ID. Shortly after we ordered, she asked me in a soft, expectant voice if I had brought her there to pop the question, and she managed to say it with such a perfectly innocent, Shirley Temple smile that for a few excruciating moments I was convinced she meant it. The food hadn't arrived yet so I had nothing to choke on, but I remember my shock and I also remember being terrified that I wouldn't have the courage to say no. In the end, though, she couldn't keep up the pretense, and I was saved from answering by her sudden paroxysm of laughter that drew the eyes of everyone in the restaurant. Later she told me how much she regretted not having brought a camera. What a delight it would have been, she said, to have captured for all eternity the "frozen pallor" of my face.

We got back to my loft around eleven, where I was foolishly counting on going to bed at a reasonable hour, having arranged with Elijah to pick him up by nine, but it was nearly dawn when we finally got to sleep. As usual, it wasn't the sex that kept us up but the conversation, as varied and as endlessly unpredictable as a good jazz solo. Diana wasn't into Buddhism yet but we eventually ended up there, knee deep in Huang Po's doctrine of universal mind. I was no Kerouac when it came to talking Zen, but I was enthusiastic and my experience during the recital made sense to her in a way she thought could translate to her own poetics.

"It sounds a lot like Jack's spiel about spontaneous prose. You know, it's always been the poet's dream to be possessed by the muse. I never connected the dots before but maybe it's the same thing. It always seemed like a conceit to me, a fanciful way of talking about the creative process, but maybe the muse is the universal mind and that was just how they described it. After all, poets are not philosophers. They're poets. Maybe they were describing the same experience the only way they knew how — with their poetic imagination. But I never heard of any technique to summon the muse at will — other than opium and excess, and neither of those actually work, at least not for me. So tell me again, how did you do it?"

"It's a kind of meditation. You listen to the silence behind the music until you're not there any more, until there's no one playing. There's just the music coming out of the silence like an echo from the depths. At least, that's how Elijah puts it."

"You know that doesn't sound logical," Diana said, shaking her head. "They're your fingers on the keys."

"I know, but as Jack would say, logic is overrated. Experience is everything. The moment I stopped being aware of myself the music literally took off. It was almost like magic, the kind you read about in fairy tales. You can say that my fingers were moving by themselves, or that the universal mind was moving them, but it comes to the same thing. The moment I had no more conscious intent the geyser erupted. All I had to do was to get out of the way and there it was. Of course, getting out of the way is a bear. You have to work at it."

"I think the only way I'll be able to understand what you're talking about is if I experience it for myself. There should be a way to do it with poetry. Any suggestions?"

It was nearly three by then, but sleep was the furthest thing from our minds. We were both excited by the possibility of a Zen poetics that could tap into the endless creativity of the universal mind.

But how to get there? I kept going back to Elijah's advice: seek the silence from which the music arises and keep your attention focused there. It should be the same for literature, I reasoned. Diana was a poet. She knew language the way I knew music. The trick was to allow the language to seek its own expression without trying to direct it or shape it or control it in any conscious way, to remove all intentionality from the picture. But in order to do that, she would have to be able to quiet her mind, so I grabbed a couple of firm cushions and did as Elijah had done with me. First I had her listen to the sounds around us: the occasional car, the wind rattling the window, the muffled squawk of a distant foghorn. Then we shifted our attention to the one question that is at the heart of all Zen practice: Who is the thinker behind the thought? What is this mind that apprehends the shifting phenomena of existence? From there it was only one short step to the universal mind in which everything rises and falls like waves on the surface of the ocean, not only our thoughts but the world itself, its sounds and colors and shapes. Or as Huang Po put it: "It is right before you, right now; start thinking about it and you miss it."

After half an hour or so of this sinking into silence, I handed Diana a notebook and a pen and asked her to try to maintain the same meditative awareness but this time to transcribe whatever words the ocean kicked up. No judgment, I reminded her. There are no good or bad words. There are just waves in the universal mind that sometimes take the form of language.

I wasn't a poet but I also grabbed a notebook and a pen and joined her, doing my best to divert my attention from the words my mind threw up to the source from where they came, the all-pervading silence of Huang Po's universal mind. Occasionally I would notice Diana scribbling away, and sometimes it would be me, and by the time we looked at each other and wordlessly agreed to end the experiment, I had filled two pages in my notebook and Diana four. Then we each read to each other what we had written. I don't know that what I wrote made much sense, but then I wasn't a poet, or any kind of a writer, not yet. But Diana was and it showed. Her four pages of inspired scrawl were full of the kind of unexpected images and daring language she would later become known for. I don't recall the content, but I remember that the voyage made me dizzy. I wasn't used to such flights of imagination. When Diana finished reading, she looked a little dizzy also, as if the experience had left her disoriented.

"I think I understand now what you were talking about," she said after a short silence, shaking her head in wonder. "I could see my intentionality like I was staring at it in a mirror. It was like a compulsion. I had to literally force myself not to pay attention. It was almost painful, it was so contrary to everything I'm used to. But you're absolutely right. The language got dammed up as soon as I paid attention to it. Actually, it felt like my whole body got dammed up, like I was tying myself up in verbal knots. But when I stopped paying attention the flow came back. And it's good stuff, hang me from a yardarm if it's not. Maybe Jack's not as crazy as he seems. The best lines in these pages are when I wasn't thinking at all about what I was writing or whether it was any good or not. It's like they wrote themselves."

"Or the universal mind wrote them."

"Well if it did, it's a lot better poet than I am … Nonintentional poetry. I think that's what I'll call it. What do you think?"

"Sounds good to me. Jazuzen and nonintentional poetry. Maybe we can combine the two. A night of nonintentional poetry with a jazz-Zen accompaniment. It can become our trademark."

"It was strange how effortless it felt," she mused, "once I got the hang of it. Writing poetry is such a struggle most of the time. Usually a line or two will just pop into my head, God knows from where. It might be some image that catches my attention that's the catalyst or some strong emotion. And if they're good lines, then I'll know there's a poem in there somewhere. The problem is the next line. I may get started with something that comes out of my unconscious, but after that I have to consciously work at it. I have to search for the right image, the right words, something that builds on those first lines and takes the poem in the direction it wants to go—or in the direction I would like it to go. Other than those first lines, though, there's never any time when I don't feel like I'm in control—I don't know if control is the right word, exactly, considering how difficult it usually is. It's more like driving in the fog down a road you've never been down before. You have to go real slow because you can't see what's up ahead. But you're still behind the wheel—it's up to you to decide if you're going to go right or left or continue on straight. This was more like being strapped into a ride in an amusement park. No control over where you're going, no idea what's coming up next, and all so fast it makes you dizzy. It was such a strange feeling, not being in control of my own words. Exhilarating but strange. Is that what it's like for you when you're soloing?"

"When I'm able to do it, yeah. But it's calming also, kind of oceanic, to tell the truth. I've only been able to do it for a few bars, here and there, but it's the best feeling I've ever had. There's a saying in Zen: when you don't hear with your ears, then you are really hearing. Something was hearing the music in those moments but it wasn't me. At least it wasn't my ordinary self with my ordinary ears. I'm not sure I can tell you what it was, but there's no way I'm going back to my old way of playing, not if I can help it. Not after my experience in that recital. No more ordinary Dan trying as hard as he can to play the right notes. That's just a dead-end street."

"I think you're on to something, Dan. I really do. If I can do the same thing in poetry—well, this changes everything. It can become a whole new approach to writing: nonintentional literature. Who knows where it will take us?"

With the benefit of hindsight it is easy to see how prescient Diana's words were. An experiment that began on my bed would one day secure for her a place of prominence in American letters. Her work with indeterminacy in literature has left a heavy imprint on a new generation of writers. As with Kerouac and his stream-of-consciousness, toilet-roll prose, her best moments bear the mark of nonintentionality—or as I prefer to think of it, the abiding influence of the Zen spirit, a taste of nirvana where the ego's flame barely flickers in the void. But all we knew then was that a road was opening up, for her as well as for me. There were still many detours waiting for us before we would understand the true import of Huang Po's words: "Not till your thoughts cease their branching, not till you abandon all thoughts of seeking, not till your mind is as motionless as wood or stone, will you be on the right road to the Gate."

22

THOUGH I WASN'T LOOKING forward to spending the summer at home, the trip down to LA nearly made up for it. We ended up leaving around ten and made Ojai a little before four, doing seventy the whole way with the top down and our voices doing battle with the wind. Elijah was in a talkative mood, and I got a chance to ask many of the questions that I hadn't had the gumption to ask before. Elijah was only eleven years older than me, though that seemed like a huge gap at the time, but he was far older in terms of life experience. Growing up black in the Deep South, six years in the army, two and a half as a monk in Myoshinji, playing the jazz clubs in New York alongside Bird and Dizzy and Miles, even his years as a Zen recluse in Berkeley—these were experiences that seemed extraordinary to a nineteen-year-old who had no life experience to speak of, and for once Elijah wasn't reluctant to talk about the past. What I remember most about that memorable conversation was how intense his life had been. It was if he had taken the experiences of two or three lives and condensed them into a couple of battle-scarred decades that had fashioned him into a man of strong convictions and even stronger determination. By the time we reached Carpinteria, I had the distinct impression that if any man could retrace the Buddha's steps in our modern world, it was Elijah. In a showdown between him and Mara, I wouldn't have given a plugged nickel for Mara's chances.

We had no problem finding the cottage a couple of miles east of town where Krishnamurti lived, but the Indian sage wasn't there. He was traveling in Europe and wasn't due back until early July. This didn't seem to faze Elijah at all, however. He talked with the caretakers of the property for a while about the protocol for asking

Krishnamurti a question once he returned and then got back in the car and asked me if I would drop him in LA, which I was more than happy to do. The extra hour and a half in the car with Elijah was like a reprieve before the execution of my sentence, and we continued our conversation all the way into the city, where I dropped him off at a friend's house in South LA. Five weeks later, at seven in the morning on a Sunday, I was back in front of that same apartment building near the corner of Slauson and Vermont to pick him up and drive him to Ojai, an unplanned excursion that gave me my first glimpse of an Indian guru.

Ojai was still pretty rustic back then, a sleepy hamlet of a few thousand souls nestled in the shadows of the Topatopa Mountains, surrounded by orchards and organic farms. Many of the outlying roads weren't paved yet, and the locals still had the habit of leaving their doors unlocked—the perfect place, as it turned out, for Krishnamurti to spend the better part of his life, a place where he could enjoy his leisure time without being bothered, where he could drop into the local cinema unnoticed for an afternoon matinee, and yet accommodating enough for the thousands of visitors who would turn up for his Sunday talks.

We arrived around eight-thirty and parked the car in a field just across from a gate where visitors were lining up to be let in. I was surprised to see how many there were, close to a thousand by the time we arrived and double that by the time the talk began. They opened the gate just after nine and people started filing in, strolling sedately down a long, winding, tree-lined path into a grassy clearing known as Oak Grove. There was a small wooden stage at one edge of the clearing with a chair on it, and since Elijah had made prior arrangements to have his question included among those that Krishnamurti would answer, we were able to sit right up front on the dried-out summer grass.

Krishnamurti arrived about forty-five minutes after we took our seats, walking up the path to the back of the stage accompanied by a couple of assistants. There was no fanfare, no commotion other than the increased murmurs of low conversations and a sea of heads turning in his direction. Just an ordinary-looking, clean-shaven, middle-aged man in a long-sleeved sky-blue shirt and gray slacks walking up the path, chatting with his two companions. I was surprised how small he looked, how short and slight of build, almost frail it seemed, though he was barely into his sixties then, but there was a presence about him that I noticed from the moment he sat down and looked out over the crowd with a childlike, almost mischievous smile. One of his assistants handed him a mic that he clipped to his shirt, but for the next two or three minutes he sat in silence and scanned the audience. I was instantly affected by the aura of composure that enveloped him, the calm radiance of a man who was entirely at peace with himself and with the world. Elijah had spent two and a half years with an enlightened master in Japan, but for me it was a revelation. This was the first time I had ever been within shouting distance of a man of his spiritual stature, and it made me realize how fortunate I was to be sitting there. Up and down Ventura County, hundreds of thousands of Southern Californians were lounging around on a Sunday morning, reading their newspapers, working in their gardens, or sitting restlessly in the pews of their local church, having absolutely no idea that a great soul was sitting in an oak grove only a short drive away, giving freely of his time to whoever came to listen. No idea and no interest as well. And up until a few months earlier I had been one of them. Whatever had brought me there, whatever stroke of luck or stroke of karma, I was profoundly grateful, and it's a feeling that has never left me, even till this day.

Before he turned to the questions, Krishnamurti gave a short talk about the chaotic state of world affairs and the self-engendered suffering that seems endemic to our world. How is it that people cannot see, he emphasized, that we will never achieve peace on earth as long as we divide ourselves along nationalistic lines? Then he related this state of affairs to our state of consciousness, both collective and individual, a state of consciousness that was entirely within our power to change—through deep introspection, meditation, and uncompromising honesty. The clarity and power of his thought astounded me, as well as its relevance to everything I had experienced in the past six months.

Elijah's was the second question he answered, each of the questions written out on a piece of paper that rested on his lap. After reading the question Krishnamurti asked Elijah for clarification.

"My question relates to a recurring dream that I've been having for the past few months. It is such an unusual dream—an unusual experience, I should say—that I decided to see a psychic about it, a man who has been practicing meditation for many years, and after giving me his interpretation he suggested that I come see you."

"What is so unusual about this dream?"

"I think it is the intensity more than anything, the feeling it generates, but I suppose I should first describe it. Several nights a week I dream that I'm sitting on the floor in a room in front of a man who's sitting on a wooden bed, much like I'm sitting in front of you now. The man's dressed in white, in clothes that appear to be traditional Indian clothes—a long-sleeved shirt and what I'm told is called a dhoti. He has glasses and olive skin and he's gazing at me. He doesn't say anything but the attraction is very powerful. I can feel him drawing me toward him. Sometimes it's so strong it wakes me up. It's only a dream, but in some ways I feel more connected to him than to anyone I've ever met. The psychic I saw thinks that this man may be my spiritual guide, an Indian guru that I am somehow destined to meet. A friend of mine, Alan Watts, who's been down to see you, thinks it may be a past-life experience rather than anything to do with the present or the future. Either way, it feels important for me to figure out what the dream means. It feels like a spiritual puzzle that I somehow have to solve."

"And you would like me to solve it for you, to interpret your dream, to get a third opinion, as it were?"

"I think what I'm searching for is an enlightened opinion, from someone with a deeper understanding than my own."

"First of all, you have to ask the right question. If you look to somebody else to interpret your dream, then you open yourself up to dependence on an external authority, and that is a dangerous path, a path that leads inevitably to conflict and suffering. A man divided from himself cannot be happy, and a man who looks to others for the truth can never be whole or at peace."

"Are you saying that if I want to understand the dream, then I have to find that understanding within?"

"Before we can begin to talk about understanding your dream, we must first understand the nature of consciousness and not let ourselves be confined by any preconceived ideas. Your consciousness is the totality of your thoughts and feelings, those you are aware of and those that are hidden from you. Your secret motivations, your hopes and fears, the values that society has imposed on you through your family, through your education and religion, values that in many cases are not real values but more like superstitions that you have swallowed without being aware of it. It is your character, your temperament, your virtues and your vices, even those you hide from yourself, but it is far more than that as well. It is also your racial and cultural memory, the entire legacy of all the lives that have been lived before you, what some people like to call the 'collective unconscious.' And if you believe in God or the atman or the soul, then it is also the thought of a supernatural, supersensible entity. Do you follow?"

"Yes, I think so."

"Most people are only aware of a small portion of the totality of their consciousness. The greater portion is hidden from them, and this is what creates the divide between the conscious and the unconscious. Actually there is no divide. Consciousness is one, but since we give attention only to a small portion of it, the greater part remains inaccessible to us. Nonetheless it is still there, churning away beneath the surface, influencing our behavior, controlling our lives in ways we are generally not aware of. We may resist its influence, but the unconscious keeps quietly working, pushing us in the direction it wants us to go. One of the ways it does this is through what we commonly call dreams. When the conscious mind goes to sleep, so to speak, when its activity becomes somewhat calm, then the unconscious portion of the mind can communicate with the conscious portion through a parade of internal images and scenes that sometimes appear to be highly symbolic—thus the urge to seek out their meaning. The problem is that whatever meaning you arrive at will be conditioned by the needs and fears and conceits of the conscious mind. And what our conscious mind wants above all is to feel safe and secure. Have you not noticed this?"

"Yes, I suppose I have. It seems like a natural tendency."

"We are conditioned to accept this as natural, but a mind that is conditioned to cling to some seemingly safe mooring, whether it is a set of religious beliefs or secular values or the sense of ego itself, cannot be free. Rather, such a mind is a slave to its prejudices, and there is nothing natural about slavery. Does it not stand to reason that if we want to find out the meaning of the urgings of the unconscious mind, then we must be willing and able to set aside the conventions and convenient explanations that the conscious mind depends on for its sense of identity and open ourselves up to something that may be uncomfortable or unsettling, something that may in fact undermine those very beliefs and values that the ego looks to for its sense of security?"

"Yes, that seems absolutely right to me. It may require courage, though."

"Facing the unknown always does. But that is the path to freedom, the path beyond the dualism that makes our consciousness into a prison. Now, if one may ask, might it not be possible to maintain this communication that we were speaking of during the waking state? To break down this illusory barrier between the conscious and unconscious minds, to bring all that is hidden within us to full awareness?"

"I believe it is possible, though very difficult. Such a person would be what I would call a sage, a Buddha, an enlightened being."

"Let us not be too quick to fall into categories that may have the effect of halting the journey of inquiry. Rather, let us continue the journey and see where it leads us. Let us be alert and see what we uncover as we go along. Now, what would happen if, when you board a bus or you go to work, you were able to be completely aware of the workings of your consciousness, of all your responses to the endlessly changing situations that present themselves before you, both your obvious conscious responses and those in the subtle depths of your mind that were hitherto hidden to you, what we have called the unconscious? What if you were able to be aware of your racial memories and traditions, the whole of your culture and all of its teachings as you have absorbed them over your lifetime, aware of how this vast tableau of human history affects the way in which your consciousness responds to the world around you? What if, at the same time, you were also aware of the clouds and the sky and the wind and the trees and the birds and all the other living creatures that inhabit this field of consciousness, both human and nonhuman? Do you agree that in such a state of full awareness your dreams, if they did not cease altogether, would lose their mystery for you, that you would cease to feel the need for interpretation?"

"Yes, that makes perfect sense. If we could be fully aware of the inner workings of our mind, then it stands to reason that it would lead to full understanding."

"Such a mind, if it were constantly aware, constantly observing, without judgment or self-interest, would no longer be a slave to convention or beliefs, whether self-imposed or socially imposed. Do you agree?"

"Absolutely."

"Does this not inevitably lead us to a different question than the one we started out with, a question that might be framed quite simply as: What is the path to freedom? Instead of falling back on some conventional or convenient explanation, as we would be likely to get with any dream interpretation, especially one supplied us by an external authority, we have allowed ourselves to be open to the unknown, and in the process we have discovered that the right question was something altogether different."

It didn't seem like the answer Elijah was looking for, but maybe Krishnamurti was right. Maybe it wasn't a matter of finding the right answer but of finding the right question. Was that then the question Elijah should have been asking all along? What is the path to freedom? It almost sounded like a Zen koan, something a Zen monk would keep struggling to solve for days and months and years until it finally led him to satori. Had Elijah come all this way just for Krishnamurti to remind him to keep working on exactly what he had been working on all along? In other words, to not get distracted by the distractions of the mind, which after all are endless, but to cut them off at their source.

I could see that Elijah was deep in thought. Krishnamurti fielded several more questions before the program ended, and each of his answers was as long and as exacting as the one he gave Elijah, but I doubt Elijah heard much of what he said. His gaze seemed to be fixed inward, following the thread the Indian sage had woven. When the program finished, I drove Elijah to the Greyhound station in Carpinteria so he could catch the afternoon bus to San Francisco. Unlike the drive up from LA, he remained silent, seemingly still pondering the import of Krishnamurti's words. I didn't want to interrupt his thoughts, but when we pulled up to the station, it seemed like an appropriate moment to ask him what he made of the experience.

"I'm glad I came, I can tell you that much, brother. I should have known better than to think he would give me a direct answer. That's not the way masters work. If I had asked Zuigan-roshi the same question, he probably would have thrown me out of his room and told me to come back when I had the answer to the sound of one hand. Krishnamurti's style may be different, but it amounts to the same thing in the end. Still, he gave me a lot to think about. Now I need to go back and meditate and see where it leads me."

I left Elijah at the station and drove back to Northridge in a similar state of quiet reflection. Krishnamurti's very presence seemed to command that in people. The powerful aura of tranquility that enveloped him and the unerring precision and depth of his thoughts went far beyond anything I had ever experienced. My only reference up until then had been Elijah, whom I had accepted as my teacher in the Buddhist sense of the word. But meeting Krishnamurti and listening to him speak forced me to recalibrate my fledgling sense of the ladder of spiritual attainment. Elijah, I could see now, was closer to me than he was to Jiddu Krishnamurti. He wasn't exactly a mere mortal—nine years of dedicated Zen practice had given him access to spiritual realms that most of us don't yet know exist—but I could sense that Krishnamurti inhabited a plane of consciousness that was as yet unknown to either one of us, though Elijah was obviously far closer to it than I was. He not only had nine years on me, he was more dedicated and more determined than I would ever be—and, I suspect, more gifted in spiritual matters as well. All of which made him eminently suited to be my first teacher, the man who opened the door for me to the interior life. But there were areas of his consciousness that were still hidden to him, whereas I sensed that Krishnamurti looked out on an inner vista that was, if not infinite, then very nearly so. He was one of those rare beings whose influence extends far beyond the people who come into his contact, which in his case numbered in the tens of thousands. It radiates outward into the culture, directing it down pathways it might not have otherwise taken. The spiritual life of California and Californians owes a great deal to his presence among us. The same is true to a lesser extent for the rest of the country, and indeed, the West in general. We would not understand the spiritual path as well as we do if it were not for his many years of teaching in a language tailored to our occidental culture and the numerous books that have resulted from those unflagging efforts, books that you will find on the bookshelf of virtually every serious Western spiritual aspirant from San Francisco to Stockholm. That was my first taste of what it was like to be around a genuine Indian sage, and I found it so palatable that I would return again and again in the coming years, not only to Ojai but also to the ashrams of the other Hindu gurus who in the sixties and seventies would help to make California a land of ashrams second only to India itself.

23

THE TRIP TO OJAI was the high-water mark of an otherwise stultifying summer. I managed a few excursions to the jazz clubs with my brother, sat for zazen in my room every morning and evening, despite the off remarks and raised eyebrows, and did my best to practice both the piano and the sax as if they were an extension of my sitting meditation. But I couldn't help feel that I no longer belonged there, like a fish trapped in a glass bowl who longs to be back in the ocean with the rest of his fishy tribe. I had only been at Berkeley for two semesters, but it didn't take two days in Northridge to realize how much the experience had changed me. The sheltered suburban culture I had grown up in seemed like a frozen relic from a glacial age. In the nine months I'd been gone, I had become so acclimated to the Bay Area counterculture and the regarding wave of history that seemed to be propelling it forward that Northridge appeared by comparison unbearably provincial and narrow-minded, a straitjacket society of closed doors and closed minds. My impatience to escape eventually grew to the point that I resorted to subterfuge. I asked Diana to write me a letter explaining why I needed to return a week earlier than planned—a nonexistent notice from the music department involving extra credit for selected students—and it bought me the week's reprieve I so badly desired. Three days later I was back at the apartment in Berkeley where Diana was waiting for me with a surprise that made me promptly forget my summertime trials: a gig at The Purple Onion on Columbus in three weeks' time; an evening of poetry and jazz in a dreamlike ambience of tinkling beer mugs, as good a present as anyone had ever given me.

Diana had been working on her nonintentional poetry throughout the summer and she was dying to tell me about it. Though it was almost six when I arrived and I was ravenous after the long drive up the coast, I flopped down on the bed and let my stomach growl while I gave her my full attention. "Do you realize," she said, "that nature itself is nonintentional? In fact, it seems to me that it's our very intentionality that cuts us off from nature. It's our effort to control things that makes them artificial. Do you know that a few hundred years ago the word 'artificial' meant 'artful,' 'full of art'? Think about it. That shift in meaning is an indictment of our entire contemporary culture. Instead of perceiving the grace and artfulness in things, we've become obsessed with how contrived and fake everything feels, including and maybe especially our art. Look at our poetry. I think if you ask most people what they really think of it, they'll tell you that it's nice and all, but the poems don't have anything to do with real life. How many times have you heard someone say that life isn't like a novel? They wish it could be but it's just not. Nor is it like a poem that's striving for an effect or a symphony with three predictable, satisfying movements. There's always something in it that feels contrived to us, that feels artificial in the modern sense of the word. But life isn't like that. Life is completely unpredictable. Nature is unpredictable. It doesn't follow human logic, or any kind of logic—unless nature has its own logic that's too complex or profound for us to understand. So what happens when we take the intentionality out of poetry? It becomes part of nature again. It becomes real—not lifelike but real life."

"Do you know how Zen that sounds?"

"What do you expect with half of North Beach running around spouting Zen koans? With you guys contaminating the water, it's no wonder I've gotten infected. Anyhow, why not? If it helps my poetry, I'm all for it. And it's definitely helping."

Diana spent the next forty-five minutes sitting on the bed, reading me the poems she had written that summer, most of them composed right there in my loft. It was an experience I'll never forget. Part of it was the immediacy of a private performance, that husky, warm contralto of hers overwhelming me the way a jazz combo in a small club could overwhelm me through the sheer resonance of the instruments. But jazz that isn't musical can't cut it, no matter how good the instruments themselves sound up close and personal, and Diana's natural flare for rhythm made her flights of nonintentional verse as musical as a good solo. But there was more to it than the music. The images and ideas seemed to defy any effort to fit them into an identifiable pattern. Whatever threads bound them together, they were not the kind you could just pick up and explain in a high-school essay. But they did make sense, the way nature makes sense—a rich, complex, fecund mixture that baffles the intellect but thrills the soul. And though I couldn't have told you why, I felt the truth of Diana's words: these poems *were* more like real life. They had the feel of true spontaneity to them, the way Elijah's solos did, an organic rightness that bound them to the soil and made them beautiful in a way I couldn't put my finger on. I wasn't a poet, but since moving to Berkeley I had been learning to appreciate poetry much the same way that I had first learned to appreciate music—with an instinctive, nonintentional delight—and it was enough for me to feel their power. I didn't need to understand them.

But Diana had something more in mind for our performance, something that seemed to stem naturally from her experiments with nonintentionality: onstage improvisation. Extemporaneous poetry was nothing new, of course. The one time we had performed together she had had to improvise the last ten minutes of our set when she ran out of memorized material, and other poets in the area had experimented with improvisation during their readings—Bob Kaufman, for one, was better known for his improvisational talent than he was for his written compositions—but no one, to Diana's knowledge, had ever opened their doors to the purely spontaneous. The extemporaneous poetry she had heard had been thematic, even if the theme was chosen by the audience. It had been intentional, tied to the dictates of the poet's logic. What she intended was to carry her nonintentionality onstage with her and put it to the ultimate test. Her plan was to begin the performance with the poems she had written over the summer, all of which had undergone minor or major revision. But for the finale she wanted to let the words choose their own course, without any conscious intervention on her part. And she wanted me to do the same on piano. Rather than consciously choose an accompaniment that seemed to suit the text, she wanted me to seek the silence and let my fingers go their own way. It sounded audacious. If our performance turned out to be too chaotic or unintelligible, the audience could turn unruly, especially in a place like The Purple Onion that was used to professional musicians and accomplished poets. But I was game. A few boos or catcalls and no return invitation would likely be the worst we would face. San Francisco audiences were not above razzing performers if they didn't consider them up to par, even in the hip environs of ultratolerant North Beach, but they didn't overturn tables or throw things at the performers as happened on occasion in New York or Chicago. And Diana was prudent enough to save the experiment for the finale. If catcalls ensued we would have our escape route all marked out.

We finally did get something to eat at a nearby café, but we spent the rest of the night carousing on my bed and making plans for the future. What a delight it was to be back! After nearly ten weeks of parentally imposed exile, I was back where I belonged, back in what seemed to me to be the center of the known universe, the cultural heart of what would soon be a new and better America. Lying in bed with the self-proclaimed queen of bohemia, I was now without question an initiated member of the cultural renaissance that we all foresaw sweeping east from North Beach and west from the Village until it inundated the American heartland, a tidal wave of change that owed its genesis and its impetus to our soon-to-be-famous beat generation. Before we went to sleep that night, Diana and I managed to convince ourselves that The Purple Onion would be only the beginning — the beginning of a melding of Zen-inflected, nonintentional poetry and jazz that would enable us to leave our mark alongside Kerouac and Ginsberg and Snyder as artists of con-sequence in a time when a handful of artists were destined to change the world. Perhaps we allowed ourselves to give in too easily to the giddy joys of self-delusion, but given the sixties I rather think that our grandiose ideas were not altogether divorced from reality. Even if we were only footnotes in a cultural upswell, we belonged to a generation that rerouted the river of history. Each of us had our respective roles to play, some greater than others, but the real credit

goes to the entire ensemble, not just to the Kerouacs and the Gins-
bergs. It was a collective effort. Lying there on the bed, dreaming
of the impact we would have as artists at the forefront of a cultural
tsunami, we could feel ourselves rising with the swell. Just a couple
of drops, perhaps, in a mass of surging water, but oh … the energy
of that wave! Just to be carried along in those days was a righteous
intoxication, and we were as inebriated as they came.

24

THE NEXT AFTERNOON, AFTER a late lunch and a long walk by the marina with Diana, I dropped by Elijah's to let him know I was back and join him for evening practice. Though I had meditated regularly over the summer, I hadn't been very successful in my efforts. The inspiration simply wasn't there, and I couldn't seem to generate it on my own. There was too much of my old life in my parents' house, and even when no one was around to openly distract me, it usually found a way to undermine my concentration. But within a day of my return, I felt almost entirely recharged. Elijah's cottage, the Berkeley Marina, even my little garage loft—they were all safe havens, the cradles of my nascent spirituality, and the passage from one to another in the space of a few hours made me keenly aware of how fortunate I was to be back.

Elijah was sitting out on the porch when I arrived, reading a Japanese text that turned out to be Huineng's commentary on the *Diamond Sutra*. After explaining a little of its history, he quoted a couple of lines from the sutra: "All that has form is an illusive existence; when it is perceived that all form is no-form, then the Tathagata is recognized." It was like being home again, at home with myself. Diana was the embodiment of my newfound sense of belonging, the hunter-goddess who had guided me through the wilderness to my tribe, but Elijah spoke straight to my sense of purpose.

"I've been meditating on these lines for the past couple of weeks," Elijah said. He picked up another text that was lying beside him on the bench and opened it to a bookmarked page. "Now listen to these words from Bodhidharma, the First Patriarch: 'One who thinks only that everything is the void but is ignorant of the law of causation falls into everlasting, pitch-black hell.' Now tell me, brother, how would you reconcile the two quotes, one from the Buddha and one from the man who brought his teachings to China?"

"Does this have anything to do with what Krishnamurti told you?"

Elijah broke into a munificent grin. "Very astute, Brother Dan. I can see that you were paying attention back there in Ojai. But leaving that aside for the moment, tell me how the two teachings fit together."

I thought about it for a few moments and something seemed to click. "It sounds like the Buddha is talking about the goal," I said, "while Bodhidharma is talking about the path."

"Very good, my dear brother. Very good. Go on."

"Okay … well, the goal is to perceive the void, to perceive the emptiness at the heart of form. If we can do this, then we perceive our own Buddha nature. But believing in the void or thinking about it is not the same as experiencing it. One is thought, which is essentially illusory, while the other is true insight, direct perception."

"And he who is ignorant of the law of causation falls into everlasting darkness?"

"The universe is an infinite web of cause and effect. If we don't know how to navigate the web, we are bound to get ensnared. At least, that's how you put it when we were driving down to Ojai."

This drew a smile from Elijah. "It is nice to know that you were paying attention. Yes, you're exactly right. As long as we are caught in the web — and we are all caught in the web until we achieve full enlightenment — then we have to learn how to decipher its weave so that we can eventually work ourselves free. Thus the precepts, the sutras, the philosophy — it's all designed to help us become adepts in the world of causation, even as we are trying to find our way out of it through our Zen practice."

"So how does that tie in with what Krishnamurti said?"

"That's what I've been meditating on. That whole conversation was aimed at getting me to ask the right question, remember? Not who the figure is in my dream or whether or not I should go to India to search for him, but rather, what role, if any, does the dream play on the path to freedom? Is it a distraction, an illusory form like all the others created by my karma, clouding my mind? Or is it a spiritual highway sign telling me what route I need to take to stay on course? Once you ask the right question the game changes."

"So which do you think it is, a distraction or a highway sign?"

"Both," he said, with a playful gleam in his eye. "That's the key to the riddle. A highway sign may point in the right direction, but it's still a distraction if you forget that the whole idea of direction is essentially an illusion. You can be going in the right direction and still get lost. It happens all the time. Moving in the right direction won't get you anywhere if you lose sight of what you're actually looking for."

"I'm not sure I understand."

"What are we looking for, brother? What's the goal?"

"To realize our Buddha nature."

"And is that something you can find outside yourself, out there in the world?"

"No, it's inside."

"There's your answer. Let's say this guru actually exists, and I go to India one day and find him, but I reach the end of my life without realizing my Buddha nature. And what if the reason I don't reach enlightenment is because I allowed myself to believe that I had found what I was looking for, that the guru was going to do it for me? In that case, the pilgrimage would have been nothing more than an elaborate distraction, another weave in the web of maya."

"But how can you know?"

"That's the wrong question. The right question is exactly what Krishnamurti said it was: What is the path to freedom? And that starts with the recognition that all form is no-form, even that of an Indian master who comes calling in your dreams. No interpretation, no fascination — that's the key. It is what it is. It's a dream. You can search if that's your karma, but even if you find what you are searching for, it's not going to open the door to freedom. You open that by leaving maya behind. You navigate the web while you are in it, and if that includes a journey to India and an apprenticeship with a yogic guru, then well and good, but it's still the play of maya and the goal doesn't change. The goal is to leave maya behind and court the emptiness. If you think that a pilgrimage and a guru is the key to enlightenment, then maya has you by the balls. No interpretation, no fascination, just the path to freedom. Whatever direction you walk, you can walk it blind or you can do your best to keep your eyes open. You can go to India fascinated by what you might find when you get there, or you can go to India like you practice *kinhin*—observing your breath, concentrating on your koan, turning each footstep into Zen practice. If you can do that, then it doesn't really matter what you find when you get there. What matters is what you find *as* you get there. In other words, the sign points inward."

"Okay, I think I understand. But does that mean you are going to India?"

"I don't know yet. Until it happens, it hasn't happened, and what hasn't happened is just an illusion. But that does seem to be where the arrow's pointing. Though if I do go, it won't be because I believe a spiritual master is calling me through my dreams. He may be calling me—I have to be open to all possibilities—and it may be my karma to meet him and learn from him, but that's not why I'll go, if I go. I'll just be following the arrow, knowing that wherever I end up, nothing really changes but the venue. You could say the same for the whole wheel of birth and death: nothing changes but the venue. Not until we learn to perceive that all form is no-form and get ourselves off the wheel."

It took most of my evening practice to let go of my desire to see Elijah stay. But eventually it went floating off into the void with a caravan of other thoughts and images, and I gave up trying to chase it down. I didn't stay for dinner—I had promised Diana that we would go out to eat when I got back—and as I walked back to the apartment I felt unusually detached, carried along by a windless calm that allowed me to recognize that however long Elijah remained in my life it would be exactly as long as it should be. No more, no less than a perfect expression of Buddha mind, leading me with flawless footsteps along the path to perfection. It was a testament to the power of meditation that I could take my karma as it came. The feeling wouldn't last, of course. Like everything else in life it would wax and wane as my mind got tossed upon the world's waves, but the Zen alchemy was clearly at work, gradually freeing my mind from its years and perhaps centuries of conditioning.

While Diana and I walked to the restaurant, she asked me if she could stay a few days longer—the Fillmore apartment had gotten crowded over the summer, and she had rather grown to like my little loft. Without bothering to hide my glee, I told her to stay as long as she liked, and I could tell that it was exactly the answer she'd been hoping to hear. When the conversation finally got around to Elijah, she lamented that everyone interesting seemed to be leaving. Gary had left for Japan in May, Ginsberg had shipped out on a merchant marine in mid-June, and three days later Kerouac had taken off hitchhiking for the Pacific Northwest, where Gary had gotten him a summer job as a lookout on Desolation Peak. None of the three were expected back anytime soon, and now there was the very real possibility that Elijah would be added to that list. But I was still buoyed by the same windless calm. "Ah, but just think of how cool it was while they were here," I told her. "It's like a published poem or a great solo on vinyl. They live forever in the mind. And may I remind you, Elijah's not gone yet. There's still some magic left in Berkeley."

For once, Diana had nothing to say. She just grabbed my hand with a contented smile and swung it back and forth in the Berkeley night.

25

Diana had only met Elijah those two times. The night of the Berkeley reading she had found him intriguing but exasperating, highly intelligent but too Zen for her tastes. But as she pointed out at Gary's farewell party, Elijah got more interesting the better you knew him. And because I talked all the time about the things he was teaching me, Diana had gotten to know him better than she realized. Very often when we were together he was the third person in the room, an invisible presence that made us both look over our shoulders. So it came as no real surprise when Diana told me a few days later that she wanted to visit Elijah, to see what he thought of her nonintentional poetry. She had been studying the Dada manifestos as part of her ongoing poetic experiments, so I suspected she wasn't entirely finished with their discussion from the Berkeley reading, either. As I said to her while we were walking over to Elijah's cottage that afternoon, it wasn't too often you came across a jazz saxophonist, ex-Zen monk who could debate the merits of Marcel Duchamp's famous urinal.

It was about five when we got there and Elijah was seated on the porch, as he usually was at that hour, either receiving guests, if there were any, or just enjoying the tranquility of his garden before he sat for evening practice. I could see an amused smile flash across his face as we walked up the path, and I was sure it was due to Diana's presence at my side and the prospect of another unpredictable conversation. He gave Diana an effusive welcome before ducking inside to prepare some fresh-squeezed orange juice, but I could tell by his smile that she was in for a challenge.

"Do you like gardens, sister?" he asked after he returned with the juice.

"Sure," she said, seemingly surprised by the question. "Who doesn't? Especially a garden as beautiful as this. Dan told me that you learned gardening in Japan while you were a monk?"

"I did. I was an assistant gardener for a couple of years in the Myoshinji monastery in Kyoto. It was an apprenticeship in more ways than one. Gardens occupy a very special place in the history of Japanese Zen. The external landscape of a Zen garden is considered to be a reflection of the internal landscape. By cultivating the external landscape, we also cultivate the internal landscape; thus the garden becomes a kind of map of our inner journey. There is a saying in Zen that you can tell the depth of a gardener's realization by how his garden affects your mind. The greater the sense of harmony it induces, the greater his realization. It's his gift to the world. I learned a lot about plants while I was there, but that inner understanding was the real essence of my apprenticeship. I like to come out here at the end of the day and let my garden show me how far I've gotten and what I need to work on. It always has something interesting and useful to say."

I could see the spark of interest glowing in Diana's face, as if she had just been offered a dish whose taste and texture were entirely new to her. "That's an unusual way to look at a garden," she said. She paused for a few moments and then said, "I wonder if the same might not be true for people's houses."

"Of course. Space has its own poetics, its own aesthetic language, whether it's a house or a cave or a garden. The more we cultivate any external space, the more its language reflects the inner spaces of our mind. The question for a Zen practitioner is whether or not we can become aware of that reflection and thus use our gardening or our interior decoration as a means to purify our inner self. It's like shaving in a mirror or putting on makeup: the mirror allows you to see what you are doing. I'm not a poet, I am a musician, but I would contend that the same holds true for poetry. A poem is also a type of garden, just as a melody is. If you look carefully you can see the artist's inner landscape reflected in the landscape of the poem, and if the artist is a Zen adept, then you may even be able to catch a glimpse of your original face."

I interrupted momentarily, intending to explain to Diana what Elijah meant by one's original face, but the look she shot me made me bite my tongue. I had seen that look before. She had latched on to something in Elijah's words, or perhaps it was just the uncommon conviction that gave his voice a weight few voices had, and I knew that anything I said would just get in the way.

"But what if that poem is completely nonintentional?" she asked.

"That depends on what you mean by nonintentional."

Whenever Diana became really excited about something she would speed up, as if her brain possessed another gear, talking so fast sometimes it would make me dizzy. This was one of those times. The words started pouring out as if she were intent on capturing the prize for the most words in the fewest minutes, and as I listened to her describe her attempts to search out new pathways for poetry, I saw a side of her I hadn't fully appreciated before: the hunger for experience that was actually a hunger for knowledge, a hunger for truth, coupled with a willingness to go wherever the truth took her, even if it meant jettisoning cherished ideas and convictions. The kind of instant adaptability that one rarely encounters in other members of the species. Some people just have less ego to begin with, and it surprised me to think that Diana might be one of them.

When she finally came out of her loquacious rapture, Elijah was looking at her with a newfound appreciation. "That is what art is all about, sister, no matter what the medium. It's that reaching beyond the ego in search of our Buddha nature. If you can take it all the way, if you can take yourself completely out of the picture along with your intentionality, then your poem becomes a reflection of the universal mind — or big mind, as I like to call it. That's the perfection of art, the place where art and Zen merge. Different words, same experience. That said, it's very difficult to achieve. Until we actually get there, we are still reflecting the contents of our small mind in our work, in this case the deeper contents. Mind has space, you know. You have the surface and you have the depths. The further aside the ego stands, the more you see the depths of your mind reflected in your art. And the deeper you go, the closer you get to universal mind. It's like what I was saying about the garden: the closer a gardener gets to his Buddha nature, the more you see it reflected in his gar-den—in its sense of harmony, the sense of tranquility and wisdom it radiates, that feeling of it being in tune with the universal order. We may not understand what the poem is saying at an intellectual level, but we can feel how it resonates with the creation. Does that make any sense to you?"

"It does, actually. I don't know that I could explain it like you did, but I think I know what you're saying."

"Explanations are overrated and mostly superfluous. Your expe-rience is what matters."

"You know, I've been thinking lately about how the ancients would talk about the muse and how the muse came to them and inspired their poetry or their music. Maybe what they were talking about was actually the universal mind."

"Of course it was. What else is there to talk about? All there is is big mind. And within big mind you have small mind, that tiny reflected facet that looks out on big mind and wonders what it all means. Artists look out on the world and use their art to express what they feel. That's small mind looking out on big mind. But if they keep digging, keep searching, then eventually they come in contact with something beyond themselves, something whose cre-ative powers dwarf anything their small mind can imagine. That's the real intoxication. That's what coaxes them out of small mind. That's why you're so excited about your experience. You're getting close to something real, something great, something that is ultimately indescribable. In the end, art is just a method, like religion. It's a bridge to take you out of your small self and into the universal self. And if you make it, there ain't nothing like it, sister. You make it to big mind and you've hit the mother lode."

Diana was nodding emphatically now, her eyes aglow in the twilight. "Okay. I'm convinced … Now that we are sort of on the subject, can I ask you a question about Dada?"

"Sure, go ahead."

"I've been reading a lot of the Dada writings this summer. I know the movement's pretty much died out now, but it seems like it's had a pretty big effect on the art avant-garde and on modern art in general. The thing is, it seems almost like an offshoot of Zen Buddhism in some ways. In one place, Tristan Tzara actually says that Dada is quasi-Buddhism, so I was thinking that they must have been influenced by Buddhist ideas. Either that or they arrived at it on their own and then noticed the resemblance. I wrote down a few quotes from Tzara's Dada manifestos. I didn't want to get them wrong. Is it okay if I read one?"

"Sure."

Diana pulled out a piece of paper from her pocket and unfolded it. "Here's one from 1918: 'Logic imprisoned by the senses is an organic disease.' Don't Zen Buddhists consider the logical mind to be a kind of prison, an obstacle to enlightenment?"

"They do, and it is."

"Here is another one I really like: 'Dada: absolute and unquestionable faith in every god that is the immediate product of spontaneity.' It's almost like a koan — a Dada koan, not a Zen koan."

"I don't know that it would make a very effective koan, but I think I see what you're getting at. Correct me if I'm wrong. You want to know if the spirit of Dada's crusade against traditional, conventional values is essentially the Zen spirit in disguise, a Western approach to freeing oneself from the oppression of the logical mind."

"Exactly! How can you say there is any meaning or virtue in society's values if we just end up killing each other? You can't. It's all a crock, including the art. That's what the Dadaists were getting at. What other explanation is there for a world war? You don't need any other proof that society's insane. And is it any different now? We've had a second world war since then, Joseph McCarthy, no end in sight to racism and segregation, or to capitalism and corporate greed, and on top of that we have a military government that disguises itself as a democracy. When you come right down to it, we live in a sociopathic society. And if our art is just going to promote the same values that got us here, then we might as well do away with it altogether — or else invent new ways of making art that subvert those values instead of reinforcing them. At least that's how I understand Dada, and that all seems very Zen to me, using non-sense and non-logic to break us free from our conditioning. I'm not a Buddhist, of course —"

"Not yet," I interjected, unable to stop myself from butting in.

Diana flashed an annoyed smile. "Anyhow, like I was saying, I'm not a Buddhist, and I've never tried working with a Zen koan, but they seem to defy logic and favor spontaneity, and I was thinking that might be the whole point: to force us beyond logic and convention and all the bullshit needless suffering that goes with it. Could that be what Tzara meant when he said that Dada was quasi-Buddhism?"

"Yes, it very likely was. You could say that Dada reeks of Zen, to paraphrase a famous Zen story. But the point of that story is to show that you can't realize Zen by thinking about it or talking about it. In other words, you can't get there through the mind; you can only get there by emptying the mind of its contents. That's why Zen is essentially a practice, not a philosophy. You could say that the Dadaists had a similar goal in mind, but they weren't practitioners, and without some kind of meditative practice you can't break free of the logical mind. In the end you will still be defined by the walls of your prison."

"But wasn't their art their practice? Or their anti-art, as they put it."

"Sure it was. But they were going about it the wrong way. They were trying to think their way to spontaneity, to think their way beyond the logical mind, and that can't be done. It can only be done by quieting the mind, not exercising it. By putting the ego to bed. They made an important contribution, but there was a limit to how far they could take it because they weren't able to get beyond the mind. Honestly, I wouldn't be surprised at all if you go further with your nonintentional poetry than Tristan Tzara and his comrades ever did. As long as you combine it with zazen. Put the two together and you might even become a modern-day Basho."

"Basho?" Diana said, shaking her head.

"One of the great Zen poets. His specialty was haiku — one of his specialties. His poems don't reek of Zen at all. They just are. And that's what makes them so very, very Zen."

"Now that I think about it, I think I actually have heard of Basho. I'm pretty sure Gary was reading him, although he was mostly into Han Shan."

"Another great Zen poet. What made them both so great was the quality of their zazen. Because they were able to touch their Buddha nature, their poems reflect the vastness of the universal mind. If you want your poems to get to that level, then you have to take your mind to that level. And that's very hard to do through poetry alone. Or through music alone. *Unless* you can turn it into practice. And for that you need zazen or some form of meditation training. You need to train your mind to stillness and bring that stillness to your poetry. That's the true state of nonintentionality. When small mind stops and big mind takes over."

Before we left, Diana invited Elijah to our upcoming performance at The Purple Onion. She was anxious for him to hear her poetry and tell her what he thought. As for me, the invitation made me a little edgy. I remembered how tough Elijah had been on me after my semester-ending recital, and this performance was going to be much more of a challenge. Nor was I entirely sure how Diana would react if Elijah was as honest with her as he was with me. But what was done was done. Elijah promised he would be there, and Elijah never reneged on his promises. Diana went back to the apartment while I stayed for evening practice, but I spent most of that session thinking how much Diana and I needed to practice our set if Elijah was going to be in the audience. It wasn't the most successful of meditations, but it did help to cement my determination. If Elijah was going to be there, then I was determined to be at my best.

26

Two things happened before our gig at The Purple Onion that would significantly alter the course of my life: Diana officially moved in with me—the indefinite became definite—and a few days later she asked me to teach her zazen. In a sense, we both became each other's mentor. She taught me the laws of human attraction, and I reciprocated by teaching her how to quiet her mind and tap into a deeper layer of her already prodigious creativity. In a world of polar opposites we were the perfect pair. Though I never once heard Diana refer to me as her boyfriend—she was too identified with her bohemian persona to acknowledge such a bourgeois idea—we would cohabit for the next two years, meditating together, performing together, learning to decipher the world together from either side of a two-way mirror, until the decline of the San Francisco Renaissance and her own unserved karma returned her to the streets of her birth, where she would remain till the Summer of Love brought her back to the Bay Area for good.

It was my first romantic relationship, and in many ways it served as a blueprint for what a relationship could and should be. The conversation that had begun rather awkwardly in the smoky haze of Bop City, listening to Frankie Foster trade choruses with Sonny Stitt, would continue uninterrupted until the day I put Diana on a Greyhound bus for New York, insisting on paying her ticket when she would have preferred to hitchhike. To this day, whenever we meet, we seem to pick up that conversation right where we left off, whether it's been two days or two years since the last time we saw each other. There were no areas that were under guard or off limits and very little subtext, apart from the kind we weren't aware of. We exorcised our traumas in that open-air arena and drew holographic images of the future, and I think that much of the unexplored landscapes we were able to visit in our individual journeys — she through her poetry, I through my music, both of us through the sheer drama of living human lives on a precarious planet — only became accessible to us because that shared flow of ideas and experience provided us with the key to the prison of our past. I think it is no accident that my inability to resist the cruder temptations of the jazz life began not long after Diana moved back east. Without the unpredictable riches of our ongoing conversation to anchor me, I was soon cut off from my moorings, adrift without provisions on a seemingly unnavigable sea — though from where I sit now, I recognize that the free fall I experienced was a kind of arduous baptism that eventually cleansed me of the crudest form of egoism: the sense of privilege that deludes the mind into believing it is unique and indestructible when in fact we are mere wind whistling through the void, the empty breath of the Buddha.

The morning after Diana brought the rest of her stuff from the Fillmore Street painters' colony, she wiped the sleep from her eyes and plopped down next to me on a cushion as I was preparing to do my morning zazen before leaving for school.

"So what do I do?" she asked. "I know there's more to this than just contemplating your navel."

That was it. No ceremony, no sheepish look or admission I had won, and no hesitation. I showed her how to sit, how to find her center of balance by swaying side to side and back and forth, where to focus her eyes, how to count her breaths. The rest came later, when I got back from school: what to do when thoughts assail the mind; how to seek the source from which those thoughts arise; the signs of progress she could expect to see in the coming weeks, beginning with the unsettling discovery of how agitated our minds really are, which is the true initiation into the meditator's life. I was still a beginner, but sometimes a beginner is the perfect teacher. My initial struggles were still fresh in my mind — indeed, I was still going through them — and so I had no difficulty describing the bruises and the triumphs that result from those first steps when a toddler stands up and tries to walk on his own.

Diana was a fast learner and her stubbornness was her greatest ally. Once she set her mind to something, she refused to give ground, no matter what stood in her way. In her case, as with all of us, she was her greatest obstacle—or rather, the chameleon-like ego that holds us in thrall with its false sense of self. But as with any seemingly sheer rock wall, there was always a handhold or a foothold to be found if you groped long enough. In the days that followed, she peppered me with questions and started devouring my books, beginning where I had, with *The Gateless Gate,* which she loved as much for its literary merits as she did for its cryptic wisdom and overt challenge to the logical mind. We set aside some portion of each day to study those texts together, searching for clues that would hasten our journey down the twin paths of jazuzen and nonintentional poetry, saving up our queries for our afternoon visits to Elijah, who seemed in no way disconcerted by the presence of another unsolicited disciple. I sort of fell into Zen by accident, seduced by Elijah's horn, but with Diana it was a conscious decision whose roots went back to the Celebrated Good Time Poetry Night. She saw a logic in Elijah's arguments, especially the link between Zen and the practice of art, that convinced her she had found her path in life. I don't believe a day has gone by since that Diana hasn't sat on her meditation cushion and breathed stillness into her mind. That, as she will be the first to acknowledge, is the real source of her poetry.

Our gig at The Purple Onion was on a Wednesday, typically a slow night for the club. That suited us just fine—if it didn't go well, the less people in the audience the better. But it did go well, better than either of us expected—so well, in fact, that Elijah was almost laudatory in his comments when we joined him afterward at his table. Diana opened with a short monologue, welcoming everyone to an evening of nonintentional poetry and jazz, but her introduction could just as well have been called "The Zen of Poetry." What was supposed to be a few words to help the audience get their bearings ended up sounding more like a dharma talk, poetry as a path to enlightenment, her way of preparing us for the journey we were about to undertake. We began with the set pieces, the nonintentional poems

she had honed over the summer, whose landscapes were as familiar
to me by then as my favorite recordings, but the last twenty minutes
were pure improvisation. Neither of us had any idea where we were
going, but that was exactly what made it so exhilarating. It was as
if Diana had been taken over by the muse, serving as a borrowed
mouthpiece for voices that were not her own, and the same muse
that borrowed her vocal chords borrowed my fingers, coloring her
figures of speech with the hues of a world beyond our understanding,
the same world we all inhabit without beginning to comprehend
its silent majesty. As the evening neared its conclusion, I felt as if I
were floating up and out of my body, looking down on the scene
in a state of tranquil wonder, as delighted by the unexpected twists
and turns of that evolving tapestry of words and music as anyone in
the audience. I remember trying to describe all this to Elijah at his
table and hearing Diana complete my sentences as if we were a single
person describing a single experience. I remember also the quality
of our smiles — lighter and richer than we were used to — and how
they were reflected in Elijah's face, which was lit up like a ceremonial
Buddha during a temple ritual.

We performed at The Place a couple of weeks later, and by then
word had gotten around of Diana's exploits. The room was as crowded
as I had ever seen it, and it seemed like the audience was mostly
poets who had come to see the new technique in action. There were
a few musicians in the crowd as well, but the poetry was definitely
center stage, and deservedly so. Diana was extending the borders of
modern verse in a hitherto unexplored direction, and I am sure her
colleagues recognized this, at least at an unconscious level. Nothing
she read that night or improvised was as powerful as "Howl" or as
incendiary, but those first experiments in nonintentional poetry were
just as groundbreaking. Allen would go on to become the spiritual
counterculture's most prominent spokesman, but as Diana would
prove in the years to come, her nonintentional poems weren't merely
written by a Zen practitioner: they *were* Zen, the meditator's experience clothed in poetry, a true outpouring of her Buddha nature.
Elijah would be long gone by then, but I have often wondered what
he would have made of Diana's mature work, how close he would

think she had come to Basho on whatever invisible Zen scale he used to weigh artistic creations. Pretty close, I suspect. For me, Gary and Diana are the true American Zen poets of our era. Neither is easy to understand. Their work is too subtle, too far removed from our everyday ego. But for those who are able to enter into the spirit of their work, the recompense is greater than any other contemporary poetry I am aware of.

Elijah wasn't at The Place that night, but I could feel his presence brushing up against me as I played. I hadn't stopped thinking altogether—thinking as a musician thinks, in melody and harmony and rhythm—but I was able to observe my musical mind at work as I inched closer to the spirit of jazuzen, strengthening that sense of mindfulness that lies at the heart of Buddhist practice. When we made it back to the loft that night, Diana's eyes were shining with a sense of wonder. "Did you feel it?" she asked. "It was almost like we weren't there at all." Nothing could have summed it up better. In those few words she articulated what has been our artistic credo ever since: to step aside and let the void speak for itself.

27

IT WAS AROUND THE time we first played The Purple Onion that Diana conceived the idea of starting a literary newsletter, a forum where local poets could share their work and ideas with the public and with their fellow writers. Articles about the San Francisco Renaissance had been appearing in the local media for some time, but the Bay Area poetry scene suddenly became national news when Richard Eberhart published his article "West Coast Rhythms" in the *New York Times Book Review* on the second of September. That article lit the fuse of what soon became a full-blown literary explosion. Ginsberg returned to the city unexpectedly a week or two after the article came out, one month earlier than planned, and *Howl* was sitting on the shelves of the City Lights bookstore to greet him, the reviews starting to pour in from around the country along with laudatory comments from poets as respected as William Carlos Williams and Mark Van Doren. Gregory Corso was in town, negotiating with Ferlinghetti for the publication of his first volume of poems; Rexroth and Kenneth Patchen were doing the same; and Kerouac was back from his mountaintop, bursting with energy after what he lamented was a thoroughly boring summer. *Life* and *Mademoiselle* even sent reporters to do photo essays on the movement. And in the middle of it all was Diana with her nonintentional poetry and her inspired idea for a biweekly newsletter where this patchwork alliance of disparate poets could meet on the fencing grounds of the written page.

I can claim at least partial credit for the title — *The Diamond Review*, inspired by our studies of the *Diamond Sutra* — but the rest was all Diana, apart from some of the grunt work, which I was more than happy to help out with. The first thing she did was to solicit submissions: poems, articles, short prose pieces, event notices for the calendar section, whatever people were willing to contribute. Within days my post-office box was flooded with material: major and minor poems from virtually every recognized poet in the San Francisco area, many of which would later go on to be anthologized; articles on the important "literary questions" from self-styled theoreticians like Rexroth and Robert Duncan; and a whole slew of submissions whose only claim to poetry was the dubious fact that they had arrived in the mail addressed to *The Diamond Review*. We even got a couple of submissions from Bob Kaufman, though Diana had to collect those in person—the US mail was too nefarious for him to risk using it himself, though he didn't object to others doing so.

Once the trash was disposed of and the editing done, Diana typed the accepted submissions onto Gestetner mimeograph stencils with an old IBM that she set up on the kitchen table, a venerable colossus that could have anchored a fair-sized boat. Ferlinghetti agreed to let her print the newsletter on the City Lights mimeograph machine and to sell it in the store on consignment, seventy-five cents an issue—those that weren't mailed out to the more than one hundred subscribers that Diana personally signed up by tracking down her friends one by one. The first issue came out a week or so after our performance at The Place and every two weeks thereafter until the following summer when the workload got to be too much for Diana to handle and she turned it into a monthly publication. With that inaugural issue my social circle began to expand exponentially. I had already met many of Diana's poet friends, but the *Review* literally brought me into contact with hundreds of artists of every stripe imaginable—not only poets but dancers, actors, painters, photographers, and those unique characters who would later be known as performance artists. Though I still didn't know that many musicians, apart from the students and professors at Berkeley, the poetry scene and the jazz scene were undergoing mutual changes that were bringing them closer together, and the access to the world of the avant-garde that I gained from being with Diana soon made me a recognizable figure in the local jazz world. In effect, I had enrolled in a crash course on how to live the life of a contemporary artist—not a commercial artist, mind you, though that whole concept was far less polarizing in the fifties, but a "real" artist, as we used to say, the kind who are in full-out rebellion against contemporary society, who flaunt their poverty as a mark of distinction and treasure their lack of public recognition for the freedom it affords them to be true to their calling. We were our own public in those days, and that was good enough for us, though the national notoriety that Ginsberg and Kerouac and a few others were beginning to enjoy would soon put a serious strain on that idyllic self-image. The pictures taken by *Mademoiselle* are a testament to that. Instead of the group photo the magazine requested, McClure and Duncan demanded to be photographed separately, Rexroth didn't bother to show up at all, and the published photo of Kerouac, Ginsberg, Corso, and Whalen reeks of the artists' egos — except for Whalen, who seems to be enjoying a Buddhist joke about the absurdity of it all.

This ever-expanding whorl of activity and community brought an understandable element of instability into my life. Though my traffic with the artistic counterculture afforded me a far more useful education than the one I was receiving in the classroom, it made it difficult for me to keep up with my studies, and it put a strain on my daily zazen practice. But though I wasn't able to join Elijah as often as I wished, two days in the week remained sacrosanct: Tuesdays and Thursdays, the days of my afternoon sax lessons. It was during one of those lessons in mid-October that I had the breakthrough I had been hoping for since I'd first read of satori, without ever quite believing I would actually get there.

Most of the Zen stories I love depict satori as a sudden flash. All of a sudden a door opens, the infinite lifts its veil, and the mind is flooded with a luminous understanding, a joyous recognition of the emptiness at the heart of all form. That's how I know that my breakthrough wasn't true satori, at least not the satori of the classic Zen stories, but it was more than I had realistically thought possible, and it was enough for Elijah to give me an unwritten certificate in the practice of jazuzen. Diana had gone to San Francisco that morning to print, collate, and mail the newsletter, after which she was planning on taking in the new Jackson Pollack exhibit at the Museum of Modern Art. She wasn't due back until late that night, if then, and I was happy that I would have a chance to sit alone with Elijah on his porch after the lesson and join him for evening practice. We started off with the usual routine: breathing and fingering exercises, extended notes, scales, arpeggios, and patterns—each an exercise in mindfulness with the instrument serving as the medium. As always, Elijah pushed me without respite, forcing me to stay alert, to maintain my concentration in my *hara*, to focus every fiber of my being on the source from which the notes arose, the infinite sky of big mind. Indeed, my lessons had become like mini-sesshins, but instead of a stick Elijah used his relentless southern drawl to prevent my mind from wandering. When it came time to put down my instrument he would test my understanding of big-mind music as if I were sitting before the roshi in *dokusan*. I have participated in many sesshins over the years, so I know exactly what Elijah was doing. He was using the menace of his voice and the intensity of his own determination to push me as hard and as fast as he could. But he was clever about it. If he had been that severe with me from the beginning, I might have turned tail and run, no matter how powerful the spell his horn had cast over me. But he turned up the pressure gradually, almost imperceptibly, and like a frog in a cauldron gradually being boiled alive, by the time I realized what I had gotten myself into, it was too late to turn back.

I spent the last half hour of that lesson blowing over changes while Elijah held down the bass line with his tenor sax. He couldn't use his voice to prod me while he was playing, but I could still feel his unspoken vigilance pressing against me like an enormous weight, his watchful eyes threatening to burn a hole in me should I relax my attention, even for an instant. In one of the great paradoxes of the Zen tradition, he was forcing me to relax, forcing me to let go, compelling me to use my breath to break free from the ego's domineering grip and shift my attention to the source of the music, the source of all thoughts. Goading me as surely as if he had a stick in his hand. It is an equation that belies explanation. How is it that ratcheting up the tension to its zenith point can force us into the insight that erases all tension? But it is a tradition that dates back to the days of Bodhidharma, and it remains alive because it works, because a long line of disciples have been forced out of their complacency and into the mysterious, life-altering glimpse of the truth that we call satori. And even though what I experienced that afternoon may not have been the true satori of Hakuin or Wumen, it wasn't that far off, either. Elijah called it a beginner's satori, the kind that loosens the soil for the deeper excavations that follow and serves as proof that jazz can be just as much a vehicle for enlightenment as the tea ceremony or the art of archery.

Looking back, I'm convinced that my biggest difficulty until then was learning to trust. Trust in Elijah's teaching, trust in myself, trust in Zen. No matter how much I thought I was taking my ego out of the equation, surrendering to the sovereignty of the breath, there was always an unconscious voice within me that kept insisting that if I truly put my mind out to pasture the result would be mindless drivel. Without the "me" to direct my music, how could I play any music at all? For all Elijah's talk of big mind or no-mind, for all the stories I had read and marveled at, fully accepting their premise in the illusory confines of my intellect, there was a part of me, unconscious still and for that reason virtually all-powerful, that refused to accept that the world beyond the ego was anything more than a smiling Buddha's colorful invention. But that afternoon Elijah's implacable assault on my ego finally broke down my resistance. He wasn't talking, he was just playing his horn and staring at me with eyes that seemed to have taken up residence inside my skull. But it was as if those eyes were talking, as if the relentless barking had a life of its own that no longer required ears or a voice to sustain itself. With every note, I became increasingly conscious of my ego, painfully aware that it was no longer a welcome presence in my mind, that the only possible relief was to break down the wall that it had spent a lifetime building up. Then the levee broke. Something rose up and battered against that wall until the force of the sea itself collapsed it. A liberating flood of music flowed over me, but inexplicably there was no "me" to get drenched. No agent and no observer, just a flood of music from a vibrating horn filling the circumambient space, and nothing more.

"That's it! That's what I'm talking about, brother!"

Elijah's voice seemed to come from a great distance. At some point he had put down his horn—exactly when, I had no idea. I opened my eyes and found them wet with tears, but I saw nothing unusual in this. Like everything else in my field of awareness, they occupied their natural place in a universe where nothing was out of place or ever could be. A universe in which everything seemed to be dancing—Elijah's graceful bulk, the horn I cradled in my hands, the carefully tended garden receding into the repose of autumn, the vaulted sky with its eternal gaze—all smiling as they danced, a revolving concert of momentary forms against a backdrop of the timeless and the formless. For several minutes I took it all in, breathing quietly, my mind an empty vessel, without latching onto anything and for that reason able to appreciate the entire tapestry—its radiance, its immense, unspeakable beauty. Gradually a sense of awe started to take hold of me, a sense of wonderment, which I soon realized was my ego becoming aware of its temporary absence.

Elijah was smiling, seemingly content to let me soak up every bit of my achievement in silence. But I was back from wherever I had been, dazzled by what I had witnessed and beginning to bubble over with questions. We put up our horns and sat on the bench, and Elijah asked me to describe my experience. When I finished what seemed to be an awkward, inarticulate summing up of what could not be described, Elijah confirmed what I already knew to be true.

"What you experienced was a kind of beginner's satori, brother. You had a taste of the ocean, a dip of your toe, but you still have a long way to go before you can dive in. But that's the way it works. Your first experience will lead to a second—as long as you keep practicing—and that will lead to another and then another, and each a little deeper. But the first is the most important. Now you know what it's all about—not with your mind but in your bones. From here on out it's just a matter of reaching for the same place every time you play, every time you sit. And when you get there, gradually going deeper."

"But, Elijah, I don't know how I got there. It just happened."

"That's how it is: when it happens, it just happens. But you know how you got there: by practicing zazen and extending that practice into everything you do, beginning with your music. Don't worry, brother. As long as you keep practicing, keep pushing, that experience will lead you back to itself. It will pull at you every time you sit for zazen, every time you pick up your horn. And when you can't get there—and most of the time you won't—then it will be like a ten-stone weight on your head. Unless you want to walk around the rest of your life with that weight on your head, then you'll keep sitting and you'll keep watching your breath, and eventually you will get back there. And each time you do, it will get a little easier, a little deeper."

To be honest, it seemed like inadvertent magic at the time, and I was no magician. But of course Elijah was right. There would be a lot of ups and downs after that and one extended detour, but my beginner's satori would not leave me alone. Whenever I went too long without tasting the freedom that lies beyond the ego, life would start to seem insipid. It would begin to lose its inherent charm and that loss would drive me back to my meditation cushion, back to my breath, back to the work of fixing my internal eye on the source from which the music of life arises. But none of it would have happened without Elijah, for without him I never would have set foot on the road that led me to the Buddha's teachings, to Suzuki-roshi and Zen Center, to the search for the self, without which life is nothing more than an out-of-tune channel whose static drowns out the music.

28

I DON'T KNOW IF IT had anything to do with my beginner's satori, but after my next lesson Elijah informed me that he had booked passage on a merchant marine shipping out for Japan in three weeks' time. I was in an ebullient mood—the afterglow of my little taste of Zen hadn't completely dissipated, and with Elijah's prodding I was able to recreate a little of that jazuzen magic during the lesson that I hadn't been able to recreate at home or at school—but the shock of his announcement seemed to wipe out all trace of my achievement.

"I suspected you might eventually decide to go," I said, feeling instantly unmoored, "but I never imagined it would be so soon. You're really going to look for this guy in your dreams?"

"Like I said when you came back from LA, that's one way to look at it, but it's not the only way. It's time for me to move on, that's all, and that's where the sign points."

I didn't know what to say so I kept silent. Elijah had become in many ways the center of gravity in my life, and the prospect of losing him hurt. I made no effort to hide my feelings either, slumping down on the bench and staring at the floorboards. Elijah was also silent for a few minutes, but when he finally spoke I could hear the affection in his voice.

"I remember Zuigan-roshi telling me once that in Zen there is no difference between coming and going. It was the day I went to his room to tell him I was going back to the States. I remember, I was really apprehensive about telling him. I thought he would be disappointed in me because I wasn't willing to stay the course, to solve my koan and achieve enlightenment. But it wasn't like that at all. When I told him I was leaving, he broke into a huge smile and patted me on the shoulder. I can't tell you how surprised I was.

He called the head monk and asked him to bring tea, and while we were sipping our tea he told me how proud he was of all I had accomplished. It was a very special moment, brother, straight to the heart. Just before I left his room, he said, 'Physically you are leaving this monastery, but actually the monastery goes with you wherever you go. The whole world is a monastery, and wherever you are your training continues. You woke up from a long sleep while you were here, and after this you will never fall asleep again.' I'll never forget those words. Never. Whatever apprehension or guilt or uneasiness I was feeling, it all melted away with those words. You know, they're just as true for you, Brother Dan."

"But I'm not leaving, Elijah, you are. In this case it's the teacher who's leaving, not the student."

"It's all the same, brother. I threw a little cold water in your face to help you get the sleep out of your eyes, like Zuigan-roshi did for me. That can't be undone. Whatever teachers are waiting for you up ahead, they'll appear at exactly the right time. You can be sure of that. And that's all that really matters. After all, there's only one teacher. He just puts on different masks at different times, that's all."

"You mean the Buddha."

"Who else? It's all designed to get you home. It's like those jigsaw puzzles. I'm just one piece in the puzzle, and a tiny piece at that. But when you put the whole puzzle together, you'll see the Buddha sitting in meditation, directing your footsteps without even needing to open his eyes."

"I'm still going to miss you, Elijah."

"I know. But don't let it go on too long, okay? You've got Diana to take care of, some revolutionary fires to stoke, and a whole lot of sitting to do. And then there's this garden to think about. It's going to need a new caretaker."

"A new caretaker?"

"Of course. Do you think I'm going to let my landlady rent this place out to somebody who wouldn't know Zen if he tripped over Bodhidharma? This is a Zen monastery in miniature, brother, in case you hadn't noticed. It deserves to be left in the right hands. I've already talked to her about it and she's agreed. As long as I trust you, she will too. It's rent free. All you have to do is take care of the garden and keep up the Zen tradition."

"But I don't know anything about gardening."

"We have three weeks. That's almost an eternity. You make the time and I'll get you ready. The most important thing is to keep sitting. In gardening, as in jazz, it's all about the zazen."

29

I was still awake when Diana came back, and we ended up spending most of the night talking. Neither of us got much sleep, but this was one of those times when sleep is overrated. I needed to work through my feelings and I couldn't have asked for a better sounding board. By the time we finally closed our eyes, my spirits were almost back to normal. As Diana summed it up in words that any Zen practitioner could appreciate: "It's not how much time you have that matters; it's how well you use the time you have."

I was a bit bleary-eyed when I showed up at Elijah's the next morning to start my apprenticeship as a Zen gardener, but I was determined to absorb as much as was humanly possible before he left. For the next three weeks I didn't make a single morning class. I even forswore my weekend trips to San Francisco. I sat with Elijah for both morning and evening practice, learned as much about Zen gardening as I could cram into that short span of time, and counted my blessings every time he barked at me during sax lessons, frightening my ego into fleeing long enough for me to get another taste of the elixir he called jazuzen. He gave me his small library, which included several excellent texts on gardening, and the number of a Japanese gardener in Sausalito who he assured me would be happy to answer any future questions I might have. Diana was as busy as always, but she joined us in the afternoon whenever she could for some twilight conversation and a little zazen. To the best of my knowledge, Elijah hadn't told anyone he was leaving, but the word got out anyway. I was reasonably sure that Diana was responsible, but I didn't say anything and Elijah didn't seem to mind, even though he had a more or less steady stream of visitors to contend with. I would have preferred to have had him all to myself for the little time that remained, but I got to see a side of him that I hadn't often seen. Elijah was no social butterfly, but he was a study in interpersonal equanimity, and the varied conversations, which ranged from intriguing to downright fascinating, added some welcome leavening to my education. Ginsberg and Corso were the first to show up — they were getting ready to hitchhike to LA, where Allen had a poetry reading scheduled for the following day, the famous reading where Allen stripped naked halfway through and hurled his clothes at a drunken heckler. Watts was the last to visit and the one I enjoyed the most. He was deep in conversation with Elijah when I arrived after an afternoon class that I couldn't skip without putting my entire semester in jeopardy. As I remember, they were discussing the future of Western spirituality, and after a quick hello I could as well have been a shadow for all the attention they paid me. But I didn't mind. Just being there was its own reward. Though I don't remember much of what they said, I remember realizing at some point that I was in the presence of two brilliant minds. It was a strange observation. After all, I had spent hundreds of hours with Elijah over the previous ten months. I had heated my brain to boiling trying to understand his explanations of Zen and cooled it back down again whenever we sat for meditation. His words had had a profound impact on my life and on how I had come to view the world, and yet I had never really thought of Elijah as having a brilliant mind. He had learned Zen from his master and now he was passing it on to me. That was all. There wasn't anything he was teaching me that wasn't in the books he gave me to read (although I know now that there is a world of difference between reading the words of dead masters and seeing an example of those same teachings in a living human being). But as I sat there and enjoyed his face-off with Alan Watts, it suddenly hit home that I was in the presence of two heavyweights. There was no denying Watt's intellectual abilities. I had read a couple of his books by then and attended several impressive and entertaining lectures at the American Academy of Asian Studies. But what surprised me was how easily Elijah parried Watt's provocative assertions and guided the British philosopher down channels that were not on any of his maps.

I'll never forget the conclusion of their conversation—in part, perhaps, because the conclusions they drew were so diametrically opposed, but also because their words seemed to have a faint ring of prophecy. In those days most of the bohemian crowd that Diana and I ran with were anarchists of one sort or another, none more so than Alan. I had never actually talked politics with Elijah, but I was well aware of his dissatisfaction with the system, and I just assumed that he saw no more need for a government than the rest of the San Francisco counterculture. But I couldn't have been more wrong. Alan had been talking about the coming end of churches and religious institutions and the birth of a universal spirituality where every individual was self-contained and self-inspired. "And that, my friend," he said, "will be the end of government, and none too soon. A self-inspired human being is a self-governing human being who doesn't need a policeman patrolling his streets or a group of politicians deciding what he can and cannot do to know how to relate properly to his brother. When that happens the state will become unnecessary; it will simply drop away." Alan wasn't trying to convince anyone of anything. He clearly believed that he was seeing into the future, and for that reason his words seemed to be the pronouncement of a sage. Especially when Elijah didn't answer right away, allowing Alan's words to hang in the air with their overtones of destiny.

What Elijah did do was smile, ever so slightly, and nod his head, settling even deeper into his kimono. But just when I thought he was in complete agreement, he surprised me (though I don't think he surprised Alan, judging from the wry smile that appeared on his face). "I should like to see that, brother," Elijah said. "Unfortunately, I won't, nor will you or anyone else, now or ever. As long as duality is the nature of the universe, there will be ignorance; and as long as there is ignorance there will be injustice, exploitation, and self-serving human beings. There's only one way to turn this earth into the paradise it could and should be, and that's to defang the tiger. Make sure that self-serving, ignorant individuals don't wield any significant social power. I do agree with you in one respect: Eventually humanity's going to figure this out. Eventually we'll grow enough in our collective awareness to ensure that the wisest and largest-hearted among us are entrusted with the administration of this planet, those whose only motivation is the welfare of every living being who makes his home here. There's nothing inherently wrong with government, brother. As long as human beings live together they need some form of organization, some form of administration, no matter how self-governing they are in their individual lives. The problem is the people who make up the government. We've done a very poor job up until now of choosing them. Let's just hope we get it right one day. And for all our sakes, let's hope it doesn't take too long."

The conversation didn't end there, but for me that was the climax and the one thing that has stuck with me all these years. What indeed would this planet look like if the wisest and most compassionate among us were guiding the show, the Buddhas and the Bodhisattvas, those who have risen above selfishness to a place where the welfare of all living beings has become their sole motivation? Probably as close to a terrestrial paradise as one could hope for in this world of relativity. But we are still light years away from that happening, trapped in a netherworld of our own making. Or perhaps not. Both Alan and Elijah were convinced that the human race was evolving into something we would all be proud of one day, no matter how different their conception of that future spiritual society was. As I've grown older, Elijah's words have coalesced into my most enduring aspiration: the hope, for all our sakes, that it doesn't take too long.

30

The Sunday before Elijah left, his landlady, Doris Abernathy, came up from LA to say goodbye to him and meet her new tenant. She was an elderly woman in her midseventies, a gentle, soft-spoken matriarch with glittering eyes, and I was surprised to see her light a stick of incense and bow before the statue of the Buddha. Though perhaps I shouldn't have been. Who else but a practicing Buddhist would have welcomed a Zen temple in her backyard? In the years that followed she would become a trusted friend and confidante who continued to shuttle back and forth between California and Japan until she became too frail to board an airplane. Doris was a friend of Nancy Wilson Ross and had met Elijah in Japan when he was living at Myoshinji. In fact, she had been directly responsible for him taking up residence in Berkeley, offering in effect to sponsor him in the monastic life that he had begun in Japan and temporarily abandoned. She was also the only link I had to Elijah after his departure that Friday, in the early morning of November 9, the morning of my twentieth birthday.

What I remember most about that morning was the fog. It was already beginning to grow light when Diana, Elijah, and I arrived at the dock shortly after six, but the fog was so thick that the world never came into view. We could hear the sounds of voices and machinery and stamping boots from the deck of Elijah's ship, but it was as if it were hidden behind a curtain that only sound could pass. I could see the outlines of a large heavy chain descending into the unseen water and a planked gangway that disappeared into the mist, as if into some cloudy heaven, but the rest of the ship's existence was pure supposition. It was cold, in the high forties at best, and the fog creeping beneath our clothes left us wet and shivering despite the sweaters that both Diana and I wore underneath our jackets. But Elijah seemed oblivious to the weather. I remember him peering up at the invisible ship with a huge smile, as if he had just been set free from prison and was still marveling at his good fortune.

"Do you want to come up?" he asked. "We're not due to leave until eight. I have to sign in, but we should have time to walk around the ship before they blow the horn and hustle you off."

That was how I spent my last hour with Elijah, the three of us exploring a hulking vessel in the fog like bright-eyed children in an exotic playground. There was no mention of Zen, no last-minute advice or admonition, no talk of the future or the past. After Elijah signed in and threw his stuff on his bunk, we peered around bulkheads, climbed slippery ladders, examined lifeboats, checked out the engine room and the dining hall and the holds, and introduced ourselves to the captain and the first mate, who let us look at some sea charts. Three oversized children married to the moment. Thinking back, I wonder if that wasn't the ideal Zen leave-taking. Chop wood, carry water. Be there, wherever you are, and revel in the moment as you wander through the playground of the world.

When the first horn blew, signaling visitors and family to leave the ship, a deep, powerful blast that rumbled in my entrails, I handed Elijah an envelope stuffed with twenty-dollar bills.

"What's this?" he asked.

"I owe you for the lessons. You never did collect."

"You don't owe me anything, brother. They were a gift — and a duty."

"Then this is also a gift. Diana and I put together whatever we could spare. A few others chipped in as well. We want to make sure you make it to India without starving along the way."

Elijah laughed and slapped me on the shoulder with his meaty hand, the same powerful hand that was so fluid and so graceful when it fingered the keys of his saxophone. "Fair enough," he said. "I'll think of y'all every time I use it. Now you'd best be going. This ain't no place for stowaways." All said with more of that Alabama drawl than I had ever heard from him before, as if his cultured speech was one more restraint that he could now throw off.

"Be sure to write, Elijah. I want to know how it's going."

"If you say so, boss."

Elijah kept his promise, but only to a point. I got a letter from him a couple of months later that Doris brought me when she returned from a trip to Kyoto. He was staying in Myoshinji and the letter was sprinkled with stories about temple life and his re-encounters with Zuigan-roshi, but despite the breezy tone I got the sense that he was already looking toward the horizon. A couple of months later I got a postcard from Calcutta with a picture of the Dakshineshvar temple complex on the front and a few barely intelligible lines on the back about the search for Hindu gurus and Tantric yogis. And that was the last I heard, either from him or about him. No idea of where his travels had taken him from there or what had happened along the way. No idea if he was even alive. Until just a few days ago.

But that's another story.

About The Author

Devashish holds an MFA in fiction from San Diego State University. He divides his time between Ananda Kirtana, a spiritual community in the Brazilian countryside, and his farm in Puerto Rico, where he has a yoga center and a tropical-fruit plantation.

You can reach him at: www.devashishdonaldacosta.com

The two excerpts from "Howl" quoted in chapter 15 are taken from: Ginsberg, Allen. _Howl and Other Poems_. San Francisco: City Lights Books, 1956.

The excerpt from Cold Mountain Poems quoted in chapter 17 comes from: Snyder, Gary, "Cold Mountain Poems," _Evergreen Review_ no. 6 (1958)